A. N. Steinberg is an American who divides her time between London, New York and her permanent home in St Louis, Missouri. She has had a varied and interesting career as a radio presenter, a boutique owner and a counsellor at a crisis centre. Her first novel, MANROOT, was also published by Headline.

Also by A. N. Steinberg

Manroot

An Eye
for an Ear

A. N. Steinberg

First published in 1995
by HEADLINE BOOK PUBLISHING

First published in paperback in 1995
by HEADLINE BOOK PUBLISHING

A HEADLINE REVIEW paperback

10 9 8 7 6 5 4 3 2 1

ISBN 0 7472 4814 1

Printed and bound in Great Britain by
Cox & Wyman Ltd, Reading, Berks

HEADLINE BOOK PUBLISHING
A division of Hodder Headline PLC
338 Euston Road
London NW1 3BH

With love
to
Mark Steinberg
and
with gratitude
to
Joan Deitch
and
Wyn Martello

PROLOGUE

The woman who answered the advertisement for the Vanderlee residence was a Mrs Sylvia Antree. Her voice on the telephone was a slow Southern drawl.

She stated clearly that the house must have an attic, and when Evan March from March Properties glowingly described the house, her inquiries returned again and again to the attic. How many windows did it have, was her curious question, and when the realtor explained that it only had one, some flash of brilliance made him add that it was heart-shaped.

Her questions ceased, and she made an appointment to see the property the following morning.

March hung up the phone and his salesman's instincts flared with hope. Curious, a woman calling; it was usually the husband who contacted them. More curious still in 1932; few people were looking for large, expensive houses, and his ad clearly stated the cash price.

He dusted off the sales brochure, which was yellow with age; this house had been on the market since the Stock Market crash. The newspapers carried the story of the Vanderlee tragedy with all its gory details, and the smiling faces of the young children and the beautiful Mrs Vanderlee captured every front page, followed by a harrowing account of how the failed businessman had murdered his children and wife before committing suicide.

The fact that the bodies had lain in the attic undisturbed for months added to the horror. They had remained unfound until a burglar slashed a screen, broke a basement window and began looting the place. It was on the second floor when the sickly-sweet smell of rotting flesh made him drop his full burlap sack, open the small attic door and creep up the narrow staircase to investigate. The carnage he found there rendered him honest. He left the sack where it was on the landing and fled from the house, leaving the front door wide open. Several days later a policeman on the beat investigated.

The attic floor had been scrubbed again and again by the cleaners, yet the stains remained. In desperation the agent even had the floor sanded, but vague pools of darker colours had seeped down into the very heart of the oak planks.

As a last resort the floor was painted a dark brown.

No buyers appeared.

On winter days an indistinct, vague odour was noticeable; even in summer with all the windows open, you could sometimes catch a whiff of an unpleasant smell you couldn't quite identify.

Evan wouldn't say it, for he was not an imaginative man, but secretly he thought it was the scent of terror and madness, and this house made him very uncomfortable. He wished desperately to sell it.

In the morning, Evan March dressed carefully. He changed his tie three times; he must look prosperous. To himself he muttered sentences, proclaiming the desirability of this property, its wonderful six acres of woods, the spaciousness of the rooms, the fact that it had three bathrooms, four fireplaces, a mammoth kitchen, and a foundation of stone.

He rehearsed like a man auditioning for a key role: after all, he hadn't shown the property for almost two years.

He was early for the appointment, so he parked the Ford at the bottom of the hill and looked up at the house, wishing the sun would come out; a bit of sunshine on the hills and glittering on the snow-covered branches of the many trees would render the property picturesque. Instead, gloomy

2

grey clouds hung low with the threat of another snowstorm on the horizon.

He glanced down the narrow road, contemplating how she would arrive – alone, in a taxi, perhaps?

He did not expect the shiny black sedan, driven by the woman herself. She pulled up, almost parked correctly, but at the last minute the wheels caught a patch of ice and the car slid to the right. Not correcting it, she turned off the key and climbed out of the car and walked cautiously towards him, looking down to avoid other patches of ice.

He cursed himself. He had forgotten to have the drive rendered safe by spreading cinders. Anxiously, he glanced towards the house and was relieved to see that at least the long row of steps had been liberally sprinkled with ash.

He studied her as she approached. She was dressed entirely in black with a veil covering her face, so that at this distance he could not see her clearly, nor could he tell the ages of the children who followed her.

'It never snows in Atlanta,' she said curtly.

He nodded.

She stopped before him, but still he couldn't see the children. He knew that sometimes a flattering remark about the youngsters could help a sale, but like obedient ducklings they stood behind her.

Beyond the veil, he saw her clear, angular face, large, dark eyes glittering behind the net, but it was her mouth that he seemed to rest on. It was a slash of vivid red, thin and wide like a wound.

The sun burst through the clouds and they both turned to look at the house high up on the hill. The snow glittered like diamonds, and seemed to hide the faults of the rooms that jutted out haphazardly. The place had been designed with no particular style in mind, as if the architect had added a room here, omitted one there . . . and pasted the turrets on as an afterthought. Mrs Vanderlee's input, he thought.

After shaking her gloved hand, he realized her grip was firmer than his. In confusion he spoke; 'Well-built, this house. Will last for ever.'

3

She answered; her voice, while soft with a Southern twang, carried an edge of ice, a carefully controlled anger at something or someone. 'I don't need it to last for ever.'

March looked down and saw his reflection in the patent leather of her black snow-flecked pumps, his face stretched out at an awkward angle.

She turned and began climbing the stone steps leading up to the house. He saw them now, as obediently they followed – a girl of about ten, who was a mirror reflection of the woman, and a boy of about eight, who, like the girl, had raven black hair, but eyes of the most startling blue. The two handsome children were dressed entirely in black as well. He assumed she was a recent widow of means.

Inside, the scent of a successful sale eluded him, especially when she ran her gloved hand over the edge of the dining-room fireplace, and looked extremely annoyed when a dark streak of dirt stained her glove. March decided he would fire the cleaners first thing when he got back to the office. He gave a running patter in each room, but she seemed not to hear or care.

Nervously, he fumbled with the latch on the attic door. Briskly, he climbed the narrow steps and felt her presence close behind him. The children hung back and waited, unwilling to follow.

She paced the floor, stopping in places as if she knew or sensed what was beneath the paint.

He almost gasped with surprise as she knelt before the heart-shaped window; unmindful now of the snow-white gloves, she traced on the glass the shape of a heart.

His hopes rose as she stood, and he seemed to see a small turning up of the cruel mouth, almost as if she were smiling.

At the bottom of the stairwell, she stopped, turned back, and stared up at the narrow steps.

Even with her attention riveted, she heard it, the boy's nervous shuffle. She turned, looked down at him, and without a word, she drew a bandaged hand from his pocket and squeezed hard. A warning look passed between them.

Only a slight wince betrayed his pain, and when she

released his hand, immediately he hid it again deep within the safety of his pocket.

Surprised at himself, March offered, 'I'm sure we could swing it at a thousand less than the asking price.'

He tried to see her eyes, but this time the thick veil cheated him; he saw only her lowered lashes as she looked down, studying her ruined gloves.

'I shall require bars.'

'Bars?'

'Yes, bars for the windows.'

His heart sank. Widows, always imagining danger. Mentally, he calculated, then consulted his sheet. How many windows were downstairs? 'That's eleven windows. I guess we could do that.'

'Eleven? Surely, Mr March, this house has more than eleven windows.'

'That's what it says here on the sheet. The downstairs and the basement – no, wait, you're right. With the basement it makes sixteen.'

'No, no,' she said, as if correcting an idiot. 'I shall require bars on *all* the windows, both upstairs and down.'

He gulped. An extra expense like this brought the house down to well below market value ... but he would give anything to unload this white elephant.

Finally, he said, 'I guess we could do that.'

She nodded, satisfied.

The new owner had been in the Vanderlee house for four weeks now, and the weekly calls from Mrs Antree did nothing to help March find the required bars for her windows.

He haunted builders' yards, frantic, as the final payment on the house would not be made until the bars had been obtained and were in the process of being installed.

With luck he finally was called to a construction yard downtown; a Catholic old folk's home had burned to the ground and enough bars had been salvaged from it to fit out the house.

March was a bit uneasy with his purchase as the ironwork was fancy, with small cherubs and angels decorating the bars. Mrs Antree didn't strike him as one who would be drawn to anything religious.

He was pleasantly surprised when a sample load was delivered and she smiled at the figures, as if they shared a secret. With her approval, he had the ironwork dumped into the back yard. She agreed to pay him the remainder of the money in cash and left him standing in the entrance hall.

He stood shifting from foot to foot, the crystal chandelier above his head shuddering slightly as a soft rhythmic pounding reverberated through the house. He could not tell if it was the wind or something else as a cry – *a howl* – seemed to rise and fall to accompany the other sound.

That scent that no amount of soap or fresh air could cover seemed stronger now.

He started as she returned. Carefully she counted each bill into his hand.

He mumbled a thank you, and promised a date for the completion of the window installation, knowing he would have to pay a lot more for the workmen to turn out in these weather conditions. The he left, heaving a sigh of relief. Evan March was not a superstitious man, but he felt this woman's presence rendered the house more terrible somehow.

As he turned the car in the drive he looked up and saw a small figure at the strange heart-shaped window. The boy's mouth was in a tortured 'O', and March shivered, for he knew now that the howl he had heard was not the wind.

Inside, the boy heard the sharp staccato of her heels on the wooden attic stairs. He bit his lip. No matter what, he would not give her the satisfaction of crying.

A draught skated along the floor. He heard the sputter of the candle she had left him.

'Bobby Lee,' she whispered, 'you've been a bad boy again. Whatever will that Mr March think?'

She turned the huddled child towards her, studied her son's face in the flickering light. She saw an older, mature face, the husband who had stolen her money, left stretchmarks on her stomach, and slowly she unwound the bandage on her son's right hand.

With satisfaction, she surveyed the blisters. Slowly, she reached for his left hand, studied the smoothness there, and held it above the candle's flame, until he howled – an unearthly sound. Downstairs, his sister covered her ears and thanked God that she was a girl.

'Good – good boy – let them out, all those devils. You think about it, while you're up here in the dark. It's just like the attic back home.' Carefully she laid the cheese sandwich down beside him.

She took the light and left him in the darkness. He held his scorched hand against the frozen windowpane and hate roared through his small body.

Later, he sensed a twitch next to him and in the gloom saw a small grey mouse nibbling at his sandwich.

Swiftly his hand slammed down, and he felt the scratch of tiny claws against his blisters. With his other throbbing hand he sought the tail, grabbed it, and held the tiny rodent aloft as it struggled and swung in his grasp.

He felt it, her Power – *something smaller, something little*.

With fury, he dashed the mouse against the window until its frantic struggle quieted. But the creature's legs still jerked slowly.

Bobby Lee felt the urge to lean forward and clamp his even white teeth around the small head. He resisted, until the small leg jerked close to his lips and then, without thinking, he did it – the unthinkable. He felt the toughness of it, and the tickle on his tongue as he snapped the tiny leg off, spat it away, now seeking the other hind leg. His act completed, he dropped the creature and watched as the mouse struggled to pull itself away with its remaining front limbs.

Bobby Lee watched. Sweat beaded up on his forehead;

his heart thundered with excitement. It felt good witnessing the pain, and he warily looked towards the locked door before he slipped his hand down into his trousers. He caressed his penis, stroking it slowly. His palm burned as the blisters burst, but another part of him felt comfort and pleasure. He watched the mouse; the small, dark eyes glittered as it dragged itself away to safety.

'I hate her. I hate her, and I hate you, too,' he whispered as he masturbated in the dark. 'I hate everybody,' he corrected himself, as he shivered and drew himself together to wait out the endless hours in the dark.

Downstairs, Sylvia stood above her daughter, listening to her prayers.

'Remember about being sorry. I know it must have been Bobby Lee's fault, but you must say you're sorry.'

'I'm sorry, Mamma, real sorry.'

'Don't tell me – tell God.'

Satisfied that each of her children were where they belonged, Sylvia went to her bedroom.

She sat down, retrieved the photo album and slowly, page by page, she relived her life in the South. The pictures of the plantation, the big sprawling house surrounded by an iron fence, gave her a pang of nostalgia.

'I have a new house,' she said aloud, as if that could transport her back to another time, before John Antree came into her life.

Thank God, her parents died before they knew what he had done. He had made a fool of her, given her two unwanted children, stolen her money and disappeared.

That was why she had moved north. She couldn't face them any more – her friends, who knew, and snickered.

She laughed to herself. He had left too soon; she still had annuities.

Taking the cuticle scissors, she checked the pages in the album again, satisfied that John Antree's head had been cut out of all the photographs. Now she searched for Bobby Lee, for his seemed to be the same face – only smaller. Starting at the first page, she looked carefully and when she found them, one by one, she removed the face of her son as if he didn't exist.

The house was quiet now, only the ticking of clocks. She missed the thump of his tiny fists beating on the floor and the howl of his screams.

Going to the window, she watched the falling snow. It had almost covered the iron bars stacked in the yard. She felt safe. The bars would keep the world out, and it would keep him in. She was sure that like his father, eventually in some way her son would disgrace her.

Two floors above, the boy watched the falling snow, too, and with interest he noticed a ginger cat picking its way across the blanket of white. His burned palms throbbed, but he imagined how pleasant it would be to stroke that soft fur. He imagined how wonderful it would feel to caress that warm, furry neck. Would it make a sound if he twisted it violently? Would it crack?

The cat jumped up and sat on the highest pile of stacked iron that wasn't covered yet by snow. It caught the movement in the small, heart-shaped window and looked up.

Bobby Lee saw the glint of red as the cat's eyes searched the window.

He felt real pleasure as he imagined what he would do if he could touch it, this soft bundle of fur; it would soothe his burning hands. It would quiet the bubble of hate within his stomach. He thought of pain – *not his, no, not his*. His own pain gave him no pleasure.

But in his eight-year-old mind he discovered a truth as he touched the twin trails of blood that the mouse had left behind. He discovered the feeling of power.

Bobby Lee whirled round in sudden fear. He thought he'd heard a whisper, a voice too soft to hear. He felt her presence right outside the locked door of the dark room. He strained his ears. It was the same message – the one he had heard so clearly in the attic in Atlanta: *giving pain is pleasure – pleasure is pain*.

He pressed his burned hands to his ears, but still he heard

it, and he was never sure ... was she really out there beyond the door, or was it simply a lesson he was meant to learn?

It wound down, slower and slower like a record at the wrong speed.

Silence thundered through the attic now. He imagined he could hear the distinct *ping!* of snowflakes falling, and then finally he heard them – small children, crying. The sound was strangely comforting. They were sobbing with such anguish he didn't have to. The sobs his lullaby, he finally slept.

He felt rather than saw the velvety blackness above him, like giant wings beating. He opened his eyes to the morning brightness, as the sleeves of her black satin kimono moved impatiently, motioning to him.

'Come now, Bobby Lee. Breakfast is on the table...'

CHAPTER 1

Addie Priest silently thanked the Lord several times that day for sending him to her. Her many trips across 14th Street with her two girls, dressed in clean starched dresses, had finally paid off. 'No,' she protested to herself. 'Paid off' sounded wrong, even to her. Her need for a nest for her girls and herself made her conversion to the Reverend Roy's mission brand of religion easy. Giving up her job – hours spent standing behind a counter at the Five & Dime selling cheap jewellery to young girls smelling of gardenia perfume – was no sacrifice. She'd trade it in a minute for the Reverend's kitchen.

Just last week, right before he proposed to her, he had given her a Bible the date 1948, inscribed on the flyleaf and on the cover – *ADDIE*. She felt it was telling, for he hadn't included her surname. In some odd way she felt her name 'Priest' had been part of her attraction to him. Exchanging it for 'Grimes' was okay with her, for the pretty nice name had never done her any good.

Thoughtfully, the Reverend had brought presents for her daughters as well. He had given her oldest girl, Stella, a pair of roller skates, and her youngest, Jenny, a doll. He called on her tenement flat, drank chicory coffee at her round kitchen table, assessed her cramped quarters and decided that this woman would do.

He had no inkling that twelve-year-old Stella already despised him, thought him false, and vowed never to call him 'Pappa'. To herself and her little sister Jenny she secretly referred to him as 'that crazy Reverend'.

Stella, who loved all the trappings of women, noticed with alarm when her mother threw away in one massive clean-up her hair curlers, pancake make-up, and even her lipstick. That preceded her announcement that she was marrying the Reverend and she and the girls would have a new home across 14th Street in the crumbling old building that was called the Mission.

Several nights before the wedding that was to take place in the city hall downtown, the girls lay in bed whispering.

'Maybe Pappa will come back and stop the wedding,' Jenny said hopefully.

'Pappa's dead.' Frustrated that Jenny was only ten and didn't really understand, Stella's words were cruel and unadorned.

'I know, but if he's in heaven like the Reverend talks about, maybe he can if heaven's such a nice place. Maybe they can give him a pass or something, like in school when I need to go to the toilet.'

'Jenny, Jenny . . . Pappa's dead. He's not coming back ever.' But she knew Jenny's fascination with her books of fairy tales made her sister yearn for, maybe even believe in, miracles.

They turned in their bed and burrowed deeper under the covers.

'I threw those skates down the sewer,' Stella confessed.

Jenny bolted up in bed. 'You did? What will Momma say?'

Stella never turned towards her, just mumbled into the pillow, 'I don't care, those skates were rusty. That crazy Reverend just picked 'em out of his donation stack, and that don't count. It's not like it was a real present. Now go to sleep.'

Jenny still sat up, her back against the headboard, the room bathed in shadow. She heard the quiet rhythm of her mother's breathing from the front room where she slept curled up on the old horsehair sofa. Soon Stella's even breath seemed to synchronize with hers, and Jenny found herself alone, afraid and awake. Everything was changing so fast. Momma was different now. She even smelled different. Gone was the smooth fragrance of facepowder mingled with the flowery scent of her lipstick; now her cheek when she kissed it felt rough, and the naphtha soap smelled clean, but harsh.

Stella stirred, and resettled further into the covers. Even her sister had changed, thought Jenny. These days, Stella simmered and boiled with anger. She wasn't fun any more.

Jenny hugged herself and shivered. The wardrobe cast an ominous shadow across the floor, and the lace curtains danced in the draught from the ill-fitting windows. And there in the rocking chair it sat – the doll.

'It wasn't really a present,' Stella had told her. The doll had once belonged to another girl. Maybe it had been a present then; maybe it had been pretty then, sitting in a crisp box with a soft dress of lace. But now – Jenny strained forward through the gloom to see it better – she knew it had a round face, spiderwebbed with cracks, one finger was missing, and when tilted, its cry of '*mama*' came out strangled and hesitant. An ugly sound. She had pretended for Momma's sake to be pleased, but she hadn't liked the doll then, and now that Stella had told her it wasn't a real present anyway, she could think about it differently. She had placed it in the rocking chair, and in the week that it had been here, she hadn't moved it; she wanted to, she wished to lay it down somewhere so its eyes would close, but Momma seemed so pleased to see it sitting there in the chair.

Jenny craned forward. She could only see its outline, the small round body of an infant, plump arms, chubby legs curved inward; only the blue-white of its sunsuit that Momma had found in the box of their old baby clothes was clearly visible.

'There, it looks like a real baby now,' Addie had pronounced with satisfaction as she dressed it. She even brought home a tiny play baby bottle from the dime store.

'It's a Betsy Wetsy, but I'm not sure that part still works,' she cautioned Jenny. It still cries, though,' and she tilted it so its strangled '*Mama – Mama*' issued forth.

Momma had ignored its eyes, but Stella said, out of Addie's earshot: 'If I had a baby that looked like that I'd kill it.' For the doll's eyes were unfocused: one murky blue eye stared straight ahead, while the other, due to a loose wire, rolled white-looking inside its own head.

With unease, Jenny's tender young heart searched, hoping to find sympathy and pity for the doll, for she was the child who liked the crippled kitten, and the mangy one-eyed stray dog that came to the schoolyard to beg.

The doll's shadow in the room seemed to be responsible for all the scary changes – her mother's harsh, clean smell, her sister Stella's anger. It was terrible to sleep next to her and hear the sound of her teeth gritting against each other, documenting the anger that grew even in her sleep.

Needing to find something to blame, she whispered, 'It's your fault,' to the hateful doll.

Shivering, she threw back the quilt. Her feet, now cold on the linoleum, drove her on. She grabbed the doll by one hand. Its tired voice called, '*Mama – Mama*.'

Jenny froze; the toy dangled from her arm, quiet again. From the next room she heard her mother shift position. Louder now, Stella ground her teeth, and a small cry of some secret anguish was released into her covers.

When it was silent again, Jenny left the bedroom on tiptoes and walked through the kitchen where a clock ticked loudly. Cautiously, she opened the porch door and went out into the dark night where nothing stirred. Theirs was the second-floor flat; above her on the third floor, she saw nothing but the shadow of an empty clothes-line swaying slowly in the night air. Below her in the brickyard, two cats on duty watching for small movements in the dark stared up at her. She saw the gleam of red eyes, which dismissed her and once again looked down, ever watchful.

Slowly, her bare feet found the steps, and she gripped the worn wooden bannister, as she eased herself down them.

14

She held the doll upright, clutched against her flannel gown so it would not cry out. She felt terrible, for she was holding it almost tenderly, all the while knowing that she meant to destroy it.

When she reached the bottom step she sat. Where? How? The brickyard mocked her; there was no earth, she could not bury it. The wooden barrels that did contain earth housed the tall, robust oleanders. Their gnarled, twisted roots left no room for a burial.

She was too afraid to venture out into the street. She yearned to have this hateful doll join Stella's skates in the sewer, but no, it was too far to go in the middle of the night.

Jenny rocked on the step thinking she had chanced so much just to go back up and replace this hateful thing on the chair. She looked down at the doll in her lap. One eye stared back up at her, while the whiteness of the other made her cry out, 'I hate you!' For it was all mixed up now, Stella, Momma, the Reverend, and Pappa never coming back from heaven.

She had to blame someone. Again she spat at the doll, 'It's your fault!' and when one of the cats jumped up beside the rainwater barrel, he provided the answer to her dilemma.

As she crept towards the barrel, the feline growled and leapt away, and with one swift motion she threw the doll in, but not before it issued one more plaintive cry. It sank for a moment, then bobbed up. She closed her eyes, thrust her hand into the cold water, and pushed the cloth under. There was a gurgling sound as the doll's body drank the water greedily and soon she felt it no longer against her small palm as it drifted down to the bottom of the rain barrel.

The surface of the water smoothed, and when she was sure, she ran noisily back up the flight of stairs. The loud click of the kitchen door woke her mother.

Sleepily, Addie called out; 'Stella? Jenny?'

'It's me, Momma. I wanted a drink of water.'

'Okay, honey, but go back to bed now, it's late.'

15

'Yes, Momma.' As Jenny crawled in beside Stella she realized it was the first real important lie she had ever told her mother.

She cupped herself against her sister's warm body and stayed awake almost until dawn.

In the excitement of packing, no one noticed that the doll was gone, not even Momma.

It was arranged that Mr Brotske, who lived in the flat downstairs, would move them. Momma borrowed one of the Reverend's canvas tents to be laid down in the truck so their meagre possessions wouldn't be spoiled with coal-dust, as his truck was usually used for delivering coal. Carrie Brotske was Jenny's best friend, and her excitement about the move made Jenny forget that it was a bad thing.

Neighbours came out and offered to help, and the other widows, while envious, drew hope from it. A widow with two children had found a man to take care of them – so maybe it could happen to them.

Jenny and Carrie skipped rope, and played hopscotch and jacks, trying to fit in all their games while the moving truck filled up. And when it was time to go, both girls' sadness at parting made Mr Brotske offer the treat of riding in the truck, which instantly dried their tears.

First he hoisted his daughter up to the tall running board of the ancient truck, next he helped Jenny.

'Girls, girls, you're only moving six blocks away across 14th Street. You'll still be best friends,' Addie soothed, but somehow both children knew this wasn't so. Someone new would move into the flat and six blocks would be too far for small friendships.

The lopsided truck swayed slowly through the streets, and when it arrived and was unloaded, each child examined her own person, looking for a parting gift that might seal the friendship.

'You can have my best barrette,' Jenny offered, and she yanked the yellow duckling out of her hair without a wince and held it out to her best friend.

Carrie took it, and tried unsuccessfully to clip it in among her blonde curls.

'Momma will do it for me,' she promised. Then Carrie's small hand rustled through the pocket of her pinafore, and found what she was looking for. She held out the half-stick of Juicy Fruit gum.

Jenny took it, put it in her mouth and chewed rapidly so she wouldn't start crying again.

For a fleeting moment Jenny had a sad thought. The yellow duckling would last maybe even till summer, but the sweet taste of the gum would fade and soon it would be nothing but a rubbery blob that you threw in the gutter or stuck under a chair.

The truck backfired twice as it prepared to leave and Jenny, with some other children, ran alongside it, waving frantically.

It was when Carrie bent down to pull up her stocking and her small face disappeared from the frame of the window that Jenny did it. She had to have one more look and she needed to wave, so she caught the handle of the truck's door as her small foot sought the tall running board. The truck coughed and lurched forward violently.

Jenny's small sweaty hand lost its grip and she felt herself falling back, endlessly falling back. Her head hit the edge of the kerbstone, and the sound was like a ripe, juicy melon dropped on a stone floor.

Pinpoints of colour spun before her, and the sound of screams and cries split the air before the blessed blackness swallowed her.

'*Concussion*.' It was the word she heard through the fog.

The warm, fuzzy sleep was filled with the scent of candles, and when Jenny finally opened her eyes some hours later, the first thing she saw was the crucifix on the pale green wall before her.

'Heaven,' she thought, and she moved her head slowly to look for him. 'Pappa?' Was he here?

She saw black everywhere. The blackness moved like coveys of birds accompanied by small, collective sounds of clicking. Later on she saw it was the nursing nuns, moving silently through the halls, the sound of their rosary beads clicking with an unknown message.

'Oh honey, thank God you're awake.' She heard her mother's voice. Through the haze she saw her sitting on a high-backed chair, and next to her was Stella, nervously twirling and twisting a strand of knotted hair.

Momma handed her a present. It was a diary, a small green book with its own tiny key. 'I didn't know what to get you, but Stella thought you'd like this, as you're always reading and writing,' her mother finished awkwardly, hoping her daughter liked the present, for she had displeased the Reverend with this purchase. He felt the thirty-nine cents was quite a waste. Jenny nodded and smoothed the cover, tracing the gold letters that proclaimed it was *My Diary*.

'Doctor thinks maybe you'll be going home in a day or two,' Addie comforted, certain that that would be the case. Again, Jenny nodded and closed her eyes, for she was so tired. She thought of her barrette and wondered if she had swallowed the gum.

'She's tired, Mom, let's go,' Stella whined.

Jenny kept her eyes closed, for she didn't want to see her sister's scared white face again. Fear like that transferred.

That night she had the first dream. She was lost in a large, dark house with a curious, heart-shaped window. Jenny found herself running through the rooms, screaming, but not really screaming, for no one heard her, and her mouth was open, but no screams came out.

She woke up bathed in sweat.

'Bad dream,' the young nun guessed correctly. 'It's gonna be okay. Doctor said you're fine. I know it's scary being in a hospital. You'll be fine once you're home in your own room with familiar things.'

Jenny nodded in agreement, but she knew she wasn't going home to a familiar place. Already she missed the three-room railroad flat, and the sparse brickyard where the only soft things were the poisonous oleanders that bloomed in their wooden barrels, and the two tough tomcats guarding the night.

No, she was going to the Mission – that large, shabby house surrounded by tumbledown bricks, that was uglier still than the tenements across 14th Street.

Jenny still felt tired and her legs were rubbery, like the time she had the measles and stayed in bed so long.

Even the taxi waiting at the kerb did not chase the flatness away, but Stella waiting at the Mission door to meet her, did. She was happy to see Stella's face smooth again, with the look of anger put away.

Their bedroom recreated the other; it contained the same bed, same dresser, and same rocking chair – and at night when they stared up at the water stain on the ceiling, they agreed that it looked like a map of Africa. They liked that funny stain and both hoped that no one would come and repair it.

A certain sense of resignation placated Jenny. Finally she had accepted that her father wasn't coming back and that her mother was stern and forever busy now with the black lady stirring endless pots in the kitchen.

Even Stella was different, but it was a difference that Jenny could not explain.

It was when her mother said, 'Sorry, honey, we must have lost it in the move,' that Jenny's brows knitted. 'The doll – she's gone,' Addie clarified. Guilt came back swiftly and terribly, and more than once Jenny tried to tell Stella about what she had done. When she was convinced she couldn't tell, she took the small key, opened the diary, stared at the blank page and finally wrote; '*I did a very bad thing. I killed her.*' It leapt off the page in its simplicity, and quickly she locked the diary and hid the book under the mattress.

The Mission was a busy place. It rang out with Bessie's singing, it shouted with heartrending testimonies at evening prayer meeting, and the pots in the kitchen constantly bubbled with different smells of cooking. Jenny slivered into a sort of contentment even though Carrie never walked the six blocks to see her, and the few times Jenny got her mother's permission to go back to the tenements where they had lived, with numerous warnings about how many times to look before she crossed the street, when she arrived there was always a gang of children playing jacks and jumping rope, and Carrie with the yellow duckling firmly clipped in her hair would say, 'Oh ... hi,' in that voice you reserved for visiting cousins that you didn't like.

Jenny knew it, even then, because of the gum. It didn't last.

She went back carefully across the streets, she looked both ways, and finding no other of her age who lived near the Mission, she sought the friends that she needed among the pages of the many books she borrowed from the library.

She liked sitting at one of the kitchen tables, reading while Momma and 'Nigger Bess' peeled potatoes or snapped beans.

'It's not right calling her that name,' Momma scolded her daughters.

'Everyone calls her that.' Stella was irritable.

'"Nigger" is an insult,' Momma explained patiently.

'She don't seem to mind,' Stella argued. 'What should we call her?'

'"Coloured" – that's the proper thing to call her.'

Stella smirked, made a face, then sassed, 'I can't see me saying "Coloured Bess". That sounds stupid.'

'Why can't we just call her Bess?' Jenny offered.

'That's right, honey. After all, they's human just like we are.'

With that Bess came through the kitchen carrying a bag of flour from the storeroom. 'Who's talking about Bess?' she asked.

Momma flushed red. 'We're just straightening out the name.' she offered.

'I know. It don't hurt my feelings any more. I heard it all

20

the time. "Nigger, Nigger". It's supposed to mean no account, but I ain't no account. I work for my food, just like you do.'

'Of course you do,' Momma soothed, as she threw a cold look towards Stella, who flounced out of the room.

'Can you move those papers, child?' Bess asked. 'Don't want to mess 'em up with all the flour.'

'Sure,' and Jenny carefully moved her drawings to the other side of the table.

Bess fingered the paper. 'Look there, Miz Roy, how that child done drew them trucks, almost like a real picture.'

Both women huddled together and examined the drawing of two trucks, each with their names carefully lettered on the side and men with bushel baskets emptying the contents.

'That one's got potatoes, and that truck's got onions and cabbage,' Jenny explained as she carefully detailed the glasses on the truck driver's face.

'That's nice, honey, real nice,' Addie crooned as she smoothed her daughter's tangled hair, suddenly remembering how little time she seemed to have for her daughters these days.

Within the hour, the real trucks pulled up and the Reverend and Sam went out to unload.

Some time later, the Reverend came into the kitchen wiping his sweat-soaked face, gulped a glass of water and told the women, 'Thank the Lord we got onions, potatoes, and cabbage. We can feed 'em good with this lot. New driver seems nice enough.'

Bess looked up and found Jenny's eyes. 'Lemme see them pictures.' She went to the window holding the paper. The sketch was a remarkable likeness of the new driver. Silently, with her heart beating fast, Bess studied the drawing carefully. It was the same real scene outside the window. The new driver's hat, glasses, even his union button clipped carefully to the collar of his shirt.

When she turned back, the look on her face made Addie ask, 'What's wrong?'

'How'd she know?' Bess said, her voice just above a whisper.

'Know what?' Addie asked.

'Know,' she repeated as she waved the paper. Suddenly Bess turned to the girl, still bent over her drawings. 'Child, how'd you know?'

Pleased, Jenny smiled, 'I don't know, I just did. I saw it in my head a while back.'

Heavily, Bess sank into a chair and began fanning herself with the paper.

'It happens like that sometimes,' Bess said as if she were talking to herself. 'It tears – tears a little hole in the curtain,' and she frantically began crossing herself.

'What is it, Bess? What you talking about?' Addie pressed.

'There's a man, I heard about him on the radio. He had it torn, the curtain, and now he sees things. After he fell off a ladder and cracked his head, he sees things – ships sinking, trains crashing, airplanes falling from the sky. God knows it's a bad thing, Missus, seeing all that and he cain't do one thing about it.'

'Ssh, Bess, you're talking foolish, scaring the child.' And they both looked at Jenny, who was listening to every word.

'Jenny, off you go now,' Addie said briskly. 'We're busy here and you're messing up the table. Go on, you can draw in your room.'

Her mother's harsh words stung, so Jenny gathered up her things and left, tears springing to her eyes. Grown-ups were funny. First they were happy about her drawings, now they were suddenly mad.

In the hall she stopped to pet the cat who was in the broom closet with a litter of new kittens. She had known they were going to be two black ones and one black and white. She sat down and stroked their soft fur. The voices from the kitchen were distant, but she heard Bess saying, 'It's not a good thing, no sirree. I heard about people who had it. It's just a small tear, and they get a peek. No,

22

Missus, tell the Reverend to pray for her, and comes Easter tell him to dip her – maybe that will stop it. No sirree, it's not a good thing.'

'Hush, Bessie, you best be seeing to those onions.'

Jenny went up to her room. It was true. She'd seen that driver and truck long before they came. She knew about the colour of the kittens, too. There was no one she could tell – they'd just get mad at her again.

Finally, she fumbled under the mattress, found the tiny book, opened the diary and wrote: '*Bessie said I had a torn curtain and peek through to somewhere, but I don't believe her 'cause I see that house with the Valentine window sometimes, and the shadow who chases me in my dreams. But it's not real, none of it, for there is no house like that, and Momma once said all children are afraid of the Boogie Man and he's not real.*'

Jenny closed the book, slid it under the mattress and went to the window to examine the lace curtain to see if she could find a tear. She couldn't.

Restless and uneasy, she paced the room. Stella was out, and she was banned from the kitchen. Suddenly remembering, she pulled out the box of broken jewelry from under the bed and sat on the rug, sorting the beads until she was satisfied. When she found one large creamy pearl that would be suitable for the centre of a necklace she began stringing the beads.

CHAPTER 2
The Dream

Rapidly I smooth her limbs for they are turning now, cold as marble. I cannot warm them for I have no fire – I have left it on the altar of Bobby Lee; nor can I cry for he owns my tear ducts and my pity is for rent.

But I can work ... when tasks are set before me. This sacrifice must be anointed; so carefully I remove them – the flannel gown, the tiny shirt, the soiled diaper. She lies before me, waiting. I think of it as incense and precious oil and lovingly I anoint her, holding back my bile.

By the lamplight I am every mother tending to her child. I map the contours of her body and gently close her unseeing eyes.

Fabric whispers, so I touch the silk and it matches perfectly the texture of cold, smooth skin. I feel the bond of Tutankhamen as I wrap her in the silken cloth, round and round until she is a cocoon waiting for the butterfly that I am certain she will become.

It's difficult closing off that tiny, still face. I look, I stare, needing to see her one more time. My lips touch but only once this imposter of a child.

The cloth swirls. I have erased her, a metamorphosis of sorts. A bundle of silk, I tell myself ... no less ... no more.

I open the French doors to find the night air crisp, cold. I welcome the freshness of dew on the soles of my trembling feet as I cross the wide lawn seeking the protection of tall trees. At the edge of the woods I pause, for a nightbird sings. I drop to my knees and like an animal I begin digging under the leaves until I have a hole big enough to welcome her, this unloved child. I cannot say goodbye, nor can I say her name, for I have forgotten it. It was not chosen by me, but by my finger running down the pages of a book.

I look up at the amber moon and yearn to lift my head and howl. But I am civilized. So instead I walk back to the house, finding the path lit by tardy fireflies.

Inside, I stop and listen to the hollow heartbeat of the house and climb the stairs and bite my lips until I suck the bitter taste of blood. I see the mound of him under the covers and the burning taste of vomit rises in my throat as I creep into bed beside him. He has infected me, this man riddled with disease. I feel it now gnawing at my insides, his cancer, now mine. He stirs deep in satisfying sleep, he's finally satiated and I begin the sustaining daydream – the way I always begin, it's like a movie.

I see him standing before me. I am kneeling, subservient. 'Do it! Pretend you like it, you bitch – you love it,' he rasps. He plays his part well, now it's my turn . . .

I reach for him. It. The penis, limp before me. My fault, he says. He cannot see them glinting – the hedge-shears, sharp and shiny. I lift it, that hateful thing and in a moment, IT WILL BE DONE. My hands finally strong, I clasp it, hold it between the blades and squeeze – the moment surreal, so simple, so quick. It lies on the floor between us. I imagine it flops like a fish gasping on a pier. There is only a black hole left, no blood, no gore, just emptiness, and the most satisfying thing is his scream – inhuman, high, piercing agony, a twin of the feeling that I feel, stuffed in my vocal cords, mute for ever.

The light flickers and the screen goes blank so I turn off the movies of my mind, like turning off the lights or putting out the garbage. I know I have one more chore. I rise and leave the prison of my bed. The shears gleam reflected in a patch of mirror. With each snip I shiver, and like pennies in a bank, the pile grows, cross-stitching each other, uneven lengths of light brown hair gathering like storm clouds in the bathroom sink.

My shift is over. I punch the time clock and return to the hollow space waiting in the bed.

I wait, I sleep, I dream: it seems an eternity until the alarm clock rings, like a starting bell. I scream over and over realizing the horror is real. It echoes, bouncing off walls, picking up volume. I follow its zigzag path that leads me to the nursery, to stare into the empty crib. It is real, it really happened.

I feel the house shift, an earthquake in my mind. I welcome the pain as my head hits the edge of the table. Pain is good, it can pull down the shade and close out the real world. Through the buzzing in my ears I hear the sounds of the Mission and Reverend Roy's loud bass voice leading the children in song:

> 'The Devil is a sly ole fox.
> If I could catch Him I'd put Him in a box.
> Lock that box and throw away the key,
> And that would be the end of He.'

CHAPTER 3

The summer of 1953, when Jenny was approaching her sixteenth birthday, was a turning point for the family. Stella's impatience to be grown-up, to be gone, and the wedding in Piggott, Arkansas, these things planted the seeds of murder, madness, and vengeance – and of Jenny's terrible dream.

They still lived at the Mission then – Addie, Jenny, Stella and the Reverend Roy, the man Momma had married when Jenny was seven. With all that happened subsequently, it's eerie, yet comforting, that the Mission is one place where Time has stood still. The huge ramshackle house is surrounded by the same sagging fence. The yard still has the two rusting refrigerators with their doors torn off, and the picnic table that always gave the children splinters still nestles under the oak tree. Further back in the yard squats the old tin swimming pool where the Reverend baptized his sinners...

By dint of sheer ignorance and persistence, and pure dumb luck of being chosen by a reporter writing articles on the poor, the Reverend Roy Grimes had embarrassed and convinced the large chain stores to donate food to his Mission. On most days, trucks would deliver items that were close to their sell date, or stale bread and pastries, and in summer, there were plentiful deliveries of vegetables and overripe fruit.

The building had a sign across its front, painted in clumsy

29

white letters that had run a little, proclaiming itself: *The Needy Man's Mission*.

The huge kitchen was always painted apple green, for in the cellar a donation of gallons of paint waited, assuring that no matter how many paint jobs it survived, the kitchen would always be green. There was a sense of permanence about that.

The old house at some date in the forgotten past had settled, and furniture and pictures all tilted slightly to the right.

The kitchen contained ten tables covered in oilcloth; on each one Jenny put a mayonnaise or pickle jar full of flowers, pretty weeds, or in the autumn, coloured leaves.

'To cheer them up,' she told Momma, who'd nod and smile and later gently argue with the Reverend, 'It don't hurt none.'

He'd shake his head and mutter that Coming to Jesus was the only cheering up anybody ever needed.

The room called the chapel was two rooms made into one; if you looked up you could still see the rough plaster where a previous wall had been. No sense of order could ever create even rows for the sinners, as the mismatched chairs in here were all different sizes, shapes and colours.

At the front of the chapel a rickety platform held the wheezing organ, a lectern of sorts, a small table for the Reverend's electric guitar, and several other tables of different heights for the candles. This was the Reverend Roy's one extravagance; the candles all had to be white. He made no exceptions to this rule.

Tacked up on the back wall was an assortment of small velveteen throw rugs, purchased at the dime store and depicting the Life of Jesus in different scenes. The reds, blues and purples fairly pulsated in the flickering candle-light.

In the summer the chapel smelled of unwashed hair and sweat as the ceiling fans slowly stirred the humid air. In winter it reeked of Vick's Mentholatum, and the stuffy heat from old oil heaters encouraged the sporadic sound of muffled coughs.

Across the hall was the kitchen, where Momma, her two girls and Nigger Bess cooked the suppers for those that came for mandatory religion and a free meal.

Stella was almost eighteen now and had only one goal in life to get married and leave the Mission. Jenny and her sister were as different as night and day. Jenny listened to everything her sister said, and believed it, while hoping some of it wasn't true. But Stella's constant oath 'Gospel truth' made Jenny push her doubts away.

Jenny was barely listening now though as Stella rattled on about Rodney. He was a truck driver, who delivered food to the Mission donated by one of the chain stores. For six months now, she had been sneaking out at night to meet him.

'You're not listening, are you, Jenny – and it's important! I'm trying to tell you about guys. I've got experience – I know how to handle them. Why, I've got Rodney—'

Her excited flow was interrupted by Addie sticking her head in the kitchen doorway. Their mother gauged the amount of food in the boiling pots and announced: 'We need more potatoes, girls. Why, the Reverend must have at least fifty in there tonight,' she said proudly.

'All right Maw, we know,' Stella answered impatiently.

They opened another sack and began peeling more potatoes, and once Stella was sure her mother was out of earshot she said, 'Jenny, the first rule is, you gotta act hot.'

'How? What do you mean?'

'Well, you know,' she began importantly, 'when you're necking and they get their hands on your tits, you breathe real fast and act like you really like it, then if it's going further, and you feel a hand up your dress, pretend you really, really like that, too, and you want to – but can't let 'em simply because you're a good girl. You make 'em think you want to, you know, with loud breathin' and sighs, but—' she stopped and waved the potato peeler '—but never, I'm telling you, NEVER let them get their fingers in your pants.'

Jenny felt shocked. She was blushing furiously, embarrassed by her own sister.

'Do you do that kinda stuff with Rodney?' she asked, hoping the answer would be no.

'Yeah – and it's working. I'm sure he's gonna ask me to marry him real soon.'

'Do you like him, Stella, or love him?'

'Well, yeah, I guess. I want outta here – the smell of the poor, the greasy potatoes, all that crazy singing ... You're too young, but I remember Momma when she wasn't so nuts on religion, before *him* – the Reverend Roy my ass.'

'What was she like?'

'Normal-like. Why, we used to go to the movies. She wore make-up, worked at Woolworth's. She always brought us candy – they let her take home the bits when the bags broke, don't you remember?'

'Sort of.'

'Well, I want outta here. Truck drivers make good money. Why, when I marry Rodney I'm gonna get a little house – he can buy one on the G.I. Bill. God, I can sit around and read *True Confessions*, not like that outdated crap you bring home from the library. *Jane Eyre, Rebecca* – shit, people like that don't exist!'

'Maybe they do.'

'Now look here, little sister, if you listen to me I'll tell you things how they are, so's you can get out of here, too.'

Jenny looked down at her hands, hoping Stella was wrong. 'Maybe I don't want to get married; I might be a nurse.

'Oh, so being a candy-striper's got to you. Well, it's a long way from being a nurse – four whole years. Momma'll never get the money to let you study four years. Between her and that crazy Reverend they want free help,' and Stella threw the last potato in the pot with a vengeance.

'The nurses seem so nice. People all love them, they're so grateful, and the babies ... Last week I worked in the nursery and they're so sweet, those tiny little babies.'

'Not me,' Stella shuddered. 'I don't want no tiny little babies. I wanna have fun.'

'It was so sad. One of them died last week, for no reason. That little baby just died in his sleep.' Stella didn't answer, for the bell rang then and they could hear the guitar being tuned.

'Turn that fire up,' Stella urged. 'Damn, the potatoes ain't near done.'

They hurried with the dinner preparations and in fifteen minutes they took off their aprons, opened the door, and let the people file into the makeshift chapel. Service first; the Reverend made them sit through that, and he demanded testimonials from somebody – how they'd seen Christ or the Virgin Mary, and if there weren't enough stories he'd tell his own again, about how the devil made him drink and one day he saw Christ's face on a sewer lid, and Christ told him to start a Mission.

The girls set out the plates on the long oilcloth-clad tables. Addie filled the takeaway boxes and they stood ready.

Sounds of the guitar, mating with the wheezing organ, filled the building and the energetic singing reverberated. It was a half hour of ranting and raving before the congregation filed out of the chapel, took their places at the tables and bent down protectively low, shoulders hunched, eating whatever was on offer.

It was always an assorted crew – unshaven men and shabby women, some of them young, with grubby-faced kids, who ate quickly in gulps. No threats of starving children in India were needed here to make them clear their plates. These were the poor, the maladjusted, the unfortunate ... and it was years later before Jenny realized that the Reverend with his shabby Mission was really doing something that was good.

Stella's scorn hid the truth from her then. 'Look at that,' Stella nodded towards a young blonde with lank hair, stomach bulging and two small children sitting next to her. 'I ain't never gonna end up like that.'

That night after lights out, Jenny watched her sister put on make-up, smear her lips together, and glance into the small mirror. 'Like this colour?' she asked. 'Stole it from the dime store today.'

'Yeah, I guess, but you shouldn't do it,' Jenny said.

'You sound just like Momma: "God's watching"! Why, He must be as busy as a one-armed paperhanger, watching me steal lipstick, when babies at your hospital are dying for no reason. Where was He then?'

Her argument was fair, and it scared Jenny.

'I found this in the clothes giveaway today.' Stella held up a shimmery satin dress. 'I'm surprised Momma didn't throw it out. It looks too sexy,' she continued.

Stella wiggled into the dress. Jenny couldn't help but admire her; she seemed to know everything about life.

'On the cover of *Photoplay* this week there's a picture of Elvis Presley with some girl and this dress is a dead ringer for the one she's wearing,' she commented.

A board somewhere in the old house creaked.

They listened for sounds. Their room faced the back of the house. Momma and the Reverend's room was in the front, and usually they were in bed and asleep by ten.

Stella put her ear to the door. 'It's okay. I thought I heard something.'

'Be careful,' Jenny warned.

Looking at her sister in the eerie light from the street lamp that cast shadows in the room, Jenny felt sad and afraid, for she knew she was losing her.

Later, struggling from sleep, Jenny tried to focus. A mixture of whisky and perfume assailed her. Stella shook her gently. 'Jenny – *Jenny!* It's happened.'

'What? What's happened?' She sat up and looked at her sister. Stella's face caught by the street lamp looked ghostly and strange.

34

'He asked me to marry him!'

Caught in a hug, they felt the rhythm of their heartbeats.

'I'm glad,' Jenny said, but her insides were jelly. It was a mixture; fear, jealousy, anger, happiness. 'I'm glad,' she repeated, as if saying it would make it true.

'We're driving to Arkansas – to Piggott,' Stella went on excitedly. 'You don't need to wait until you're eighteen there. I could pass for eighteen anyway.'

'When are you going?'

'The Saturday after next. You gotta cover for me, Jenny. You gotta make sure nothing goes wrong.'

Jenny crawled back into bed, and listened to the sound of Stella undressing, a sound she would always recall with pleasure. They lay warm against each other, knees bent into knees.

'The perfume – Momma will notice,' Jenny whispered.

'I'll wash it off in the morning. It was just like I told you, Jenny. Act hot, but not *too* hot. Rodney couldn't stand it – he can hardly wait. He's my ticket out of here.'

Their silence deepened. 'Don't worry, little sister,' she yawned. 'I'll get you out of here, too.'

They slept with the promise warm between them. The clang of the bell rang harshly at 5 a.m.

'Bastard,' Stella muttered. 'Do-gooder bastard. He wants to save the world, let him. I don't. I wanna save myself.' The sisters huddled together in the cold room, their sleep precious.

The thudding on the door accompanied Addie's cheerful call: 'Rise and shine, girls. Truck's a-coming!'

Jenny got up first, crawling over Stella. 'Might as well get up or she'll keep knocking.'

Reluctantly, Stella sat up. 'Fuck – shit – goddamn – fuck – shit – bastard – bitch – motherfucker. It makes me feel better cussing in this goddamn hole of a Mission.'

'God's watching,' Jenny teased. 'Sorry, I mean God's listening.'

The first truck pulled up to the side yard, leaving a load of

35

overripe peaches to be sorted. The donor stores were doing their bit for the poor, while taking a heavy write-off on their tax.

Reverend Roy in his undershirt unloaded the trucks with Big Sam, the reformed drunk, his assistant.

It was gonna be a long, hard day, with Addie, Stella and Jenny sorting the good from the bad. The bad would be put aside for the pig farmer.

'Better eat something first,' Momma said.

'Just toast,' Jenny answered.

'How about some oats? We'll need stamina for this job,' she cautioned. 'Peaches – thank the Lord!'

'Just toast,' Jenny repeated.

'Where's that lazy sister of yours?' and before Jenny could answer, Stella came in.

'Coffee, Maw.'

Addie's tired shoulders straightened and she seemed to sniff the air, but that thought was lost as Stella lit a cigarette.

'You know how the Reverend feels about smoking – ladies smoking, anyhow, and especially in the Lord's House.'

Ignoring her, Stella took a deep drag. 'Just coffee, Maw.' Jenny could see the effort it took for her sister not to say more.

'Peaches, we got peaches today,' Addie said brightly.

'Don't matter; it all stinks.'

'Stella, it's food, good food for them that needs it. The Lord provides.' She stared at her daughter with dismay. 'Don't let the Reverend hear you talking like that.'

'He's your husband, Maw – why call him the Reverend. He ain't no real Reverend anyway. He got that piece of paper for ten bucks by the mail order.'

The sass shut Addie up. She turned to the stove, poured more coffee and left the room.

'Why talk to Maw like that, Stella? She can't help it.'

'Sure she can. The Reverend – why, she acts like that

phony is Somebody. Can't she see he's a little man that only seems big down here with all this riffraff?'

'It's a whole truckload – I better start.' Jenny rose and left Stella sitting there smoking furiously.

The sun was warm in the fresh, crisp air of early summer. Jenny tried not to think of the musky smell of the rotten fruit they'd have to pick through. She went to the weathered picnic table in the side yard, where stacked in an orderly pile, the baskets waited.

'Someone's gonna have to sign the delivery slip.'

Jenny looked round to see that a man had come up behind her.

'You work here?' he said.

'Yes,' she nodded.

He offered a pink slip, and when she didn't reach for it, he put it on the table. 'Here,' he indicated, holding out the pen. 'Press hard, so it shows on the carbons.'

'What should I sign?'

'Your name.'

Feeling stupid, she took the pen he offered, pressed hard and signed Jenny Priest. He read the slip, tore them apart and handed her the copy.

'Jeannie with the light brown hair.'

'No, it's Jenny,' she corrected, and looked up into the bluest eyes she had ever seen. He smiled a dazzling smile, reached over and gently touched her hair.

'It's Jeannie to me.'

She felt foolish for blushing, for she didn't know how to be flippant like Stella.

'Priest – pretty appropriate,' he smiled.

Jenny was relieved to see her sister.

'Not appropriate at all,' Stella quipped. 'That crazy Reverend ain't our father.' She was looking him over carefully.

He looked back at her, still smiling. 'Another Jeannie with the light brown hair.'

'No, I'm Stella who might be red, or blonde, or whatever colour I feel like.'

He turned back to Jenny. 'I prefer Jeannie with the light brown hair.' Then he folded the paper, put it in his pocket, winked and strode back to his truck.

'Who in the hell was that?' Stella asked. 'Good-looking bastard. Why, I do believe he was flirting with you, little sister.'

'No, he was only teasing,' Jenny said as she reached for the first heavy bushel, took it to the table and began sorting the peaches.

Stella sat next to her, absentmindedly throwing peaches into the different baskets.

'He's gotta nerve – why, he's old enough to be your father. Good-looking bastard, though. I'll ask Rodney if he knows him. All those truck drivers seem to know each other.'

'He was just teasing,' Jenny repeated.

Stella worked faster now. 'Thirteen more days,' she mused, 'that's all. We're gonna get a house. Rodney talked about St Ann's – it's a community way out in the suburbs. You'll come out and spend time with me. It'll be clean and pretty – we'll have steak and asparagus. We never *ever* have had asparagus. We'll have all kinds of goodies, not this rotten shit people throw away.'

Looking up, she saw Jenny's face, stricken with the sadness of losing her; she always led and Jenny always followed.

Reaching over, she ruffled her sister's hair. 'All right, Jeannie with the light brown hair, I'll take care of you. I won't forget. I'll get you out of here, too, I promise.'

Tears just started coming, and Jenny wasn't exactly sure why.

'There, there, honey.' Stella reached over and smoothed away the tears.

'What's the matter?' Momma called from across the yard.

'Nothing, Maw. Jenny caught a splinter from the table. It's okay, I got it out.'

She lied so easy.

'You're pretty,' Stella said fiercely, 'real pretty. Ain't filled out yet. Somebody's gonna love you, you'll see. Why you're almost sixteen. Maw got married when she was that age.'

'I wish the world wasn't like this,' Jenny whispered.

'Like what, honey?'

'You know, everything depending on men.'

'That's how it is, can't change it. That's how it's always been, always will be,' Stella said, and a sadness come over her face, and for once you could see beneath her crisp exterior.

'Do you love him, Stella, really love him?'

'I guess so, I don't know what love is. I love you. I try not to, but I guess I love Maw. I'm disappointed in her. I'm gonna be different – I'm gonna be a person, not just a shadow tagging Rodney. Of course I love him. He's my ticket out of here!'

They both laughed, tugged the next basket over, and began sorting in silence, each caught in her own thoughts.

'We're lucky, so lucky,' Maw always said. 'Gotta roof over our heads, food on the table, and a good man to take care of us.'

Looking at the humanity that came through the doors of the Mission each night told the girls that she was right. Still – there had to be more to life than sin and salvation. Like Stella, Jenny yearned for beauty, clean new things, music, art; she yearned for things that must exist somewhere away from the brick tenements, the littered lots, the graffiti walls.

Sitting in the back of the chapel that night, Jenny listened to the testimonies, the tearful cries. Like Stella, she wondered why God didn't hear their pleas? Or if He heard, why didn't He answer?

'*The Devil is a sly ole fox.*' Voices rang out loud, angry, more shouting than singing.

They slipped out to the kitchen, to begin on the dirty dishes.

39

'There must have been fifty again tonight. Maw was right,' Stella said.

She washed. Jenny dried.

'Someday, this place will seem like a bad dream. Like I said, you're too young to remember, but it didn't used to be this way. Why, Momma had a radio, she even used to dance.'

'I wish I remembered,' Jenny said sadly.

'Never mind. I'll get a radio, even a record player, and we'll pick us some dance records. Rodney's even talking about buying a TV.'

Rodney, the Reverend . . . it all depended on men.

They went up early to their room. It was barely nine, but they had sorted and given out over 300 bushels of peaches. It was hard work. Jenny crawled into bed, not minding the light as Stella tried on clothes, chattering endlessly about Rodney. She talked, but she required no answer. Surrogate mother, sister, friend . . . Jenny was losing all of them in thirteen days.

On Sundays, when other churches were having services, the Reverend slept late, sometimes till one or two in the afternoon. Jenny asked Momma why.

'Honey, Reverend Roy, he works hard all week, so he figured just like the Lord he'd rest on Sunday.'

Those were the mornings Jenny would see her mother in the kitchen, sitting at one of the worn tables, drinking coffee.

'Morning, Maw.'

'Morning, honey.' She'd get up and pour the coffee.

Today, looking at her youngest daughter as if she hadn't seen her for a long time, Addie remarked, 'Gosh, you're getting pretty – all growed up and I hadn't noticed. Have you—' Embarrassed, she paused. 'Have you had the curse yet? I meant to talk to you about it.'

'Yeah, Momma, Stella explained it.'

'Good.' Relief was plain on her face. 'Sometimes I get so

busy doing the Lord's work, I forget that I got two fine girls right under my nose.'

Jenny scalded her tongue on the hot coffee. It was almost a warning not to ask, but it came out anyway. 'What'd you do before you did the Lord's work?'

'Oh, my,' Addie blushed, 'it seems so long ago. I worked in the dime store, selling things.'

'Did you like it?'

'I thought I did, but that was before I knew the Reverend. Silly, useless work it was.'

'What was my daddy like?'

'Oh,' her face softened for a minute, then closed up tight. 'He was a weak man, really, your pa. Sold ladies' stockings, travelled a lot, but he fell off the path. Drink; it was the drinking that killed him. He died in a poker game. Don't get me wrong, honey, there weren't nothing about him that a little religion couldn't have helped. I was young then; I didn't know how to lead a good Christian life. Thank the Lord, I found the way. Rather, the Reverend showed me the way.'

The Reverend, the Reverend ... always he was between them. Stella and Jenny had lost her a long time ago. And as Jenny left her standing at the sink rinsing out the cups, she heard her mother's clear soprano voice singing, '*He is trampling out the vintage where the grapes of wrath are stored* ...'

Passing the storeroom, the telltale meow drew her in. The cat had found the burlap sack, curled up and deposited another six kittens on it. 'Silly cat. He'll only drown most of them, anyway.'

The cat looked up and licked her hand. Jenny sat on the floor, and one by one she held the tiny creatures. 'Which one will be lucky? Who will take you, or you?' she asked. She couldn't watch those times when he – the Reverend – tied the rest in a sack, weighted it down with a rock and drowned them in the pool.

It always reminded her of the baptisms which were usually held at Easter in the side yard. Candles lining the path as the saved souls were led barefoot to the round tin wading pool to be dipped under, struggling, while the Faithful wailed out the hymns, and Sam played a harmonica, trying to keep them in tune.

For a minute she felt breathless remembering that Easter, when it had been her turn, the shock of that cold water, the Reverend's firm hand holding her under. The burning in her nose and throat. He had dipped her, but it didn't fix the curtain, for that was the summer she saw Bess lying in a cheap wood coffin. She hadn't told her, for Bess had always dreamed of meeting the Lord in a snow-white box banked high with red roses.

CHAPTER 4

The boxes of broken beads and jewelry parts that some store always donated to the Mission gave Jenny so much pleasure that Momma, who was told by the Reverend to throw the whole lot out, disobeyed him and passed them on Jenny.

She kept the box under the bed. With fishing line, she spent many happy hours stringing necklaces.

'These are pretty enough for somebody to buy 'em,' Stella praised, one day soon after the peach-sorting. She reached for the long necklace Jenny had made of crystal and pearl beads. 'I'd like this one for my weddin'.' And she flung the long rope of beads over her head.

'I made it for you. I was thinking of your wedding when I made it,' Jenny lied.

'Can you make earrings, too – long ones that would dangle? I'm thinking of doing my hair in an upsweep.'

Jenny pawed through the box of parts and pieces, but could find no clips, only ear-wires.

'That's okay,' Stella said excitedly. 'I'll pierce 'em. I saw how Sally did hers – it's easy. Make me them earrings, Jenny, please. And make 'em match the necklace. Can you do it?'

''Course,' Jenny said, surprised at her confidence, but ever since she had first touched these beads, the stones of crystal, it was like a great big puzzle that she had already worked out. For some reason, her fingers could easily pick them out, the parts she needed. Her mind already saw designs and when each one was finished, she knew it was good.

It was like finding something she'd been looking for all her life. Even as a little girl she had drawn crayon flowers on the takeaway paper bags. They went almost unnoticed, but sometimes Momma would shake her head at them.

'Girls, girls, girls. I got one girl starved, wantin' anything pretty. You're a magpie, Stella, wantin' anything that glitters. You watch that appetite. Magpies steal, takin' things they shouldn't oughta – and you, my little one,' she looked closely at Jenny, 'seems your heart and your head just burstin' to make anything pretty. He don't understand,' she nodded towards the room they called the chapel. 'Just watch your step, girls – don't let that wantin' get us into trouble. We got it good here – he's a good man.'

When the earrings were done Stella was ecstatic. 'They're beautiful. I love them.' She held one up to her ears, swept her hair up and turned back and forth to get a better view in the mirror. 'Let's do it,' she said.

'What?'

'My ears. I can't wait to wear these.'

Apprehensively, Jenny followed her to the kitchen.

Stella took the ice pick and poked at the slab of ice in the refrigerator until a chunk came off. Back in their room she threaded the needle.

'I can't do it,' Jenny begged off.

'Sure you can, it don't hurt none. Pinch your ear. See? Ear lobes are almost numb, and the ice will make it completely painless. Jenny, you gotta.'

Jenny reached up and pinched her ear. Stella was right: it didn't hurt. With shaking fingers she held the cork behind her sister's ear. The needle looked so large and dangerous.

'Do it,' Stella urged, her eyes squeezed tight.

She plunged the needle through; it sank into the cork.

'Now pull the thread through,' Stella instructed.

She did. That part looked almost worse than the needle, the white line of thread turned pink. Jenny tied it and snipped it off.

'Now I gotta remember to keep turning it, so's the thread don't grow into my skin,' Stella said proudly. 'I'll be ready for the earrings come Friday.'

'You better not let the Reverend see,' Jenny cautioned.

'Naw, he won't. With my hair down, the thread ain't even noticeable.' And Stella turned to make sure.

'Now for the second one. Get 'em even, Jenny.' She swivelled her head back and forth, gauging the distance. With a firmer hand Jenny plunged the needle through and it was done. Stella now had pierced ears.

'You know that stupid Karen? Sally tried doing her ears, and that stoop fainted dead away. Imagine that, just hit the floor – and now she's only got one ear done.'

Stella stood up, tweaked at the threads, turning, admiring herself in the mirror. 'Thank you, honey.'

'Girls! Girls!' Momma's voice was calling up the stairs. 'Truck's here – we got potatoes.'

Among the delivery men Jenny spotted him. Rodney. Stella went back and forth about her work, but under the maple tree in the side yard Jenny saw them meet. Stella leaned towards him and rapid speech seemed to flow between them.

It was something about their posture, the movement of their heads, that gave them away. Jenny hoped Momma or the Reverend weren't looking, for you could see without knowing how there was an intimacy between them.

She didn't really know if it was anger, jealousy or her fear of Stella getting caught that made her call out. Stella looked towards Jenny, her face a tight mask of anger that softened, and finally smiled. Jenny saw the gentle touch as their fingers reached out to brush each other before Stella walked slowly away, her hips swinging deliberately, knowing he was watching.

The girls bent down together and carried a heavy basket to the kitchen.

'He wants to go out with you,' Stella whispered.

'Who?'

'That smartass, the good-looking one with the blue eyes.

45

Rodney knows him from the teamsters – they're both in the same local at the union hall.'

Jenny felt a thrill. She felt feverish She couldn't admit it even to herself, but she had thought about him once or twice, relived his comments, all that talk about Jeannie with the light brown hair.

Momma saw them tugging at the heavy bushels. She looked up at the sun and wiped sweat from her brow. 'Hot, it's too hot today. Jenny, you're lookin' peaked – go in and have some cold lemonade. Sam can finish up here.'

Relieved, they went inside where the shaded room felt cool and the fans above whirred slowly, shifting the air.

The lemonade was cooler yet. They sat at the table and Jenny nervously picked at a spot that was peeling on the oilcloth as Stella told her all about him, at least all she knew.

'Rodney said his name's Bobby Lee Antree, and his nickname's Bubba. He's divorced, got one kid. His ex-wife's a tramp, he threw her out. He's got a big ole house a little ways out, with a few acres. He drives long distance sometimes, makes good money, but I'm thinking he's fast track. I know his type – I don't think you could handle a guy like that, Jenny.'

She felt her anger flare, which was odd because she didn't feel mad at Stella very often.

'And you *could* handle a guy like that?' she blurted out.

Stella saw the spot of colour in Jenny's cheeks and realized she'd upset her. 'I'm sorry, honey, I didn't mean nothing. It's just—' she paused and struggled for the right words. 'It's just you only been to a couple movies with that little Jimmy what's-his-name and I bet he didn't even try anything.'

'Yes, he did,' Jenny lied. 'We necked all through the movies and he tried puttin' his hand on my—'

Stella's laughter stopped her as she spluttered, 'He couldn'ta got much of a handful.'

In that minute Jenny hated her sister. 'I'd like to go out

46

with this Bobby Lee or Bubba, whatever his name is,' she said firmly.

Stella stopped laughing and looked at her sister as if seeing her for the first time.

'Hey, little sister, I'm sorry, honest. You know, you're really pretty, almost beautiful,' she said. 'I guess it couldn't hurt if we doubled, then at least you wouldn't be alone with him.'

Her anger vanished as quickly as it had come. 'No, Stella, I was just mad. I couldn't really do it. I wouldn't know what to say or do.'

The refusal seemed to make Stella more determined. 'We can't just let you sit at home here. No, you're right – it's time you learned how to play with the big boys. I'll teach you.'

They didn't talk about it again, but Stella called Rodney and made the arrangements. It was for Saturday night and they planned on going to a drive-in movie.

'I asked Rodney to let Bobby Lee drive, so that way you'll be in the front seat. It's not as dangerous there. A guy can't do as much that way. I'll be able to keep an eye on you. If you get in too deep, give me a signal,' Stella said as she wiggled into a tank top.

In the dim light from the street lamp, she turned Jenny around. 'Want a dab of this? It's Gardenia perfume. Stole it from the dime store today.'

'No.' Jenny struggled out of her grasp. 'I don't even feel like myself now,' she said as she pulled the drawstring blouse up onto her shoulders. The low neck was bothering her.

At the last minute Stella insisted. She wadded them up into a ball, and pushed the socks into Jenny's bra.

'No, Stella, I can't do this.'

'He'll never know it. Makes you look a lot older.'

It was the sharp toot of a horn that allowed the socks to remain there as Stella hissed, 'I told him never to do that,' and she pulled Jenny along into the dark hallway. One by one, slowly they crept down the steps and paused for a minute, for the third one from the bottom always squeaked.

The house was quiet. They went through the darkened kitchen out into the summer night.

The car was parked halfway down the block, and when the door opened the overhead light went on and Jenny saw him again. His hair shone almost black, his tanned face was as handsome as she remembered, and his mouth was melted into a welcoming smile. She took the hand he offered and got in.

'Hi, Jeannie,' he said.

'Hi,' she answered, her voice breaking with nervousness.

He drove casually, with one arm resting on his door. With the other hand he juggled a beer, putting it between his legs when he shifted gear. A cigarette dangled from his lips. Once he took it out of his mouth and offered it to her. She shook her head no, and leaned back listening to the radio.

She felt unreal. He seemed so foreign. At the Mission she was used to seeing men who were down and out, shuffling along in a common sort of shame. It was his confidence that intimidated her the most.

From the refreshment stand he bought hot dogs, popcorn and soda. During the first picture, a comedy, they all laughed a lot. Jenny wasn't even sure what the picture was about.

At intermission Stella said, 'Ladies' room, excuse us,' and Jenny was surprised to see Stella's lipstick was smeared.

'How's it going?' she asked.

'I'm scared. I don't know what to do,' Jenny confessed.

'It's okay, honey, honest. Next picture is a love story. He'll get cozy, you'll see – and when he kisses, let your mouth open a little.'

'You mean French kissing?'

'Yeah. It's okay, it don't hurt nothing and it really heats guys up. That's good, just don't let him get too fresh.'

Jenny tugged at her top.

'Leave 'em in, it looks good.'

Stella was right. During the next picture he whispered, 'Come on over, little girl. I don't bite,' and his hand coaxed her across the seat; slowly she felt his arm snake across her shoulder leading her closer. The smell of his shaving soap was clear and pleasant, and the tendrils of Jenny's hair were electric as they brushed his face. She felt his warm breath against her ear, and goose bumps rose on her neck and arms.

She stayed still, afraid to move, and his warm, steady breath teased her ear for a time. When finally his other hand reached under her chin and turned her face toward his, his lips were warm and salty from the beer. They touched hers softly, moving gently back and forth. Jenny was glad she remembered, for when his tongue sought hers, her lips were slack and welcoming, and she felt a current so electric she shivered in his arms.

It was a deep, lasting kiss, and she felt cheated when it was over. A spot in her stomach felt warm and empty at the same time.

In anticipation, she waited, anxious to feel it again, those lips, that tongue that created such a light unreal feeling within her, as if her body were only made of sensation. Is this what Stella feels? she wondered.

Sitting rigid as a stone, her hand fell asleep, but he did not turn her face towards him again, his lips did not reach out for hers. It was just the gentle wind of his breath on her neck, teasing her until the picture was over.

'Jesus it's hot,' he muttered as he turned on the motor. 'Anyone for Forest Park?'

'Yeah, Forest Park sounds good,' Rodney answered from the back seat, and as before, Bobby Lee leaned against his door, kept time with his fingers tapping to the radio, and they drove through the summer night.

They parked by the fountain, where the lights changed colour and painted the couples lying on the grass in different shades of red, green, blue, purple and orange.

'Some people bring their blankets and sleep out here,' Bobby Lee said as he held her hand and led her away from the others, up the hill, near a grove of trees.

Jenny looked back, trying to see Stella. In the car it was different; alone in the dark on the hillside she felt afraid, not only of him but of herself. She could see Rodney and Stella veer off to sit down near a bank of fir trees; they weren't too far away. 'Here, sit,' he patted a spot. 'Grass's just been cut, it's soft, smells nice.'

Jenny sat awkwardly and pulled her skirt tight around her legs.

He offered a small bottle. 'Wanna sip?' She shook her head no. 'Go on – one little nip can't hurt.'

Rather than argue, she put the bottle to her lips. The sharp taste of whisky made her gasp. She handed it back; he took a long pull on the bottle. Then he stretched out on the grass, his hands beneath his head. 'Lookit all those stars up there.'

Jenny looked up into the sky, where the stars twinkled and flickered, and she began to relax.

'This is nothing,' he exclaimed. 'Why, when I drive through Arizona or New Mexico there's thousands of stars in an ink-black sky. It's beautiful, really beautiful.'

Suddenly Bobby Lee sat up on one elbow. 'Not half as beautiful as you are, though, little girl.'

'Thank you,' she managed to say, but she felt funny all over, him calling her beautiful.

'You don't have to thank me for saying the truth.' And his eyes seemed to gleam. 'Come here, little girl,' he whispered. Timidly, she moved a little closer.

He reached up to her shoulders and drew her down to his lips, and as before, his tongue seeking hers was pure magic, for time seemed to pause. Somehow she felt the tickle of the grass beneath her. Now he was looking down at her, tenderly brushing her hair back, kissing her eyelids, her cheeks, then she felt the moistness of his tongue caressing her ear.

It was when he reached for them that the moment

dissolved. 'Shit!' He sat up and pulled one out. 'Socks. I hate this kinda crap'

Embarrassed, Jenny tugged at her blouse. 'It was Stella's idea,' she said lamely.

Bobby Lee clutched his knees, and she couldn't see his face, but she could feel his anger.

'Prick-teaser, ball-buster, that's what she is. I've known that kind of girl before.'

'That's my sister! She's not what you said. She's really nice and I won't have you saying those kinda things about her. I want to go home.'

He sighed, searched for his winning smile, then said, 'I apologize. I didn't mean it, it's just I don't like tricks. I liked you just the way you were.' He turned toward her. 'I can see it now, the way you looked the first time I saw you, with that little white sun-dress and those cute sandals. If I'd wanted a girl with big tits I would've found one.'

'I want to go home,' Jenny repeated.

'Don't be mad at me, little girl. I like you, I really like you.' His hand brushed her hair. 'I bet you had pigtails when you were little.'

Charmed, Jenny confessed, 'I did.'

'Don't be mad at your Bubba.'

'I'm not,' she said softly, but his words made her feel funny, him saying, 'Your Bubba,' as if he belonged to her.

He scooted over, and again they kissed, his lips taking her to another place, where she felt apart and separate from her real self. His Jeannie was someone different from Jenny.

Before she realized it, his hand slid down and stroked the small mound of her breast; easily the peasant blouse gave, and his tongue caressed her firm nipple.

His touch created currents within her body, and she could not even think. She lay back, open and vulnerable until his hand, smooth as glass, slid up her skirt, and with a jolt she felt his caress.

'*No!*' She pushed him away roughly. 'No, stop. I can't. I won't.' She felt like crying in her helplessness.

'It's okay. I'm not mad,' he reassured her. 'It's just that you're so beautiful it's hard to keep my hands off you.'

Jenny sat up and smoothed her skirt around her legs and held on tightly.

'Have you let anybody do that before?' he asked.

'What?'

'You know – kiss your titties.'

'No, no. Never. I never let you either, you just did it.'

'Have you let anybody do the other before?'

'What?'

'You know, rub your pussy.'

With that, she began to cry. 'I never let you do that either, you just did it.'

'That's okay. I just asked—'

'I want to go home now,' and she stood up and loudly called, 'Stella! Stella!' and ran down the hill.

The other couples looked up, only disturbed for a minute, and went back to their lovemaking.

In bed in the dark, Stella asked, 'Did he try to touch your tits?'

''Course not,' Jenny muttered.

'Did he try touching you down there?'

'No – I told you.'

'Good,' she said, 'you gotta string 'em along. One little bit at a time, but you stop before going all the way. 'Member Maw's advice. She told me a long time ago, no man's buying any cows if they can get free milk!'

'That's stupid.'

'No, it's true. Guys are like that, they never want for too long what they can have.'

'Why?'

'I don't know,' Stella said truthfully. 'I guess 'cause they're different from us.' She sighed. 'Was he a good kisser?'

'Uh huh.'

'Did you like it?'

'It was okay.'

Stella sat up in bed and began tickling her sister. 'Jesus, I could shake you till your teeth rattle and you still wouldn't tell me nothing. You've always been like that, your mouth closed tighter than a zipper.'

They laughed and wrestled and finally fell back on the pillows, exhausted.

In the dim light a moth fluttered up towards the ceiling, his silvery wings beating slowly as he circled the map of Africa. It came to Stella, that memory.

'Remember what Maw told us about angels when we was real little?' she said, her voice tender as warm butter.

'No.'

In the dark her fingers reached out to search the planes of Jenny's face. She stopped and traced the indentation above her lips.

'There,' she said. 'Momma said when a baby is born an angel comes down and puts her finger right there so we don't tell. Jenny, on you the angel must have pressed extra hard.'

CHAPTER 5

During art class Jenny found herself doodling his name on the bottom of the page: *Bobby Lee, Bobby Lee, Bobby Lee*. She felt funny about what she had written in the diary. Heaven help her if Stella somehow read it.

She gave the truth to those pages. Yes, she loved his touch; just thinking about it made her close her legs tight. She didn't know what these feelings meant. Was she a bad girl? She hadn't wanted him to stop. The magic of his hands was like velvet, the feel of his lips, his breath in her ear, all produced that wonderful empty feeling in her stomach.

'It's lovely.' The voice behind her made her start.

'Thank you, Mrs Dunn,' she stammered, trying to cover the names on the page.

The teacher reached over and picked up the sketch. 'You have a definite flair for design. Have you thought about what you'll do later, is there a chance you'd be continuing your education?'

'I thought about nursing,' she lied. She hadn't thought about anything but him for days.

Mrs Dunn dropped the paper back onto the desk. 'A worthy profession, your parents should be pleased. What university do you have in mind?'

Jenny blushed, knowing it was a lie. 'None, really, Mrs Dunn. I haven't even asked my mother.'

'There are scholarships, you know, and you have excellent grades. If you like, next year, closer to graduation, I could show you how to fill out the papers to apply.'

'Why, thank you.'

She reached over Jenny's shoulder, fingered the sketch and smiled about the tell-tale name. Ignoring it, she said, 'This necklace and earrings look so real, I could almost lift them off the page. You made them so realistic they seem to exist.'

'Oh, they do, Mrs Dunn. They're real.'

'They are?'

'Yes, ma'am. I really made this set out of beads, for my sister's wedding. It was kinda fun drawing them now from memory.'

'I remember your sister. Stella dropped out, was it last year?'

'Yes, ma'am.'

'Well, give her my congratulations.'

'I will.'

She looked at Jenny carefully, almost with a wistful sadness, for she knew as well as Jenny did that there would be no further schooling.

'You have real talent for design, Jenny. I remember your other papers. Sometimes if you want something bad enough you can find a way.'

'Yes, ma'am,' Jenny said, and began to shade the drawing, for she felt uncomfortable with that kind of talk. Mrs Dunn had no idea what it was like, across 14th Street at the Mission. Dreams of being an artist of some kind were pure nonsense. Jenny never even thought about it any more. The closest she had ever come to daydreaming was her ambition to become a nurse, and now all she dreamed about was him.

On her way home, she took a detour to stop by the grill where Stella was working part-time.

'Hi, baby sister, what brings you this way?' Stella leaned closer and whispered, 'Order what you want. Mrs Meyer ain't here today.'

'No, I just thought maybe a Coke,' and Jenny reached into her pocket for a dime.

Stella yelled something to the cook through the hatch,

56

and in a few minutes a great big cheeseburger with a plate of fries was set before Jenny. 'Root beer float, was it?'

'No, Stella. I only have a dime,' Jenny hissed.

Stella cracked her gum, bustled about teasing the male customers, and shortly she set the big frosty glass in front of her sister.

Jenny's heart raced; she felt like a criminal. If Mrs Meyer walked in now she couldn't pay for any of it.

'Cover for me, Sally. I'm taking my break now.' And Stella moved the generous plate and glass from the counter over to the booth. She took the dime and put it in the jukebox, saying, 'I love this song,' and a man's voice began singing the sad lyrics to 'Honey'.

'What's up?' she finally asked. 'Go on and eat. It's good food, not like that rotten stuff we get at the Mission.'

'Nothing,' Jenny answered between bites. Stella was right, the food was wonderful.

'I know you better than that. Something's wrong, isn't it?'

'No,' and in a spurt of bravado Jenny pushed the sketch towards her.

'Hey, it's my necklace and earrings – the ones I'm wearing for the wedding.' Stella wondered why the bottom of the page was torn off.

'Yeah. I drew it from memory in art class. Do you think it's good – the drawing, I mean?'

'Sure, honey,' Stella said. 'You always could draw. Why, when you were little you were the best colourer I ever saw. You never went over the lines in them colouring books.'

Jenny looked down at her hands and picked at a hangnail. No one ever understood her. Suddenly she felt foolish.

After an awkward silence Stella asked, 'You stopped by to show me this?'

'Well, yes and no. Mrs Dunn – you remember her, English and art – she said I had a real flair, no, she said I had a real *talent* for design.'

'I agree.' Stella brightened. 'Why look so sad about it?'

'It's just that she asked about after graduation – was I going to continue my education?'

'You mean about the nursing?'

'No, she talked about art and design.'

Suddenly Stella looked so old, so much older than her seventeen years, and Jenny saw the sadness that her sister usually hid.

'Those teachers have no damned business talking like that, making a girl have dreams that ain't never gonna come true. No, baby sister, them fancy colleges and art schools are for girls with rich parents. The only way outta that Mission is with a ring on the third finger of your left hand.'

Jenny's eyes misted up.

'Finish them French fries. That nigger cook will only put 'em on somebody else's plate if you don't,' Stella warned.

Jenny looked down at the plate, her appetite gone, but one by one she dipped the fries in the ketchup and finished them.

It started on her way home. She stopped at the corner, looked up at the spires at St Rose's and with a chill realized that someone had designed it. That church – it had started as a thought, an idea in someone's mind.

At home Momma scolded, 'You're late, start shelling them peas. Reverend's expecting another big crowd tonight.'

She worked as fast as she could, but her mind was a muddle. Bobby Lee, design . . . everywhere she looked she saw the reality of design. The faded plates she set out still had the remnants of painted flowers, some with a thin gold border. She felt excited, as if she were the only one in the world who understood the significance of this new knowledge.

Stella came into the kitchen before the service was started, and pitched in with the preparations. 'Four more days, and I won't be waitin' on these scumbags.'

'Some of them can't help it.' Jenny defended the

58

nameless people who came every night to hear the Reverend, and sit down and partake of free food.

'Yeah – and some of 'em can,' Stella retorted.

Later, in bed, Stella still carried on about the Mission. 'I hate this place, the smell of sweat, half-rotten food, cheap clothes that belonged to someone else. I'm gonna have everything new, brand new. Nobody's tits will ever have been in *my* new bras before.'

'Ssh, ssh.'

'No, Jenny. I feel so low when I have to pick through the ragbags, and get one of them stretched-out, awful pink bras and put it on. My skin's fresh and new and Momma shouldn't have made us come to this dump. I hate it, I hate her. I'll get you outta here too,' she promised.

'Ssh, it's all right. Like you said, it's only four more days.'

Stella hugged her sister in the dark. 'Yeah, four more days,' and they slept.

When she awoke and looked about her, the bedroom had already assumed an atmosphere of loneliness that Jenny knew would settle in the empty corners that Stella would leave behind. Perfume, make-up, curlers – an endless array of her things were already packed and shoved under the bed in the unlikely event that Momma would come in the room. Being Sunday, the girls had no chores so they lay in bed, too lazy to even go downstairs for toast.

Stella's face was screwed up into a frown as she composed the farewell note.

She bit the tip of the pencil, concentrated – hesitated. 'Oh Jenny, you write it. I'm no good at this sort of thing.'

'Me? I can't write your note. I don't know how you feel, or what you want to say.'

'"Adios", that's all I really want to say.'

Jenny propped herself on one elbow and studied her sister. Without her make-up, Stella's face seemed very young. She was actually plain, someone who could have slipped by unnoticed, if it wasn't for her nervous energy; it lit up her face and her ability to create herself, curls, lashes, colour. She surrounded herself until you believed she was part of that vibrant spectrum. Jenny realized for the first time that they didn't know each other at all.

Now, studying her half-finished note, Stella felt uncertain. A flicker of fear showed in her hazel eyes.

'Why *are* you running away?' Jenny asked urgently. 'Momma won't care that you're getting married. You're almost eighteen, after all.'

'It's because I wouldn't want Rodney in here. I wouldn't want him to see the stained walls, smell the smells. Why, I look awful in this dump! Most of all, can you imagine that little toad Reverend Roy marrying us in that pretend church? Oh Jenny, it gives me the creeps just thinking of it. No, the Justice of the Peace sounds real good to me.' Stella sighed. 'That's why.'

She folded the note, wrote *Mom* on top. Later on, when she was in the bathroom, Jenny peeked. She had written:

Mom,
 I'm off to Arkansas. I'm getting married.
           Stella.

Jenny picked up a pen; the ink in it was blue. She searched the room until she found one with black ink and in front of *Mom* she wrote *Dear* and after *Stella* she wrote *P.S. I love you*. She folded the note and put it back on the dresser where Stella had left it. It could do no harm to leave a kindness, and somewhere down deep she knew Stella meant the words she had written.

Somehow Jenny couldn't bear to stay surrounded by the walls that she knew would soon hear her tears and feel her loneliness. She left Stella looking in drawers, behind pictures for notes or things she might have hidden there.

Jenny took the precious book, grabbed a peach from the kitchen and went to the picnic table to read – not *read* exactly, for it was a thesaurus, but she practised saying the words out loud. She was only on page nineteen and she wanted to know all the words and what they meant.

To the west, a derelict building shaded the yard. Cornflowers grew in abundance, milkweed sprang up between the cracks in the brick sidewalk, and Jenny wondered who in the world decided which plants were weeds and which were flowers. To this day when she thinks of the Mission she can almost smell the summer's newly cut grass and weeds, and the air pungent with the scent of milkweed.

Looking down again she began reading, words ... meanings ... She felt rather than saw her coming. A soft oath, her wrenched ankle, and Stella limped toward her across the grass. Jenny was afraid of the utter terror in her sister's face. Clear as a picture before her, she saw the street lamp, with no car parked beneath it, and Stella sitting on the suitcase staring out through the latticework of lace curtain, watching, waiting for the car that would never come.

Stella did not miss it; she knew that blank look on her sister's face. She sat down on the grass, rubbing her ankle, playing with the broken strap of her shoe. 'He's not coming, is he?' she said, her voice full of uncertainty and shame.

'I don't know.' Jenny left the book, its pages fluttering back and forth in the soft wind, and she sat down beside Stella in the fragrant grass.

'You know,' Stella accused. 'You know.'

Stealthily Jenny studied her sister's body. Her waist – was it thicker? She felt ashamed of her suspicious thoughts, but Jenny's mind was full of novels, tragedies, unmentionable cruelties perpetrated on the women in those stories ... women who had succumbed.

'It's his alternator – the car ain't running,' Stella said defensively. 'At least, that's what he said on the phone.'

Jenny touched her hand, and was surprised that it trembled so. She was silent despite all the questions she wanted to ask, running like small mice through her mind. And she felt ashamed of her inner relief – *Stella isn't leaving – she isn't going* – but the feeling soon passed and she reconsidered. 'No, not like this,' Jenny thought, not this Stella before her, unmasked and plain, with only broken dreams shimmering in her eyes. 'I don't need her company that much.'

'I'm calling him back later,' Stella stated, her flat voice that betrayed her belief that she had already lost the game.

'Yes,' Jenny said, as if her agreement would make things better.

Stella went back to the house to lie in bed and stare at the stain they had agreed years ago was just like a map of Africa.

Jenny looked up into the blue summer sky, where only one small cloud skittered in the wind. She imagined it was a kite that would take her message up to Him.

'Dear God, please, *please* let her have this thing she wants so badly, this wedding. I won't ask anything for myself.'

If Jenny had known what price this answered prayer carried, she would never have voiced it.

The sisters didn't or couldn't talk, so Jenny went to bed worried and tired at nine o'clock Deep in sleep, several hours later she felt the familiar tug: 'Jenny! Jenny, wake up!'

Rubbing her eyes she sat up, and saw by the door the silhouette of the waiting suitcases.

'What – are you going tonight?' Somewhere in the night, two tomcats yowled at each other.

Jenny felt her sister's breath hot and anxious against her ear. 'Plans have changed, you've gotta help me.'

Sensing urgency and fully awake now, Jenny said in a whisper, 'Sure, I'll do anything, you know that.'

'I need you to go with me.'

'Go with you – why?'

'Ssh,' Stella warned. The sounds of angry felines interrupted the night. 'Rodney's car – I told you it's not running. Bobby said he'd drive and be our witness, but he wants you to come, too.'

Jenny was speechless. Her vision, that kaleidoscope that brought her snippets of things to come, was wrong. Rodney *was* coming for Stella, after all.

'But Momma—' Jenny hedged.

'I'll fix the note, I'll tell her.'

'But, but . . .' Jenny stuttered, not really knowing how to protest.

'They'll give you shit when you get back, but Momma knows whenever we get into trouble I'm always to blame.'

Stella was right, it had always been that way.

'Hurry, Jenny. You gotta come!'

'You mean right now?'

'Yeah, they're waiting down the street. It's two o'clock. We'll be in Piggott by morning, and by noon I'll be Mrs Rodney Miller.' And Stella hugged herself with the promise of that statement.

Jenny reached in the closet, pulled out a dress, felt on the floor and found her sandals.

By the window, aided by the bluish streetlight, Stella added words to her note: '*Jenny is going with me, I'll bring her back.*' She didn't comment on the earlier additions to the note.

Safe on the dark street carrying two small suitcases, they went towards the corner and the parked car.

For a moment Jenny felt a surge of panic, but when the door opened the interior light bathed him in a soft yellow glow. He was smiling that wonderful smile and she felt weak when she heard his smooth voice greet her.

'Hi, Jeannie.'

'Why'd you bring it?' they heard Rodney complaining. 'He'll just throw up – it's a long ride.'

'She wouldn't dare,' Stella said as she petted the small grey kitten and climbed into the back seat of the car.

That night was a half-finished puzzle; pieces of it are still missing, and although they are no longer important, Jenny is certain they will never be found now.

It was a collage of different things – sights, smells, touch, sounds – that come back to her at times with the clarity of second sight. Dark trees rushing past, the throb of Nat King Cole on the radio, the weak yellow light of the headlights pulling them down narrow twisting roads, the oasis of the filling station with two pumps and the angry owner in a robe filling up the starving gas tank, his reluctant kindness of paper towels to clean up the carpets where the dizzy kitten had deposited her undigested dinner. It was champagne corks popping, toasting a wedding that had not yet occurred.

It was Bobby Lee driving fast and popping bennies to stay awake, when the car stopped by a dark road, where crickets chirped so loud it hurt their ears. The drivers switched and it was in that pause when Bobby Lee lit them – two small, crooked cigarettes, and the scent of burnt orange peels hung in the air.

Stella giggled as she took a drag. 'Hold it – keep it in,' Rodney advised.

In the dark car, in the midnight blue night, it seemed okay for Jenny to put the rough cigarette between her lips, to 'hold it in tight' and through the burning, let peace spread a stain of peaceful pink, with cool sips of champagne to dampen down her burning lungs.

The motion of the car swaying, her ears tickling as the vibration of the radio echoed, the taste of his lips, her body a bed of seedlings coming alive under his touch . . . She lay down in the back seat and above his head saw the shadow of speeding trees, taking her to a magic place.

It was when he said it, against her ear, damp words; 'That's good, little Jeannie – your pussy's real tight.'

It was then she realized what it was, that sensation of electricity coursing pleasantly through her body. She had broken the cardinal rule, the one Stella had told her about: *Never, never, EVER let them get their fingers in your pants . . .*

CHAPTER 6

Without any problem they found the preacher's house, which sat on the outskirts of Piggott. The small frame house was a neat affair, painted pristine white with bright green shutters and a copper weather vane that twirled slowly back and forth as the morning breeze changed its mind. A white picket fence and closed gate guarded the trim grass, and rows of daisies bordered the walk to the wide porch. Right above the swing, tacked neatly, was the sign:

JUSTICE OF THE PEACE. NO APPOINTMENT NECESSARY.

'Sally was right,' Stella exclaimed happily.

'No appointment necessary,' Rodney commented, looking towards the sign in the early morning gloom. 'It's pretty early, hon.'

Stella froze. That stray thought of cold feet on Rodney's part made her come out with an uneasy laugh. 'Let's open the last bottle of champagne then,' she suggested eagerly.

'Can you get it? Us guys gotta find some bushes,' Rodney answered, as both men climbed out of the car. They crossed the road and headed towards a grove of trees.

'Do I look all right?' Stella asked.

Jenny, half-asleep and still dizzy, sat up and tried to see her sister, but only caught a glance in the small rearview mirror as Stella liberally applied more lipstick.

'Turn around so I can see.'

Stella started to turn but then burst out almost in tears. 'I don't have it.'

'What?' Jenny asked.

'You know, something old, something new, something borrowed, something blue. Bessie always said it was real bad luck at a wedding to miss any part of it. I don't have anything blue! My dress is new, I borrowed your slip, and my shoes are old, but I don't have a goddamn thing that's blue. Bessie swore by it,' Stella whined.

'Hush, hush, we'll think of something,' Jenny assured her.

Stella tilted the champagne bottle and took a long swig; bubbles burst on the top of her nose. She handed the bottle to Jenny, who raised it and because she was so thirsty, kept drinking.

'Whoah, honey, that's enough,' Stella warned. 'What am I gonna do?' she wailed.

'I know! I know!' Jenny yelled, totally unlike herself, as she was still tipsy. 'Your mascara – it's blue.'

'Oh, that's right, it is. You saved my life, honey. No, you saved my marriage,' and Stella began pawing through the large purse to find it.

Walking back, Rodney said drunkenly to Bobby Lee, 'Let's make it a double. That's a sweet little girl you got there. You'd be getting a cherry, that's for sure.'

Bobby Lee stopped in the road. 'No sirree. I tried this marriage crap once and got myself a real bitch. No, I've been there.'

'Chicken, are ya?'

'Hey, ain't nobody ever called me chicken.'

They resumed walking unsteadily, leaning into each other.

'Just think of it, Bobby Lee. That's sweet meat you got there. It'd be sitting at home waiting for you. You could have it every night – two, three times. That's sweet meat all right, cherry guaranteed.'

'Hell, next to driving ninety miles an hour on some dark

road, cherry-bustin's what I like best. You're right, that little gal's got a real tight little pussy.'

Rodney stopped again in the road. 'How'd you know?'

'You don't think I had her laying down in the back seat for nothin'.'

Both men roared with laughter. It was the sight of Jenny lying across the seat, so young and pretty in the yellow dress, and her snow-white cotton pants peeking out that brought back to Bobby Lee a vivid memory of his mother's canary, so beautiful in that small wicker cage. He could almost see her, this girl-child, in his big house with the bars on all the windows, all sweetness and innocence, *all his*. As Rodney pointed out, he could have it – anyway, any time.

They passed the bottle between them.

A noisy rooster nearby announced the morning and the sun rose, a red, fierce ball of fire in the east.

'Do it, man. Here's a hundred sez you're chicken,' Rodney urged.

Bobby Lee hitched up his trousers and repeated drunkenly, 'Nobody ever 'cused me of being chicken.'

The men stood outside the car while Stella redid her make-up and straightened her wedding outfit as best she could. The long dangling earrings looked silly in the new morning, a strange contrast with her wrinkled satin dress.

'I shoulda had a corsage,' she complained to no one in particular.

Bobby Lee reached for the last of the champagne and took a long swig. Then he stuck his head in the window and smiled crookedly. 'How 'bout it? Wanna be my child bride, Baby Doll?'

The air filled with peals of Stella's drunken laughter. 'Hot damn – we're gonna have a double weddin'.'

Reaching in the window, she squeezed Jenny's hand so hard it hurt. Leaning in, she pretended to kiss her cheek, but whispered in her ear: 'Say yes, Jenny. It's happening – a miracle. We'll both be outta there, that goddamn Mission.'

Bobby lounged against the window looking intensely at

Jenny. To her, his face seemed to waver back and forth, but his blue eyes held hers steady. ' "Yes" is just one little word,' he said, letting the sentence hang. 'I mean it.'

Jenny felt the pinch as Stella reached for the soft part of her arm. 'Ouch!'

'That didn't sound like yes,' and he bent his head into the window and his lips met hers, with the gentlest of kisses. 'One little word,' he repeated. 'I want you to be my Baby Doll bride.'

It was the champagne, the unreality of the moment, or the words repeated over and over by Stella in the past that they had to get out of the Mission, or the thought of going back alone . . . It could have been any one of these or all of them, for like an unknown being Jenny heard herself whisper, 'Yes.'

On wobbly legs she got out of the car and breathed in the pure country air. She felt dizzy still, and Bobby Lee fussed over her, combing her hair, smoothing her dress. Suddenly he flopped down on the ground and took off his shoes. Surprised, they all laughed, for he took off his socks, balled 'em up, and carefully placed one in each side of Jenny's bra.

'Fix her up,' he directed Stella. 'She's gotta look older, she's gotta look eighteen.'

Stella fumbled in her bag, selected the brightest red lipstick, and smeared it heavily on Jenny's lips. She brushed rouge on her cheeks. 'Hold still, dammit, and stop blinking,' she ordered as she tried putting on some mascara.

Their preparations halted as an old woman opened the door, shook out a dust mop and yelled, 'Come on, if you're comin'. Preacher's wantin' his breakfast.'

Jenny felt Bobby Lee's arm holding hers as unsteadily they walked towards the small house.

Inside the tidy parlour was an organ, a Bible, and several high-backed chairs that were covered in crocheted doilies.

The old lady briskly played a wedding march, and they heard the jumble of hurried words, then Stella was kissing her brand new husband. Jenny was next. His firm hand held hers, and she couldn't seem to look anywhere but at the preacher's night-shirt hastily tucked into his trousers, and again there was a stream of meaningless words that made her this stranger's wife.

She looked down at the man's heavy ring that swirled around on her slender finger and threatened to drop. The kiss that sealed their marriage was different from before; it was hard, relentless – impatient for something waiting in the future.

As they left, leaning off the porch the old woman threw a scanty handful of rice, and then they heard the preacher ordering what he wanted for breakfast.

Still half-drunk, they found a diner, and suddenly silent they ate their eggs, bacon and toast – each of them caught in their own private thoughts. 'This calls for a goddamn celebration,' Rodney boomed, and before they found the motel they had bought a couple of bottles of bourbon and some beer.

The motel was clean and plain. The rooms had only a dresser, a double bed, one chair and a radio that played when you fed it nickels.

'I need a shower,' Bobby Lee said.

When Jenny heard the water running, she took the bottle of bourbon off the night-stand, closed her eyes, and drank. The whisky was harsh and it burned, but she kept drinking.

Better, she felt better, for the warmth spread, and chased her fear away. She was so tired now. She lay back on the bed, and the radio Bobby Lee had stuffed with nickels played a love song. She drifted down, down into the whirlpool like when she had her tonsils out and smelled the ether.

Sometime later, she woke to the sound of his regular snoring. The room was dark now; against the shade a red glow came and went as the *Vacancies* sign out front flickered on and off.

She was cold. Jenny reached down and touched her shivering flesh, surprised that she was naked. She sat up, and the room spun. Sick, God how sick that whisky made her feel. Unsteadily she stood and made her way to the bathroom.

Under the harsh neon light her face was grey and pinched. Her body ached, her breast throbbed with a pain. She gasped as she looked down and saw blood slowly trickling down her legs.

They must have done it, and she didn't even remember.

She ran the water and sank down into the warm bath. She closed her eyes, and tried remembering. She had no recollection of kisses or caresses, but down there she felt so sore that it must have happened. She lay there until the water cooled, and when he opened the door she automatically covered her breasts with the wash-cloth.

He knelt down. 'No, Baby Doll, you can't do that any more. You're my wife now. You belong to me.'

He kissed her and it was tender and she felt the fear draining away even when he took the wash-cloth and slowly ran his finger over her nipples. 'I like 'em. They're like little pink flowers, and they're all mine.'

He stood up. 'I'll get you an Alka Seltzer,' he said and returned with the sizzling glass. 'Drink it all up – you'll feel better,' he promised.

On the way home Rodney teased, 'Damn, if this was my car, I'd teach you to drive right now, Stella, I swear. It's not fair; I did all the work, you just laid there. I'm so tired.'

In the back seat, Jenny lay against Bobby Lee, and heard the regular beat of his heart. She felt afraid and hopeful at the same time.

In a serious voice he asked her, 'Think your mom will annul it?'

'No.' Stella turned and answered for her. 'Not if she's ruined, she wouldn't do that. Hell, Maw got married when she was sixteen. Hey, Rodney, next town let's look for a Western Union office. We've gotta send her a telegram.'

Stella looked back at Jenny, her face beaming with happiness. 'Now Jenny, don't write her or nothing. We gotta let some time go by. Just the telegram so she'll know we're okay.'

Jenny nodded in agreement. She couldn't face her mother right now anyway, for she felt a sense of shame. In one night she had smoked marijuana, got drunk and married a stranger. It wasn't like her, but as Stella said, any time they got into trouble it was Stella's fault. Funny to think of it that way – 'got into trouble'. Getting married shouldn't be thought of in those terms.

'You don't have any clothes. I could lend you some of mine,' Stella offered.

'No.' Bobby Lee spoke up sharply. 'I'll buy her what she needs.'

At the next truck stop, they pulled in to eat dinner. When the girls went to the ladies' room, Stella giggled and hugged her sister. 'We did it! God, Jenny, we did it, got ourselves married. And you even found yourself a husband that owns a house. Rodney says it's real nice.'

She turned to the mirror. For an instant, a small flicker of jealousy flashed across her face. 'Rodney's only got an apartment for now but he promised to put in the papers for the G.I. loan, comes Monday.'

'That's great.'

'How was it?' Stella asked, studying Jenny's face closely.

'Oh, you know. Okay, I guess.'

'When did you start lying through your teeth, little sister? It wasn't good – it hurt. I know. I even did, and I was loosened up a little, for the last month or so, I been letting Rodney put his finger in. Last week he did two, but I never went all the way, just finger-fucking, that's as far as I let him go.'

In spite of herself, Jenny blushed furiously.

'You're such a baby,' Stella teased. 'Who would have thought that Bobby Lee and you would have got hitched?' She went back to brushing her hair vigorously. 'Don't worry, it'll get better. Rodney sez when I'm broke in, I'll learn to love it,' she giggled. 'Broke in, sounds like a horse.'

They went back to the car. It was Bobby Lee's turn to drive. He punched it, drove a little over the speed limit, but they weren't stopped.

They were all tired, hung over and anxious to get out of the car. They didn't see a Western Union office, but at the next rest stop, Stella got some change and decided to put in the long-distance call.

After four rings, Sam answered.

'Sam, it's Stella. Put Momma on the phone.'

'She's in the chapel. It's service.'

'I don't care. Go get her.'

'It's service,' he repeated stubbornly.

'Sam, please go get her. It's real important.'

The sound of the receiver banging against the wall and the operator instructing Stella to put in two more quarters had her cussing.

Finally Addie's scared voice answered.

'Maw, it's me. You don't need to be worried. It's good news. I'm married, so's Jenny. We had a double wedding.'

'Jenny's married, too?' Her voice was incredulous. 'To who?'

'It's okay, Momma. Jenny's right here. I'll put her on.'

'Hello,' Jenny barely whispered into the phone.

'Is this true, or some kind of mean joke your sister's playing? You can come home right now. I'll fix it with the Reverend so it'll be okay.'

It was Addie mentioning the Reverend that gave Jenny a quick jolt of anger.

'No, it's true, Momma,' she gushed. 'He's a wonderful man, he has a good job, I love him and I'm very happy.'

There was silence until the sharp voice of the operator demanded another quarter.

'I don't understand. Where did you meet him? Who is he?'

'I've gotta go now, Momma, I'm out of change. I promise I'll write. We're both fine.' Jenny hung up the receiver, and turned to face her new husband. She had made her choice. There was no going back.

Several hours later they reached St Louis. In front of Rodney's apartment. Stella and Jenny parted, exchanging hugs and bits of paper that contained their new phone

72

numbers. Stella whispered, 'It's gonna be great. You'll see.'

They drove away and left Stella and Rodney standing on the sidewalk among the suitcases, waving frantically. Out of the back window Jenny saw Rodney scoop her sister up and carry her and the struggling kitten over the threshold.

'It's a short ride, about twenty minutes,' Bobby Lee said as he gently squeezed her hand. 'Tired, Baby Doll?'

'Yeah,' and with newfound courage she squeezed back.

The city lights dwindled, and the sound of crickets and the summer night swallowed up the speeding car.

When he pulled into the long driveway and she caught the first glimpse of the house, she let out a surprised, 'Oh.'

'It's a big ole house. I grew up here,' he explained. 'I never would have chosen a house like this myself, guess I'm just too lazy to move.'

She felt a charge of excitement. Politely, Bobby Lee opened the car door for her. She stepped out into the summer evening and breathed the lovely scent of roses. A soft wind rustled the trees and magically, fireflies darted gracefully in the air, dipping and rising in their game of hide-and-seek.

Far above them the house waited. He started up the stone steps and she heard the jingle of metal as he rummaged through his pocket for the keys.

Following his long strides up the steps she was breathless trying to keep up with him. She paused and looked up toward the dark house.

She blinked, and caught at her throat, surprise cheating her of air. Only one anguished cry escaped her, a strangled 'No' as she saw it. At the very top of the house under the eaves was the small heart-shaped window of her dreams.

'No, no, no!' she repeated silently in her terrified mind. For now she saw clearly that every window in this house had bars.

The inky blackness of his shadow stretched back to engulf her. She wanted to run – somewhere, anywhere – but in terror she was rooted to the spot.

Finally the sobs bubbled forth and hysterically she cried, her legs and arms trembling in a spasm of terror, for it came back to her clearly, the memory of running through a dark house with a faceless stranger chasing her.

'What's wrong?' he yelled as he turned, and two at a time took the steps back down to her. She saw only a huge black thing approaching her, and then liquid on her legs as her bladder betrayed her, and her sobs increased.

'There, there. It's okay,' she heard him whisper as he took her into his arms and the warmth of him lulled her, as he rocked her back and forth gently.

'Ssh, ssh,' he coaxed as he took a handkerchief from his back pocket and dried her tears. He felt it in the pit of his stomach, growing. *She was so little, so helpless – and she was his. He felt it singing within him – the Power*.

He took her small hand and led her gently up the steps to the house.

'I'm sorry,' she finally managed to say.

'I told you it's okay,' he said kindly.

Somewhat composed now she wondered if he would carry her over the threshold. Instead, he reached for the keys and unlocked the door. Hesitantly, she followed him into the entrance hall.

'Want a snack?' he said, as if nothing unusual had happened.

She nodded and followed him into the kitchen, a large, cheerful room that sparkled with fresh, brilliant yellow paint. The house was old, yet it had wonderful new appliances.

'It's really nice,' she said nervously. He made her sit while he scrambled some eggs.

Feeling foolish now, she sat there stiffly, embarrassed at her outburst, her damp dress clinging to her.

'I love waiting on you,' he said as he leaned over and kissed her cheek. They ate silently and lingered over coffee.

In dread, she waited for the time they would have to go up to bed.

'Jeannie, I'm beat. I gotta go to work in the morning. You can explore the house by yourself tomorrow. Do you mind?'

'No, that will be fine.'

Upstairs, the landing contained five doors, all shut.

'Here's our room,' he said as he opened the door to a large, beautiful room papered in delicate off-white with petite pink flowers. A large four-poster bed dominated the room. Its canopy of antique lace matched the curtains on the three windows.

Jenny wondered at her new husband, for Bobby Lee didn't seem to belong in this room. It was as if he were a trespasser who had opened the wrong door.

'I'm gonna take a quick shower,' he said, and retreated into the adjoining bathroom.

Gingerly she walked around the room, touching the porcelain figures; they looked antique. A particularly beautiful statue caught her eye. It depicted a young girl on a swing forever frozen in her upward glide, one dainty shoe pointed towards the leaves of the tree that shielded her.

'It must have been his mother's room,' she thought. 'He must have loved her very much.'

With his hair drenched, and only a towel around his waist, he came back into the room. 'I ran you some bathwater,' he said. He went to a drawer and took out a large white T-shirt. 'Sorry, Baby Doll, it's the best I can do for now. I'll get you some clothes tomorrow.'

Jenny took the shirt and entered the old-fashioned bathroom; thoughtfully, he had filled the tub with bath salts. She climbed into the water and lay back. The warmth took the soreness and stiffness from the long ride out of her body, but the cloying sweet scent of roses made her want to sneeze.

Unsure of herself, she prolonged the bath. Finally she dried herself, put on the T-shirt, re-entered the bedroom, and found him snoring.

She turned off the light and crept under the summer quilt, careful not to touch him or bump into him.

She lay there wondering how this had happened, this 'miracle', as Stella described her marriage. She had seen Bobby Lee twice in her life and now he was here in this bed beside her, her husband, her love.

She tried not to think of the dreams – the window, the bars. She thought instead of his kisses, his caress, remembering through the haze of alcohol his other touch – how it had been *exquisite* In spite of the newness and the fear, she almost hoped he would roll over and awaken and remember that she was his bride.

Soft moonlight bathed the room; somewhere she heard the hoot of an owl, and against the screen a moth fluttered. On the far wall, a picture faced the bed. She could see the outline of its fancy frame, but the reflection on the glass in the moonlit room shielded its contents. Yet she felt sure there were eyes looking at them. The certainty was so overwhelming, it smothered her, and she rolled towards him, and jumped as she felt his nakedness. He only murmured and finally she slept, dreaming with the sad sound of weeping children in her ears.

In the morning, his side of the bed was empty. On his pillow lay a rose and the note:

Baby Doll,
See you at 6:30.
Yours, Bobby Lee.

The names he called her were embarrassing. She guessed maybe she should have liked them, but she didn't.

Jenny picked up her dress and underwear and washed them in the sink. In the closet she found a worn work-shirt, which she put on. It felt strange against her skin. She touched the cloth, looking for the essence of him.

Remembering, she rushed back to the bedroom and gazed up at the picture. It was a portrait of an unsmiling woman. Clearly she could see Bobby Lee's chin, hairline, and brows, but the eyes were angry as if seeing something that they could not bear to contemplate.

Jenny made the bed quickly. She wanted to be out of that room and away from those disquieting eyes. Timidly she walked along the landing and opened the closed doors.

The other bedrooms were plain, almost too plain, as if any former occupant had taken everything personal away.

The last room surprised her, for it was a nursery, with cheerful plaques on the walls, a rocking horse, and a toy chest still overflowing, as though the child had only just run away and left it all behind. The morning breeze fluttered the Donald Duck curtains and a wind-chime tingled hauntingly as if it missed the child who had played here. Only the bars were out of place, casting their ominous shadows over the brightness of the room.

Of course – she remembered now what Stella had told her. Bobby Lee was divorced, with an ex-wife and a child.

Quietly she closed the door and went downstairs.

It was a beautiful house. The living room had gleaming mahogany tables, a wonderful sofa with down-filled cushions and brocade chairs. The feeling in there was one of comfort and good taste.

On the mantel in an ornate silver frame the same brooding woman stared out at her.

The dining room was an elegant counterpart to the living room. The large table had eight matching mahogany chairs, with needlepoint seat covers. The corner cabinet gleamed with fragile china and crystal goblets. She was afraid to touch anything.

The side room was different, as if someone had transplanted another room from another house. It contained a comfortable battered couch, two sagging armchairs and a rag rug. By the fireplace stood a television set; on one table, forgotten, was a half-empty can of beer.

She felt like an intruder, walking quietly through the rooms of this lonely house. There was something in its heart, vibrations of some sadness she could not readily identify. That sound . . . she had heard it even in her sleep. Soft, just below hearing, the mournful plaint of weeping children. She opened the back door, searching with her eyes the lawn, the bushes . . . thinking that perhaps it was only the wail of a lost cat.

Aware of the sharp ringing now, she closed the door and finally located it, the telephone on a small table in the hall.

Tentatively she picked it up and squeaked, 'Hello.'

'Why so quiet, honey? It's me. Did I wake you?'

'No, I've been up a while. Bobby Lee's already gone.'

'Whooo-ee!' Stella yelled. 'We did it. We're two married bitches,' and she heard her happy laughter. 'How's the house?'

'It's – it's big, and it's really elegant, like one of those houses in the stories I'm always reading.' She stopped. She couldn't say it. *The window, the house . . .*

'What's that word? "Elegant", you say,' Stella mocked.

'Doesn't hurt to improve your English,' Jenny retorted.

'I know, Jenny – or should I say Jeannie? How was it – any better?' she asked.

Pretending, Jenny responded, 'How was what?'

'You know, the fucking.'

'Oh Stella. You can be so crude.'

'My, my, little sister, this kind of talk comes from reading all those dictionaries.'

'They're not dictionaries, the book is a thesaurus.'

'Whatever. Rodney and I did it twice last night. He sez we gotta do it at least once every night till we get it right,' she laughed.

'The house is great,' Jenny said, trying to change the subject. 'It's full of really nice furniture. I think most of it's antique.'

'Oh, I'm gonna get some brand new stuff. I don't want any old junk – I've had enough of that. Rodney sez we're going out pretty soon to pick out the furniture and he promised me a TV.'

Jenny bit her tongue, and didn't mention the one she had just seen.

'What are you doing for clothes?' Stella went on.

'Oh God, Stella, I forgot. I washed out my dress and

78

stuff. I left it upstairs. Bobby Lee said he's gonna stop by the store and bring me a few things.'

'I bet you'll see some black filmy underwear. That's the kinda stuff guys always buy!'

'I gotta go. My clothes might be dripping all over the bathroom floor.'

'Okay. Later you call me so my phone will ring.'

'Sure. 'Bye.'

Jenny hung up and felt placed firmly back in reality. Stella was like that, she seemed to shake the cobwebs of Jenny's internal life, and land her right smack in the middle of reality. There *were* no soft cries; they'd existed only in her imagination.

She ran up and retrieved the clothes that had dripped on the floor, cleaned up the water then went out the back door to look for a clothes-line. On the porch she found some pegs and soon her clothes were flapping in the wind.

She sat down on the flagstone patio, and looked around with wonder at the grounds. Rose-bushes bloomed along the stone path, tiger lilies grew wild and profuse – every colour of flower blossomed somewhere in the yard and she followed the path until it stopped at a dense wood. Jenny breathed that summer air as if she was starved for it; her heart sang with the beauty of it, the place. Her eyes feasted on the green, the incredible green; even the sky here looked blue-er.

Eyes that had known only derelict buildings and tumbledown, graffiti-covered walls, could not drink it in quickly enough.

He owned it, all of this. It belonged to him, and he was her husband.

In the birdbath, robins splashed happily.

It was this sight that made her eyes mist. She cried, for what if she had missed it? What if she'd never known it *did* exist, a place like this . . .

Suddenly, Jenny felt a chill on that warm summer day. She knew she didn't deserve this place. Why had a stranger picked her to share this paradise?

With Bobby Lee gone, Jenny had a chance to think. She tried sorting out her feelings. She could not understand the jigsaw of this man, her husband. For most of the time he was ordinary, even nice, except when . . .

Her worry over the problems pushed away the strangeness of dreaming the heart-shaped window so many years ago. Often she forgot about the visions or whatever they were, for the glimpses were never of anything important – except that one time when she saw clearly Bessie at the bus stop clutching her heart, and then her smooth brown face finally at rest in the plain wooden coffin. But most of the time those peeks through the curtain were of mundane, insignificant things.

CHAPTER 7

Bobby Lee's note said he would be home at six-thirty. Jenny wanted to have a proper supper for him. She searched the ample refrigerator, and next to it, the large freezer as well. It was bursting with prime cuts of meat, frozen vegetables of every description, and gallon upon gallon of chocolate ice cream.

She smiled. Bit by bit, she was trying to learn everything about this stranger who was her husband. Happily, she prepared corn on the cob, green beans and biscuits made from scratch. He came home promptly at six-thirty, his arms loaded with packages.

'Go on, open them,' he urged, watching her eagerly.

Carefully she opened the bags to find sun-dresses, shorts, blouses, nightgowns, and even underwear. But Stella was wrong. There was no black filmy lingerie, only sensible white cotton panties and a set in pastel colours that proclaimed the day of the week.

'Saturday we can go up to the shopping centre and you can pick out what you need,' he promised.

'This is fine. Thank you so much,' she murmured, as she looked across the table at this stranger who was her husband.

'Dinner's great, Jeannie. I didn't know I got myself a great cook.' Across the table he noticed her looking at his upper arm, where he had a heart-shaped tattoo with an arrow through it and the word MOTHER below.

'Oh this,' he said with a grin. 'I did it to spite her – my

81

mother. Matter of fact, I did a lot of things to spite her. That's why I became a truck driver in the first place. I couldn't get an occupation she would have hated more, except maybe if I drove a garbage truck.'

Jenny nodded, not understanding why he thought this funny.

'Didn't you ever do anything to spite your mother?' And before she could answer, he said, 'Yeah, I guess you did. You married me.'

Jenny got up from the chair and went to the stove and asked, 'Would you like some more?'

'Yeah. You're a great little cook, Baby Doll. Everything's delicious.' And she refilled his plate and again he ate hungrily.

After coffee they went to the room he called the den, turned on the TV, and he said softly, 'Come here, little girl.'

She sat on the floor before him and he stroked her hair absentmindedly as they watched the comedy hour.

'How about a beer?' Obediently she went to the fridge, brought him a cold beer, resumed her seat on the floor before him, but he seemed to have forgotten and he didn't touch her again.

After the show, he stretched and looked at the clock. 'Almost bedtime, Baby Doll. Why don't you go up, jump in the tub and get all sweet-smelling for your Bubba?'

She nodded, excited and scared. Tonight they would finally become man and wife. Stella said it would hurt, so she'd prepare herself. Stella said it'd get better. Stella was usually right.

As Jenny washed she could hear the sounds of him moving about in the bedroom. 'Did you fall asleep in there, Baby Doll?' he finally called.

'I'll be right out.' She dried off and put on the long white cotton gown he had bought her. It was modest. She opened the door and saw that the bedroom had been transformed; candles flickered on the tables and bathed the room in a soft light.

Bobby Lee sat on the edge of the bed. He was naked.

'Come here where I can see you,' he whispered.

She came and stood before him timidly.

'Oh, you're a beautiful girl. Take it off.' His voice had changed now, was hoarse, unfamiliar.

Unconsciously Jenny clutched at the gown, looked longingly at the bed, the covers. She'd imagined it would be dark. She needed the protection of darkness.

'Move over,' he indicated with his hand, 'and take it off, I said.'

Slowly she shifted in the direction he indicated, not realizing he was placing her in front of a three-way mirror. 'Go on – be a good little girl.' With trembling fingers, she lifted the gown and let it fall around her feet.

He tilted his head back and forth, studying her in the mirror behind her. 'Ever see one?' he said, looking down between his open thighs.

She was so frightened, she could only nod no.

'Are you sure?' he questioned her in a breathless voice.

Rapidly, she shook her head no.

'Come closer, Baby Doll. You've got to look at him, look at him like you love him and he'll be real good.'

She moved closer, terrified. This was not like any of the books she had read about love; why didn't Stella tell her it'd be like this? Her eyes misted; she simply would not cry, she promised herself.

'See, Baby Doll? See, he's being real good, doing what dicks are supposed to do. He's standing up at attention.' He leaned back admiring himself. 'Ooooh – see how big he is! You know what? I'm gonna put him right in that tight little pussy of yours.'

She was having trouble breathing. The gutter words were so harsh and ugly.

'Scared, Baby Doll?' She must have misunderstood him for she thought he said, 'Good, that's good.'

Roughly he took her wrists – pulled her down on the bed, laying her across it sideways. With hands of steel, he took her ankles, pulled her legs apart, and stood hovering above her. Her terror heightened his excitement.

'Look at him, Baby Doll, look how big he is, and you're gonna have to take all of him. I'm gonna ram him right up that little bitty pussy.' The ugly words fell like dirt coating her skin.

She closed her eyes, and felt the excruciating pain, as he thrust savagely into her. The pain went on and on. 'You can cry, Baby Doll. Go on – you've gotta do it, gotta take all of him, every inch of him. Spread 'em wide.' She sobbed beneath him.

His animal grunts went on and on. She could only think *'Why didn't Stella tell me what it was really gonna be like?'*

When it was over, she heard him whistling cheerfully in the shower. She lay there stunned. The sharp pains still lingered, and in the picture on the wall those eyes glared down at her in anger. She looked away from his naked body until he put on his shorts. He blew out the candles, climbed into bed and said placidly, ''Night, Baby Doll.'

In the days that followed, in the daylight, at breakfast, at dinner, in the den, he seemed like someone else, not this cruel stranger who loved hurting her.

He brought more ice cream and boxes of candy, complimented her cooking, and on the weekend they had a barbecue, but it was on those nights when he would look over and say, 'Get yourself clean and sweet-smelling for your Bubba,' that she would delay as long as possible in the bath, dreading to come out into that candlelit room. For it was never making love, it was something else.

This time he ordered her to get down on all fours – and with shame she could see their bodies in the mirror, as he thrust over her. 'Tight pussy – ooh, it's tight now. This big dick of mine only likes it real little.' His words made her feel sick. In the night when he slept, she cried into a towel in the bathroom so he wouldn't hear her. The degradation made her listless with despair. It was her fault. Something was wrong with her or he wouldn't act this way.

It was over a week since she had even answered the phone. She hated her sister, her big sister who had betrayed her, but finally she did answer the persistent ringing. 'Where in the hell have you been? I've been calling you for days,' Stella snapped.

'Oh, I've been working in the yard. I planted some tomatoes, and strawberries. Bobby Lee brought me some plants so I've been outside mostly.'

'Well, guess what? We got a contract in on a little row house, and I've got my driver's licence, too.'

'How'd you do that?'

'Hell, it's simple. You just walk in, pay 'em a quarter. Rodney's been letting me practise in the neighbourhood. In another week or so I'll be good enough to drive farther, then I'll come out to see your place.'

'Oh, that would be nice,' Jenny said.

'You don't sound overjoyed.'

'Sure, I'll be glad to see you,' and she realized she really would be. 'What about the house? What's it like?'

'It's brand new, a real doll-house, with two big bedrooms, a great tiled bathroom, and a dream of a kitchen. Even the yard's cyclone fenced. I just love it. I can't wait till we move in.'

'Sounds great.'

'You don't. Is something wrong?' Stella asked.

Jenny yearned to spill out her confusion, her unhappiness, but all her life she never could talk about anything too personal. So once again she closed herself up tightly.

'Nothing's wrong, not really,' she lied.

'You don't sound very convincing. Is it the sex thing? Rodney was right – I'm broke in already. He just touches that little button, and I get wet as can be, and it's good. I did it the other night for the first time. I came!'

Jenny felt sick. There *must* be something wrong with her. How could Stella like it? It was so animal – so degrading.

'Listen honey, I got a feeling it is that sex thing. Make

him neck a little bit longer, make him rub it. They call it foreplay, or before play, or something like that. I read a magazine that told me all about women and what to do. You're supposed to ask for what you want.'

'I'm okay,' Jenny said curtly and hung up, and wondered if maybe what they were doing was different.

She'd try. She had to do something, for she felt the dread every night. Was it gonna be the candlelit room?

She experienced total relief when Bobby Lee said he had a long haul, and he'd be gone for about a week. She just had to get through Saturday and Sunday.

It was about nine on the Saturday morning when the doorbell rang and Jenny answered it to find a woman and a small girl standing on the porch.

The woman seemed puzzled to see her. 'I'm Raylean,' she announced.

'Oh.'

'Have I been fired?' the woman asked while studying her carefully.

'Fired?' Jenny repeated stupidly.

'I do the cleaning every other Saturday and I need to know am I fired?'

Jenny said, 'Come in,' and stepped aside.

Bobby Lee appeared from the kitchen. He seemed surprised to see them. He turned to Jenny. 'Oh, I forgot to mention it. Raylean cleans every other Saturday.' He introduced her. 'This is my wife Jeannie.'

'Your wife?' Raylean said, surprise plain on her face. 'Do we have the same arrangements, Mr Antree?'

'Er no . . .' he answered nervously. 'Actually we can cut out Saturdays. Can you come on Tuesday, every other Tuesday? But go ahead for today since you're here.'

'Yes, Tuesday's fine,' Raylean agreed, and headed for the kitchen for the cleaning supplies. The child ran up the stairs as if she knew exactly where she was going.

'I could do it,' Jenny said. 'I've got plenty of time and I have been doing the cleaning anyway.'

'No, that's all right,' Bobby Lee said. 'She needs the

work, raising that little girl by herself. We'll keep her. Is Tuesday okay with you?'

'Yes,' Jenny answered, and felt pampered. Imagine, having someone to clean the house for her. At times like these she could almost forget the dim bedroom with the candles burning.

Upstairs she found the child in the nursery, humming to herself, but when she opened the door, the girl started. 'I thought it was him,' she accused. She looked at Jenny with eyes that were far too old. 'He always gives me ice cream.'

'I'll bring some up,' Jenny offered, and while she was in the kitchen scooping up a sundae, Bobby Lee came in. He ran his hand through his hair nervously.

'Gee, Jeannie, I forgot all about it. I'm going bowling today with some of the guys from the union. I'll be back late.'

Jenny nodded, puzzled by his manner. She topped the sundae with a cherry and took the ice cream upstairs where the child was looking out of the nursery window watching Bobby Lee's car pull away. She ate the ice cream in large hurried gulps.

'Slow down, honey,' Jenny said gently. 'My momma always said it can give you a stomach ache if you eat too fast.'

The child looked up at Jenny and slowed down a little. 'I hate stomach aches,' she said.

'So do I.'

Finished, she went back to her puzzle, and Jenny felt the same helplessness she had so often experienced at the Mission, when confronted by very needy children. She left her alone to explore the wonderland that was the nursery.

Raylean was on her hands and knees waxing the floor. Her eyes were downcast. Something was wrong. The woman didn't like her and Jenny didn't even know why.

She went out into the yard to pull weeds. It felt good, the warm sun on her back, and her plump tomato plants, soon to be ripe, filled her with pride.

Suddenly she had the urge to call Maw. She went in and

dialled the Mission. Maw answered, but Jenny couldn't speak. After hearing three or four of her mother's rushed hello's, gently she put the receiver down. Maybe sometime later, she could call her. Addie was her mother and Jenny missed her. She needed to talk to a woman. She needed to know about things. Did everyone know about the ugliness that occurred between men and women, except her? What about those books, the love stories – were they all lies? And love – did it really exist?

When Bobby Lee came home that night, she could tell he was drunk; he stumbled two or three times on the stairs. She huddled closer into the pillows with dread, pretending to be asleep.

She followed his movements in sound, the flushing of the toilet, the soft whisper of cloth as he shed his clothes. Her heart sank when she heard the match scratching the side of the box, and the smell of sulphur as he lit the candles.

'Playing games, little girl? I know you're not asleep,' he slurred. In one swish, he had tugged the covers off her like a magician performing a favourite trick.

'What, Bobby Lee?' she hedged, rubbing her eyes.

'Take it off!' he thundered, the anger plain in his face. This was different. Just when she thought she knew the games, the rules changed.

She sat up slowly and took off the gown.

'Up. Get up!' he ordered. Like a snake, his fingers coiled around her wrist and he flung her out of the bed. In the flickering light she saw herself repeated over and over in the mirrors.

Behind her he lay back on the bed, his legs spread wide. 'Look at him,' he ordered. 'He scares you when he's big and terrible, doesn't he, Baby Doll?'

Remembering Stella's words, Jenny tried getting up. She reached for him. Maybe a soft caress, a kiss, her skin next to his, gentleness, tenderness . . . maybe she could change this.

He pulled away from her seeking arms and said, 'Your fault,' and he looked with fresh anger at his limp member.

88

'Bad girls need to be spanked,' and in a minute he had her over his knees, and his palm rang out, stinging her buttocks with each slap. Against her breast she felt him awaken and she prayed for it to be fast, but the spanking stopped and she felt one finger, touch and probe, in and out, in and out, slowly his finger probed her. 'You like that, little girl,' he crooned, and she felt revulsion, because her body betrayed her. He was right, she did.

'Spread 'em,' he whispered. It went on and on, the sound of a soft swish. 'But you're a bad little girl. Your cunt shouldn't feel good, when you left Dickie so disappointed,' and she felt a jolt of pain as he thrust them inside her, all four fingers.

She screamed, felt his wetness and knew it was over.

She stayed awake half the night. What could she do? It wasn't fair. The movies, the books – they all lied. There was no such thing as love. She felt sick even thinking about it. Did Momma have to do these things to keep a roof over her head? And Stella, would she trade dignity for a house and a TV? Maybe that's what she'd meant when she always said, 'It's all up to men. That's how it is, that's how it always will be.'

In the morning Jenny couldn't meet his eyes. They ate breakfast in silence.

They stayed outdoors. He marvelled at the tomatoes. 'You gotta green thumb, Baby Doll.' She felt as though they were actors in a play. He seemed so natural now, so at ease, she wasn't sure last night had really happened.

It was after dinner, in the den, when he insisted that she drink a beer with him. She did so to please him, all the while counting the minutes until tomorrow. He'd be gone for a week, then she could think, and figure it out. She sat stiffly in the chair, pretending great interest in the TV show.

He left the room and came back with his mother's picture in the silver frame and put it on the TV. He came over to her and said quietly, 'I was a little drunk last night. Sorry.'

She nodded.

'Forgive me,' he coaxed. She nodded, afraid she couldn't

be convincing if she spoke. With an arm, he pushed the recliner back, sat on the edge of her chair, and she felt his hand snaking up her dress.

Deftly, he pushed aside her pants. He reached over and gently kissed her, but she could not respond. 'Your turn. I promise I'll be good,' he whispered.

His fingers gently rubbed her. 'Your turn,' he promised again, and she saw what he was holding in his hand – the jar. His fingers were cool and slick. 'Close your eyes, Baby Doll. There, there, Baby Doll,' and one finger probed and slid in, while the other fingers gently massaged. He touched it – the button, that's what Stella had called it – and she held herself rigid.

'No, no, Baby Doll, relax. Bubba is not gonna hurt you. I said it's your turn,' and gently he treasured her flesh. 'Just like playing doctor,' he said. 'My sister and I played this game a lot up in the attic. Not this attic, the one in Atlanta. I brought the Vaseline, stole it from Momma's room, and my sister had real soft hands. "Playing doctor" we called it,' and with that he reached for Jenny's hand and she touched it; its velvet softness surprised her. It throbbed and she was deeply ashamed as she felt her legs slowly drifting apart. 'That's it, Baby Doll, touch it nice. Good, that pussy's real hot – *real* hot,' he breathed.

And in spite of herself and the disgust she felt at what they were doing, something fiery burst within her, and she emerged breathless and finished.

'I knew it,' he whispered in her ear. 'You're one of those cunts that likes finger-fucking.' He looked up at the picture of his mother and smiled. Jenny went upstairs and vomited into the sink. Life was ugly, and love uglier still.

Bobby Lee left the next morning at eight. Jenny was confused. What did it mean, was she becoming broken in? Most of it she hated, but that feeling, what he had done to her, she liked, she really liked. But was it making love? She wasn't sure, but she didn't think so.

CHAPTER 8

Lingering over coffee one morning, Jenny heard the rapid tooting of a horn. She felt a sinking in the pit of her stomach. He couldn't be back already, it was only Wednesday. She didn't expect him till the weekend.

Looking out front she didn't recognize the shiny green car until she saw her step out and wave.

Two at a time Stella took the steps up to meet her.

They hugged and a cloud of perfume hovered over their heads. Stella stepped back, held Jenny's arms out and her anxious eyes examined her sister's face. 'Jenny, are you okay? You look so thin.'

'Sure I am, I'm fine.'

'Well, give me your secret then. I've been wolfing down steaks and chocolate cake and lo and behold, remember how I always talked about asparagus? Damn, I don't even *like* the stuff!' She patted her hips, 'I've put on a pound or two, but Rodney sez he likes it.'

'You look great,' Jenny said, and it was true. Stella was dressed in a smart seersucker suit, and aviator shoes in navy and white. Her purse, her summer jewelry, all matched. She looked young and stylish.

As if noticing for the first time, Stella looked up. 'Jesus, what's with the bars?'

'Oh, those. I don't like them either. Bobby Lee said when they moved here from Atlanta this place was more remote than it is now, and his mother being a widow with two small kids, needed something to make her feel safe.'

'A dog would have been cheaper,' Stella quipped. 'You sure weren't kidding when you said the house was big.'

'Come in,' Jenny invited, and Stella followed her into the dim hall.

They went from room to room. Stella was surprised at the grandeur of the house. 'It's so big, with so many beautiful things. How on earth do you keep it all clean and polished?'

Embarrassed, Jenny admitted, 'We have a woman comes in and does the cleaning twice a month.'

'You have a cleaning lady? La-di-da,' Stella joked. They went upstairs as proudly Jenny showed her all the rooms.

In the bedroom Stella looked at the portrait. 'Who in the hell is that?'

'It's Bobby Lee's mother, Mrs Sylvia Antree. This was her house; he grew up here.'

'Well, damn, I'd take that picture down right now. She looks like an unforgiving old bitch. I wouldn't want her staring at me while I'm in that big bed gettin' it off.'

Stella plumped the mattress, gingerly touched the porcelain statues. 'It's a great house, honey. 'Course, I don't understand these old antique things. You're the artist. For me, I got it all picked out brand new. Our bedroom suite is blond, Swedish-modern, and the house – Jenny, you'll love it.' Stella stopped and looked around. 'Well, maybe you won't. This is more you, I guess.'

In the upper landing, Jenny opened the doors of the other rooms. Stella peeked her head in briefly, until they came to the nursery.

'Got it all ready,' she joked. 'You always loved babies.'

'No, no, I didn't decorate it. It's from the other – you know . . .' She couldn't say wife, she didn't know why.

In an appraising glance Stella took in the toys. 'I bet his kid's a girl.'

'I don't know; he never talks about them.'

'That's good. Let ghosts from the past stay there, in the past.'

Jenny shut the door of the nursery quietly and they

92

turned to go downstairs, but Stella spied the narrow staircase. 'Where's that go?'

'The attic; I've never been up there. Bobby Lee said there could be bats up there. There were before.'

'Oooh,' Stella shivered. 'Just like a Dracula movie. Let's see,' and helplessly Jenny followed her up the narrow stairs.

Splinters of light shone through the cracks in the frame house. Dust motes danced in the air and as Jenny bumped into a box, a tin-plate toy rolled out and started a slow journey across the dusty floor, its music mechanism rusty with age, the tune croaked out into the silence. She picked up the toy and the last frantic whirl of tight springs buzzed. As she reached into the box to replace it, she saw the toy sets, side by side – a nurse's kit and a doctor's bag, the pretend stethoscope furred with dust, and a small bottle with faded pink pills. The harsh lesson taught to a small boy.

Jenny felt her hands shake, remembering his words: 'My sister and I played nasty in the attic.'

'Brr,' Stella said, 'I don't see any bats, but it's scary enough anyway.'

As Jenny closed the door she noticed it – long tears of splintered wood. Stella's eyes followed hers. 'Looks like someone was locked in here and was trying pretty bad to get out,' Stella said.

They went downstairs to the cheerful kitchen where they enjoyed cinnamon rolls and fresh coffee.

Stella felt it was all so strange. She had planned and dreamed her life and it was turning out better than she had even imagined. But Jenny, something about Jenny made her uneasy, this girl-child sitting across from her looking even younger than her sixteen years. This man, this house ... something in the puzzle did not fit. It was too storybook-perfect.

She played with the spoon. She knew it was silly, but she wanted to ask. She never believed in it, for she was practical; other than a few silly superstitions, she knew her

A. N. Steinberg

feet were firmly on the ground. It was Jenny who had always lived with her head in the clouds.

'Did you see it?' she asked finally.

'What?'

'This house, Bobby Lee, the wedding. You know, before it happened?'

A shiver went through Jenny. The window, she had seen the window for years, but it was something she couldn't explain.

'No. I often think of Bessie, it was her talk that scared Momma so much. It scared me, too, for it was small stupid things I said. They were probably only guesses, anyway. You know, I always read so much and I had such a vivid imagination when I was little, Momma always accused me of making it up.'

'That's right,' Stella said, 'and Momma was always hollering at me for my silly superstitions. I was even frantic at the wedding for having nothing blue . . .' She stopped in mid-sentence and suddenly felt afraid for her baby sister, knowing Jenny hadn't had any of the right things.

Hurriedly she said, 'Jenny, you really lucked out. Bobby Lee has a great job, you've got this wonderful house. Maybe that crazy Reverend was right – maybe there *is* a God.'

Jenny sipped her coffee. 'Yeah, maybe,' she agreed.

Stella looked around, with envy and pride. 'It's a really big house.'

'We don't use all the rooms,' Jenny confessed. 'Mainly we go in the den, or the bedroom.' And her voice dropped with shame.

'The den – I haven't seen it.' Stella stood up, ready for another tour.

'It's not much,' Jenny said as they went down the hall. She could see her sister's surprise at the simple cluttered room with furniture that had seen much better days. Then her glance lit on it.

'A TV! Why you little brat, you never told me you had one,' and she turned it on, flicked the dial and Lucille Ball

94

smiled out at them on the twelve-inch black and white screen.

'I love this show, it's "I Love Lucy", I saw it once at my neighbour's house,' said Stella, plopping down in the armchair, mesmerized by the tiny screen.

'I'll bring your coffee in here, or would you rather have lemonade?'

'Coffee's fine,' Stella answered, not taking her eyes off the set.

When Jenny returned with the small tray, clouds of smoke hovered over the small screen, for Stella had found the ashtray. She sipped the coffee and puffed on a long black cigarette with a silver tip. 'Aren't these class?' she asked, not needing an answer.

As the programme ended she held it up, the jar of Vaseline, and said, 'I see you been makin' out in all the rooms. If Bobby Lee still gotta use this, he must be very big, or you're not broke in yet.'

That jar, that revolting jar, did it. All the tears Jenny had held back until now came forth, and she sat on the couch and sobbed, her hands covering her face.

Stella came over and tried hugging her.

'Go away,' Jenny said angrily.

'There, there, little sister. I'm sorry, you're right. I'm crude. I know I am, but it doesn't hurt none to joke about stuff.'

Her hand rhythmically rubbed Jenny's shoulder, and they were quiet except for Jenny's sobs, which diminished when she was finally cried out.

'I'm sorry,' Stella said again, and she dabbed with her scented handkerchief at Jenny's swollen eyes. 'It takes time,' she said kindly, pausing carefully to choose words that wouldn't offend.

'I hate it,' Jenny almost blurted, then she remembered not all of it.

'It takes time,' Stella repeated. 'Bobby Lee's been married before. Can't you tell him to go easy, like that article I read. It said with some women you gotta go slow and you're so young, baby sister,' and she rained kisses on Jenny's tearstained cheeks.

They held each other tight for a few minutes. Jenny longed to talk, but the zipper of her mouth stayed shut. As much as she wanted to, she couldn't ask embarrassing questions.

'Show me the yard,' Stella said brightly, and they went out into the sunny day. They sat in the lawn chairs, with the gentle buzz of bees and an occasional butterfly flitting from flower to flower and Stella said it, what Jenny was thinking. 'It's like Paradise.'

Jenny nodded silently, but thinking more intensely than ever: *'Paradise always comes equipped with a full-blown evil snake.'*

CHAPTER 9

With Raylean's cleaning there was so little left to do that Jenny found she did even less, and because of this he found the lipstick-stained cigarette.

'What's this?' He came into the kitchen holding out the offending ashtray.

'It's a cigarette,' Jenny answered dumbly.

'You smoking? I don't like girls smoking. It looks cheap.'

'No, Bobby Lee, I'm not smoking. It's Stella – she was here last Wednesday.'

'You didn't tell me,' he accused.

'It just slipped my mind.'

'I bet there's a lot of other things that slip your mind when I'm gone.'

'No,' she protested, feeling queasy, for she didn't know where this was leading. His eyes looked dark and angry.

'She's got her driver's licence; Rodney got her a car, so she just came by,' she rambled on. 'She looks real good. They're getting a new house.'

'I don't want you running around with her. Now that she's got that wedding ring on her finger, she'll probably start hanging around taverns or something.'

She wanted him to understand. 'No, Stella's not like that,' she said. 'She acts tough sometimes, but you don't really know her. It's an act. She loves Rodney. She's so happy to be making him a home – you just don't know her.'

He didn't answer, just looked at Jenny thoughtfully and in a second his mood changed. 'You've been wearing that same old dress for too long. I promised you a shopping trip – let's go.'

'Honest?' she said, feeling like a child who has been promised a trip to the zoo.

'Come on,' he urged as he looked for his wallet and the car keys.

Jenny would have liked to wash her face, run a comb through her hair. Instead, she followed him out to the car, combing her hair with her fingers and hoping she looked presentable.

As he backed out of the driveway he commented, 'We better grocery shop, too. The freezer's getting low.'

Jenny agreed, but to her who had come from so little it seemed bountiful even now.

She didn't remember the road, for when they had arrived it was dark. With surprise she realized it had been over a month and she hadn't even left the house in all that time.

Like a caged bird that didn't know about freedom and suddenly found the door open, she wanted to soar, to fly until she was breathless, but with a feeling of incredible sadness she knew she had nowhere to fly to.

The car jarred, the brakes squealed. 'Damn brat,' Bobby Lee cursed, as they saw Raylean's daughter running across the road towards a tumbledown frame shack.

'That Raylean's?' Jenny asked.

He shook his head and drove faster.

Just short of a mile, everything changed. It was the county. She hadn't realized it was so close; she could have walked there easily.

On both sides of the road small stores in the shopping strip seemed alive with cars and people.

'Grant's,' he commented. 'You'll probably find something that you like there,' and he pulled up to the bright store full of sophisticated mannequins.

Jenny felt nervous and unsure, among the racks and racks of pretty dresses. She didn't remember ever buying anything new.

'Go on,' he urged and timidly she began looking at the

dresses, examining each one of them, sliding the hanger to see the next.

'Pick out a couple, try 'em on. I'll be back, I need a shirt or two.'

Before she had made a choice, the brisk saleslady came over to assist.

'This would look great on you, honey.'

Jenny nodded no to the bright red dress the sales clerk held out. After a couple of tries she left her saying, 'When you're ready, dressing room's in back.'

Jenny felt confused. Should she try to look older? Maybe that's what was wrong. Maybe if she did, Bobby Lee wouldn't be so disappointed in her. Maybe then he would be tender and it would be all right.

Still, the garish prints of some of the fabrics didn't seem right. In the end she tried on a white cotton dress with tiny yellow flowers, and a pink one with a dainty sweetheart neckline. In the mirror she felt pretty. Her light brown hair tangled around her face in loose natural curls; in one month of marriage it had already grown longer. It now fell four inches below her shoulders. Her face that had become thinner made her dark eyes seem even larger, with her cheekbones more defined. Even without lipstick her lips were full – 'bee-sting' lips, Stella called them.

The dresses weren't exactly right. They didn't make her look any older. Her chest was still flat, with only a small mound where full breasts should have swelled.

Rudely the saleslady swung the curtain open. 'Your daddy's here.'

Nervously she looked toward Bobby Lee; he hadn't heard her.

'My husband,' she whispered.

'Oh,' the saleslady said, contempt alive in her eyes.

Jenny walked out shyly; his brilliant smile told her that he liked it.

'Yes, that one,' he said, and he didn't even ask the price.

Next she tried the white one with the yellow flowers.

'Yes.' Again he smiled.

Suddenly she felt proud to be his wife. He looked so handsome, so assured; he paid the clerk from a wallet stuffed with bills, and while the woman had looked at Jenny with veiled scorn, she tripped over herself calling him 'Sir' and putting each dress in a box.

Things would work out. She had pleased him.

At the grocer's she couldn't believe it. He piled the cart high with meat, canned foods of every description, fruit, fresh and frozen vegetables, and when he'd finished, he took Jenny's hand and led her to the freezer. 'Pick it out. The ice cream, any flavour you want. No, Baby Doll, you can have two.'

To please him she hesitated. 'There's so many flavours.'

'Take your time,' he said, and his face was excited and pleased with this gift he was giving.

'Girls always seem to like chocolate,' he said, and she reached for Dutch chocolate, and to halt the strangeness of it, she reached for a tub of cherry as well.

On the ride home he whistled and tapped his fingers on the steering wheel. He was in a good mood; this was the time for Jenny to mention it.

'Stella's feeling bad,' she began tentatively. 'With all the excitement, she forgot my birthday.'

'Your birthday? When was it?'

'The fifteenth.'

'Gosh, Baby Doll, you should have told me.'

'Tell the truth, I forgot it myself with gettin' married and all.'

'Sweet Sixteen, Jeannie,' and when he looked over, she thought she saw love in his eyes.

It gave her the courage to go on. 'Next Sunday they're wantin' us to come over to see the new house. Stella plans to get a cake and barbecue.' She held her breath.

'Sure,' he agreed, and cheerfully he resumed whistling.

It took them three or four trips to get the groceries up to the house, and when she picked up the boxes with her new dresses, it fell out of the car. It must have been under the seat.

A small barrette dropped onto the ground. Jenny picked up the blue plastic bow, a child's hairslide. Rudely he took it out of her hand, but his face was blanched of colour. 'Probably Tammy's. It's been in there a long time.'

She knew he washed, vacuumed and waxed that car every week. It was his pride and joy. How could he have overlooked it? Silently, they put away the groceries. He was hungry, so she made bacon, lettuce and tomato sandwiches.

'Baseball game's on,' he said, and took his plate and went into the den.

When she brought him the second beer, she noticed his forced cheerfulness as he said, 'Hey, Jeannie, aren't you gonna eat some ice cream?'

'Yes, I am. I thought I'd sit outside a while. I don't understand baseball.'

She served herself a dish of ice cream and sat on the patio in the early dusk watching fireflies dancing in the night. When she was sure it was safe, she took the melting dish of ice cream and poured it out into the bed of daisies. She wasn't sure why!

CHAPTER 10

Jenny called Stella to tell her about her phone call to the Mission. 'Stella, Maw seemed real bad. She's really worried. She even cried on the phone.'

'Cried? What's she crying about?'

'She's fretting 'bout why we're staying away so long. She said this absolutely crazy thing: she thought maybe we were caught by white slavers or something.'

'White slavers? Jesus, that's some wild tale from the twenties. Don't she know this is 1953 and we're two respectable married women?'

'I think we ought to see her.'

'Yeah, I guess you're right. You know, Rodney's been delivering to the Mission every week. Has Bobby Lee?'

'I don't know. I don't ask him and he didn't mention it.'

'Okay. How about tomorrow? I can run out with the car and pick you up. I'd love for you to see the new house, but I guess it can wait until Sunday. It'll look more special with your birthday cake and all.'

Jenny hadn't told Bobby Lee about her plans to visit the Mission, though she wondered if it was a day that he might be delivering there. It was curious that he never mentioned the Mission one way or another, she thought. She roamed the house, roamed the yard, she was anxious for Stella to come. Jenny realized that she yearned to see people, stores, houses, streets. Ever since it had dawned on her that she had been virtually alone in her marvellous house for over a month, she'd felt a restrictive loneliness.

She heard the horn toot. Carefully she checked the doors and ran down to meet Stella. Then she thought she might have left the stove on, and she went back to check. She hadn't.

'I've gotta be back way before six,' Jenny said nervously.

'Haven't you told him where you're going?'

'No. I think he might be worried since I'm only sixteen. He might be thinking Maw will be so angry or have it annulled or something.'

'Then he can't know Maw, or the Reverend. No sirree – once a little virgin has been ruined, ole Roy would never think a woman should be single. You know his idea of marriage: Till death do us part.'

Her words echoed in Jenny's ears, and she felt a quick surge of fear. Till death do us part – it was so final.

'I love your dress. You look so sweet, Sweet Sixteen,' and with that Stella began singing 'Happy Birthday to you, Happy Birthday to you.'

Stella parked in front, by the main door of the Mission. With relief Jenny noticed that no trucks were delivering.

As if they hadn't been gone for a month, Sam came out, tipped his soiled cap that he always wore and said, 'Morning, girls,' as he stroked the hood of the car. 'Nash, ain't it?'

'Yes,' Stella answered. 'My husband bought it for me. It's automatic, too.'

They left him standing there in the bright sun caressing the shiny car.

Both girls went through the door, where familiar smells assailed them – a vague hint of yesterday's dinner, a whiff of mothballs from the clothing room, and the undertone of yesterday's candles burning.

They both fought down a feeling of panic as Addie came towards them, arms outstretched: 'Jenny, Stella!' calling each of them by the wrong name.

'No, no, Stella – Jenny.' And she drew her daughters to her. In a circle they hugged and she cried, 'I was so worried.'

'We're okay – we're fine. No, we're great,' Stella bragged.

'Good, that's good. Addie drew Stella's hand up to admire the ring as if that one visible sign would convince her that everything was all right.

Instinctively Jenny drew her left hand behind her. 'We married with Bobby Lee's ring; he hasn't got mine yet.'

The crease of worry reappeared on Addie's forehead and she searched Jenny's eyes looking for the truth. Her gaze never wavered, and Addie sensed it: something was wrong. They sat as she bustled about the kitchen.

'Tea – we've got a whole load of fancy tea. Let's have that, shall we?' With a flourish she poured, offered wedges of lemon, and reached for some rolls. 'I'll just heat 'em up, makes 'em taste fresh again.'

Jenny felt guilty when she thought of her bulging freezer and pantry full of every kind of food imaginable.

Finally Addie sat. 'Now tell me all about it. Who did you girls marry, and where did you meet them?'

Stella told first, softening the story, glossing over the stolen evenings and trying to make the nights of sneaking out seem romantic. Once again, Jenny was grateful for her ability to alter a story, as she made it seem like they had known both men for a long time.

'Let's see . . . Rodney – don't he deliver for Kroger?'

'Yeah, Maw, that's him, the big red-head one who's always joking with Sam.'

'Sure, sure, I know him.' She turned to Jenny.

'Bobby Lee drives for National,' her daughter said.

'Bobby Lee . . . don't recall him, but you know how it gets, with trucks rolling in and out. It can be real hectic, you know.'

'I'm sure you'd remember, once you saw him. He's dark-headed, with tanned skin and very bright blue eyes,' Jenny said.

'Sounds handsome,' Addie smiled.

'Oh he *is*, Maw.' Stella answered for her sister. 'Your little baby girl's got herself a real good catch. Jenny's got a

105

great big house and acres of beautiful ground. He drives long distance, too.'

'Good, that's good,' and Addie reached over and patted each of their hands.

'Stella's going on about me, well, Maw, she's got herself one of those brand new houses in a subdivision, and Rodney, he taught her to drive and bought her that car,' Jenny said.

'Good, that's good,' Addie repeated, but her mind was already somewhere else.

'How you doing for help?' Jenny asked, really concerned for her mother as she knew how hard Addie worked even when Stella and she had been here to help her.

'Not too bad. I got a young girl staying up in your old room. She was homeless, living on the streets with her little boy, so the Reverend took her in and she's been a treasure. It gave the Reverend another good idea; he's wanting to start a shelter. You know those two buildings across the street? The owners thinking about donating 'em. We'd have to fix 'em up, 'cos they ain't livable in now.'

'That's great, Maw—' Before Jenny had finished what she wanted to say, Reverend Roy appeared in the doorway. His lank frame dressed in black, he took in the sight of his wife with her daughters, and he tried, but couldn't quite manage a smile. 'Morning, girls.'

They both nodded and mumbled something.

'You didn't have to run off. I would have married you both right here,' he said, hurt plain in his voice.

Quickly, Jenny looked at Stella and prayed she wouldn't say anything smart. She surprised her with the gentle lie: 'Didn't want to put you to any trouble, Reverend. You've got so much to do now,' she said humbly.

'No trouble, I like doing weddings. Marriage is sacred, and don't you forget it, girls. God sez it's until death do you part.'

They both nodded. He left the room calling out for Sam.

'You'll have to come out some Sunday, Maw, or Rodney or I could come and get you,' Stella offered.

'I'd like that.' And Addie turned to Jenny as if waiting for the same invitation.

Jenny looked down and picked at the same old spot where the oil cloth was peeling.

Stella, too, seemed surprised that no such invitation was forthcoming. 'Sunday we're having Bobby Lee and Jenny over for barbecue and birthday cake 'cause her birthday done passed – but maybe you'd wanna come out then, Maw?'

'I don't know, I'd have to ask the Reverend.'

Jenny saw the spot of anger flare on Stella's cheeks.

'Don't ask the Reverend, tell him.'

'I guess the truck would be okay. It's running kinda poorly. We'd need directions.'

'Oh Maw, it's not Alaska. We live in St Ann's, about nineteen miles from here. Taking the highway it's even less.'

With that Addie got up and went to the old cabinet, and brought out a package wrapped in green tissue paper. It was decorated with the stars that they gave out at vacation Bible school.

'For your birthday; I didn't forget,' she said as she held the present out to Jenny.

'If you're coming Sunday, can I open it then?'

'Whatever you want, Jenny. She reached out and kissed her daughter's cheek. 'Happy birthday.'

From the hallway they heard the sound of a child crying, and in a minute she entered the room, a thin, pale, blonde girl carrying a small boy on one hip.

'Hush,' she urged the child as she looked at the three of them seated around the table, and the boy quieted.

'I'm sorry,' she said, trying to back out of the room.

'No, Thelma, come on in. I want you to meet my girls. This here's Stella, and Jenny.'

The girls nodded. You could see the naked envy in her

glance as she took in their clean stylish clothes and well-groomed appearance.

'Sit, child,' Addie urged. 'Have a cup of tea and some cake, it's still warm.' She handed the child a piece, and he began munching, the crumbs scattering everywhere.

'Look, Scotty. Look what I found in the donations today,' and out of her pocket Addie took a small toy car, the blue paint still good, and the wheels intact.

The child grabbed the toy car, and proceeded to roll it on the table among the crumbs.

'He's sweet. How old is he?' Jenny asked.

'Almost two.'

She devoured him with her eyes. His pink cheeks were radiant, the straight fair hair fell over his forehead and the chubby fingers were busy with the task of keeping the car moving. 'Brr, Brr,' he gave a motor sound as the car curved and turned on the shiny oilcloth.

'You like kids?' Thelma asked Jenny.

'Yes, I do. I worked with them a little when I was a candy-striper.'

'Yeah, my Jenny's gonna be a good mother; she always loved the little ones,' Addie said proudly, and she looked at Stella and quickly glanced away.

Sam stuck his head in the doorway. 'Trucks coming.'

Jenny's heart raced with fear. '*Dear God, don't let it be Bobby Lee,*' she prayed.

Sam, reappeared. 'It's bread. We can handle it.'

Through the window they saw it was a truck from Kroger.

Stella jumped up. 'Wouldn't it be neat if it was Rodney?' She moved the curtain and watched until the driver alighted. 'No, it's not him.'

They spent the next hour or two talking to their mother, and Jenny felt the urge to see the other rooms. She walked into the chapel; which now seemed smaller and more pathetic somehow.

She would have liked to see their old bedroom, but didn't

want to intrude; they lived there now – Thelma and her little boy.

Jenny heard the meow, and two kittens tumbled out of the storeroom closet chasing a ball of dust. She leaned down to pet them.

Addie came up behind her. 'It's a real shame we couldn't find homes for 'em. Reverend gonna drown 'em Sunday.'

Stella reached down to stroke them. 'I took one, Maw, before I got married. She's so fat now we call her Butterball. Hey, Jenny, with all that ground you've got, why don't you take 'em? It'd be good. They'd make sure you don't have mice.'

Jenny remembered clearly the struggling sack moving under the water in that big old tin pool in the backyard and she found herself saying, 'Sure, I'd love to have them.' And she picked them up and hugged their soft bodies next to her fearful heart.

In the car when Stella started the motor they heard their soft, frightened meows. 'They're really pretty,' Stella said, 'and they'll be company. Don't you get lonely out there in that big ole house?'

'No,' Jenny lied. 'I've got so much to do, with the garden and all. No, I really love it.'

In the rearview window they could see Addie waving for them to stop. Jenny got out. 'What is it, Maw?'

'There's more. I saved them for you,' and Sam brought out three big boxes.

'You know that jewelry stuff you always liked? Well, we got more donations. I told the Reverend right out I wouldn't throw it away. I told him "I'm planning on saving it for Jenny".'

'Thanks,' said Jenny, hugging her mother tightly as Sam loaded them into the trunk.

'Be there at six,' Stella reminded her. 'Don't lose that paper; it's got the directions and phone numbers on the bottom in case you get lost.'

Addie nodded, and waved with her apron, and Scotty came and stood beside her and waved with both hands.

'They'll probably upchuck in that box,' Stella said. 'I think I smell it already.'

'I'll open the back windows.' Jenny reached over and rolled them down. 'Stella, I think I'll tell Bobby Lee they're strays.'

'Oh, why would you do that?'

'Well, you know, he might not like cats, or he might be allergic or something,' she said feebly.

'Okay. Do you want to stop for cat food?'

'No, I've got plenty of food I can give 'em and the store's not too far if I need more. It's really a nice walk.'

'Is that where you shop?'

'Yeah. It's where I bought a couple new dresses, at Grant's in the shopping strip.'

Stella glanced over. 'I meant to tell you, you look so cute in that one.'

'Thanks.'

Stella switched on the radio, and they rode in silence.

At the house Stella carried up two boxes of the broken jewelry, and Jenny carried one and the box that contained the screaming kittens.

Stella stayed while Jenny gave the kittens a saucer of cream, which they lapped up greedily, and then she let them out into the back yard. Within a minute they were happily chasing butterflies.

When she put the cream away, Stella glanced into the full refrigerator. 'With all this food, baby sister, I can't imagine why you're so thin.'

As soon as Jenny saw the car disappear down the road she began looking for a hiding place for the boxes of jewelry parts. The nursery; it would be perfect! She carried them up and stowed them in the closet.

She didn't want to tell Bobby Lee that they had been to the Mission. She didn't want to spoil anything as she was so looking forward to Sunday.

She checked the clock. There was still time, so she went

110

upstairs and sat on the floor and looked through the boxes. They contained a treasure trove of assorted beads, parts of jewelry, peacock feathers and other materials. Her imagination soared. She remembered seeing a craft store next to Grant's. She could walk there, but he never left her any money. She'd find a way. These things, these pretty things, had designs dancing in her mind. She longed to touch them and turn them into completed, beautiful creations. She lined them up, pearls here, beads, red, green iridescent ... all in little piles. Chains, small pieces, large ones, and rhinestones glittered on the floor. Mesmerized, she stroked the precious things.

Through her fog, she heard the sound of a car motor. She glanced out the window. It was Bobby Lee, and she hadn't started supper.

She raced downstairs, opened two cans of chili, and was stirring the pots when he came in.

'Hi, Baby Doll.' She felt his kiss on her neck.

She turned and smiled at him. 'Hi. Did you have a good day?'

'Yeah, it was okay. Is that chili?'

'Yeah. It's so hot, I thought we could just have salad and chili, and ice cream for dessert.'

'We had chili yesterday,' he pointed out.

'Oh, I thought you liked it.'

'I do, but as you said, it's so hot. I was thinking of something like cold chicken.'

'I can do that tomorrow if you want.'

He reached in the refrigerator for a beer, and walked to the screen door and looked out into the yard. With dread she heard the scratching on the screen.

'Damn, there's two cats out here.'

'Yeah. Bobby Lee?' She instinctively raised her voice to make it sound childlike – somehow she knew he loved this. 'Please, please can we keep them?' she begged. 'They're a couple of strays.'

'Well...' he looked down at the two kittens. 'I don't want them clawing the furniture.'

'I promise, I promise,' she almost lisped. 'I wouldn't dare let them in the living room or the dining room either.'

'If you're a good little girl, you can keep them,' he said solemnly.

CHAPTER 11

The new playful kittens and the treasure trove of beads made her feel less lonely. She needed things, so when Bobby Lee slept she went through his pockets and found small bits of change. When she had amassed a couple of dollars she started out on the pleasant walk to the shopping area.

The walk turned out to be not so pleasant, as August tended to be very hot. Waves of heat rose from the blacktop and she walked slower.

At Raylean's Jenny saw the orange crates by the overgrown driveway, and sitting importantly behind her makeshift table was the little girl, swirling a pitcher of dark purple Kool Aid.

Jenny stopped, brushed off her sweat-stained face and said, 'You're just what I need. It's hot and I'm really thirsty.'

'It's a nickel. If you want an ice cube it's seven cents.'

'Well, seems like I better have the ice cube,' and she dug into her pocket sorting the change. The child swirled the spoon rapidly trying to catch a small sliver of ice.

'It's gone,' she said dejectedly.

'That's okay – it still looks cold,' and Jenny handed her the seven cents.

She poured the Kool Aid into a large plastic cup, not stopping till it overflowed.

Gratefully Jenny drank the sugar-sweet drink, wiped off

her mouth and replaced the cup. 'I never did get your name when you were up at the house.'

The child looked at her, smirking with importance. 'I know your name. You're Mrs Antree.'

'That's right, but it's not fair I don't know your name.'

'It's Patsy. Here.' She held out the two cents. 'I didn't have no ice cubes left.'

'That's okay. Maybe next time you'll give me two.'

The girl shook her head yes, liking the compromise. 'I like coming to your house on Tuesdays.'

'Well, good, I'm glad.'

'I didn't like coming on Saturdays.'

'Why not?'

She put two dirty Kool Aid stained hands over her mouth. 'I'm not supposed to say,' and she looked worriedly towards the house. 'Bye!' and she left the table with the half-full pitcher of Kool Aid growing warmer in the hot sun.

Jenny walked on, worried and curious. There were secrets in that house, in its attic and the playroom – and she felt she would be better off if she never learned them.

At the craft shop she spent her money carefully. She bought a new clay that could be fired, and was ideal for jewelry. Already she imagined wonderful necklaces decorated with rhinestones. She also bought cord, jump rings, and clasps.

Satisfied and happy, she crossed the street to walk on the shady side going back, and saw one of her favourite places in the world – a library.

Inside, she browsed among the books and found a section on jewelry. She sat entranced, turning over page after page of pictures of beautiful pieces of jewelry, some of it going back to the Middle Ages.

When she replaced the large illustrated books she found the one that changed her life.

It was a book on costume-jewelry designers. Rapidly she flicked through the pages. Women were represented here –

114

Chanel, Schiaparelli – but closer to home right here in America were women designers like Miriam Haskell. Jenny almost quivered with happiness at the pictures of the designers' creations, their silky Baroque pearls woven into brooches with seed pearls and filigree. Jenny drank in the beauty on these pages, and new names swirled around in her head ... Hattie Carnegie, Nettie Rosenstein ... they were women and they were designers, and like fresh knowledge she began to see again the world of design, the plaque on the wall, the sleek chair she was sitting in, the sculpture in the middle of the room.

This world of design called to her in some secret language, and at that moment she did not know how, or where, or when – but she felt it waiting for her in the unknown future.

At the counter she filled out the card, desperately wanting to take home some of those books.

'Do you have any identification or anything with your address on it?' the librarian asked.

'No.'

'Well, in that case we'll have to mail you the card. That will be ten cents.'

Jenny looked in her pocket and found only one penny left.

The woman looked at her kindly, decided in her favour and said, 'You can pay it first time you check something out.'

With a new-found happiness she walked along the road appreciating all the beauty around her. She saw it in the tall majestic trees, the shy wildflowers, even in the blades of grass, the miracle of all that God had designed.

At home she put the craft supplies in the playroom and treated the kittens to liver from the chicken that she had started to prepare for supper.

'Something smells real good,' Bobby Lee said as he came in from work, reached for his cold beer and walked to the screen door to look out over the yard. It was a ritual, a habit of some kind.

'I've made fried chicken and mashed potatoes, with some of our own ripe tomatoes.'

'Good for you, Jeannie. I told you you had a green thumb.'

Jenny felt relaxed. He was in a good mood, and as she stole glances at him she realized how handsome he really was. If only things were different; maybe they'd change. To keep her mood hopeful she said, 'Maybe we could eat outside on the patio?'

He glanced at her with a puzzled look and she realized why. She had just made a suggestion all of her own. Usually she was always asking permission.

The food tasted better out there in the soft summer evening. The temperature had dropped to make it comfortable, a breeze stirred the tops of the trees and high up, small black birds like commas swooped and dipped in the air.

'Are they bats?' she asked.

'No, they're chimney swifts.'

They both lay back in the comfortable lawn chairs, and for once she felt herself drift, until in a quiet voice he said; 'I delivered to the Mission today.' She held her breath and waited. 'They seemed to know me there – at least, your Maw did.'

'Stella told her which ones you were, our husbands, I mean.' She paused. 'She invited them for Sunday, and she said Maw seemed real glad for us.'

'Is that right?'

'Yes, she said Maw seemed real glad.'

There was an awkward silence, then he said what he always said after dinner. 'Aren't you gonna have any ice cream?'

'Oh yeah, sure. You want some?'

'No, I bought it for you,' he said, looking at her.

Jenny went into the house, filled the smallest bowl she could find and went back out to join him. He stretched forward to look at the bowl. 'Aren't you having chocolate?'

'It's all gone.'

'Oh, I'm sorry, I have to get you more,' and he laughed indulgently. 'I remember little girls always like chocolate best of all.'

'That's right,' and slowly she began to eat, forcing herself to finish the small bowl, while he watched her intently.

'That's good,' he pronounced, as if praising a small child who had finished all of its spinach. Then: 'I'm tired, it's been a rough day. Guess I'll turn in early. Coming?'

'I thought I'd sit out a while,' she said.

He reached down and kissed her cheek, saying, 'Night, hon.'

The screen door slammed and she watched the kittens playing a game of chase with the numerous lightning bugs, racing back and forth across the wide lawn.

The sky deepened to purple, and one magnificent star rose and shimmered in the sky.

She squeezed her eyes shut and murmured, 'Star light, Star bright, I wish I may, I wish I might have the wish I wish tonight.'

She opened her eyes and looked up at the trembling star and said out loud, 'Please make Bobby Lee love me. Take away whatever this evil is. Make him love me, like love's supposed to be.'

CHAPTER 12

Jenny was as nervous as a cat when Sunday arrived. She had muttered silent prayers all day. *'Let it be okay, please. No scenes, let it be good.'*

Bobby Lee looked great; he had made a special effort. His light blue shirt brought out the blue in his eyes, his navy slacks had a razor-sharp crease, and he had polished his black loafers until they were like twin mirrors.

She felt touched, for it seemed like he wanted to make a good impression. He had even bought two bottles of imported champagne to toast her birthday.

'You're lookin' sweet and beautiful, little girl,' he said as they held hands walking to the car.

She felt she did look okay. Her skin had tanned to a dusty rose from all the time she spent in the garden.

After shampooing, she had brushed her hair till it shone, light brown with tints of gold from the sun. Her eyes looked dark as coals, and her face was beginning to fill out a little. She wore the pink dress with the sweetheart neckline. Regretfully when she looked in the mirror she thought, just a touch of pink on her lips would have made it perfect, but she didn't have any lipstick.

The radio played softly in the car as they drove and Bobby Lee turned to her. ''Member that song? It was playing that night we drove to Arkansas.'

'Yeah, they played it more than once.'

'Mona Lisa ... Mona Lisa ... men have named you ...' and his voice blended with Nat King Cole's on the radio.

Jenny's nervousness melted and she felt so happy. The family would all be together tonight; it was a warm feeling.

They had a little trouble finding Stella's place, as all the houses in the subdivision were alike. 'Stella said to look for the gas lamp; her address is on it,' Jenny said.

'Two-three-two-one – is that it?'

'Yes. I see it, it's the next one up,' Jenny instructed.

He pulled up to the kerb, and they were in front of a snug brick bungalow with a manicured lawn and small new shrubs that still had the tags hanging from the branches.

On the second ring, Stella opened the door; a cloud of perfume hovered over her. 'Jenny, happy birthday!' and she was caught in her sister's warm embrace.

Stella looked at Bobby Lee, hesitated, then grabbed him in a hug. 'Hi, brother-in-law,' she smiled.

He smiled back. 'Hi.'

Rodney took Bobby Lee off to the back yard so they could talk and he could still watch the pork chops simmering on the pit. The air was redolent with the aroma of delicious barbecue.

Stella took Jenny from room to room. The living room was done in rock maple – big comfortable chairs, a sturdy coffee table loaded down with magazines. Next, the dining room was blond Swedish-modern. 'I don't know why I did this,' Stella said. 'It's those furniture stores. They're so big you want everything. I guess the styles don't mix.'

'They're okay,' Jenny said unconvincingly.

'No, they're not. I should have asked you to go with me. Like the teacher said, you gotta flair for design or something like that.'

'Stella, it's great, all brand new. That's what you always wanted.'

'True.'

Next, they inspected the kitchen. A blind man could see that this was her pride and joy.

'That over there's a dishwasher, and Rodney insisted we get a Mixmaster, toaster, and a real good coffee pot. I guess that's why I'm getting so fat.'

'No, you're not,' Jenny protested, but as she looked down she could see the toreador pants stretched out over her round tummy.

They looked at each other, and Stella smiled the tiniest of smiles.

'Are you—' Jenny didn't finish, for Stella was grinning like a Cheshire Cat.

'Yes, I'm two months.'

'Two months?'

'Yeah, honey. I lied to you. We did it a couple of times before we were married.'

'You did? Why, Stella, all that talk about – you know – only doing certain things.'

'I did it for you, Jenny. I didn't want you to get into trouble.'

'Why, thank you, big sister, but what was all that about you not wanting any babies?'

'Oh Jenny, I love Rodney so much, I want a little boy just like him. I can't wait.'

'What if it's a girl?'

'Then I'll love her to death, too, and we'll keep trying till I get my little boy.'

'That's wonderful.'

Stella suddenly looked wistful standing in her bright new kitchen. 'Remember, you used to ask me all the time did I love him? Well, I didn't know, honest to God, I didn't know, but I do now. I love Rodney with all my heart.'

Jenny nodded, and Stella tugged her along to see the new tiled bathroom, all in aqua and pink.

'It's elegant, to use your word, don't you think?'

'It sure is,' Jenny agreed.

'Now for the most important room in the house, the bedroom. Swedish-modern, like the dining room,' Stella said, and Jenny could see her sister's pride as she rubbed the top of the blond dresser. 'It must have been something I read or had seen in the movies that made me pick maple for the living room. It just seems people can't be unhappy if they got chairs and couches like that,' Stella finished, and

121

before Jenny could agree with her they heard the backfire of the old truck.

They walked out to meet Addie and the Reverend, and Stella began the same tour as Jenny went out into the yard to join the men.

They were laughing and talking companionably, and Bobby Lee brought her a chair and asked if he could get her a soda or something.

Stella had already set the picnic table with a checkered paper tablecloth and white paper plates; on either end, votive candles gave out the scent of oil of citronella to keep the mosquitoes at bay.

When Stella finally brought Addie and the Reverend outside the men shook hands solemnly, and it was strange, for they were all familiar with each other, from a different time and place, and now they were all family.

Addie seemed to watch Bobby Lee as if crawling into his mind, to fathom what on earth this handsome worldly man could have seen in her very, very young daughter. She guessed him to be almost thirty.

Stella's kitten wove in and out of the various seated legs, rubbing his fur against trousers and bare legs.

'Looks just like our strays,' Bobby Lee said as he reached down to pet the cat. Jenny saw Stella's mouth open, then, remembering, she turned away and began placing the plastic forks on the table.

The dinner was mouth-watering, the meat succulent and smothered in tart barbecue sauce.'

'Great sauce,' Bobby Lee commented.

'It's not any ole sauce out of a bottle. No sirree. I add a beer, Budweiser. You pour just a little when the coals blaze up, then add a little more beer to the sauce.

'I'll have to try that,' Bobby Lee said.

For a moment there was an awkward silence as they all remembered that the Reverend was a reformed alcoholic.

Stella brought out the coffee, then after pouring she went back into the house and returned with a huge white birthday cake blazing with candles.

Their voices blended as they sang 'Happy Birthday' and Jenny felt the blush beginning in her cheeks.

'Make a wish,' Stella urged.

She closed her eyes and made the same wish as before. '*Make Bobby Lee love me, really love me, like love is supposed to be.*'

She inhaled and blew out at the flickering candles. They went out and Jenny heard the roar of approval just as one candle relit and burned brightly.

'It doesn't matter,' Addie said, 'it's just foolish superstition,' and she looked from her daughter to Bobby Lee as if she had read Jenny's mind and knew what her wish was.

The corks popped and with a flourish Bobby Lee poured, filling the glasses to the brim. He stopped in front of the Reverend's empty glass and moved on.

'To Jeannie,' Bobby Lee toasted.

'He calls me that,' she whispered to her mother, who looked surprised.

'To Jenny,' Stella repeated the toast, and they all raised their glasses in a birthday toast, including the Reverend, who brought the empty glass up to his lips.

'Presents – presents,' Stella called, and she held out a large box beautifully wrapped.

'It's so pretty, I hate to open it,' Jenny said, and carefully she slipped off the bow, picked at the sellotape, and removed the lid to reveal a black jersey dress with red feather trim.

'It's beautiful,' she exclaimed, all the while knowing it would look better on Stella than it ever would on her.

Next, Momma handed her the green tissue package she had seen at the Mission. The good conduct stars had lifted a little in the heat. She opened the box to find a crucifix on a dainty chain.

'It's beautiful, Maw, and Reverend. Thank you.'

'It's sterling,' Addie said. 'Chain is, too. I'll hook it on if you want.' And she came behind Jenny, and after struggling for a few minutes Stella offered, 'Here Maw, I'll do it,' and deftly she hooked the small catch.

Bobby Lee looked slightly tipsy, but Jenny was so proud of him; he was being so cordial.

Almost shyly he handed her a small box. With shaking hands, she tore at the tissue, and flipped open the lid. In front of her, in this tiny box, was the most magnificent ring she had ever seen.

The large square-cut diamond winked in the light; the perfect stone was surrounded by baguette emeralds. She was breathless with surprise.

'It was my mother's,' he said. 'Go on, put it on.'

Jenny hesitated and he reached over and took out the ring and slid it on her finger.

'Let me see,' Stella urged, almost as breathless as Jenny. 'Must be at least a carat.'

'It's two,' he said quietly.

Stella took her hand, pulling her around the yard to stop in front of Addie, the Reverend and finally Rodney.

'When are you gonna get me a rock like this?' she teased.

'Probably never,' he joked back.

'It's been a wonderful birthday. I thank all of you. I can't remember any birthday as wonderful as this,' and Jenny continued to stare at her hand in disbelief.

When the cake was eaten, Addie said they had to go; it was a long drive home. After promises to do it again real soon, they left, the truck smoking and backfiring as it pulled out of the driveway. It was a perfect evening. They were all full of good food, and slightly tipsy from the champagne.

'Come on, I've got something else to show you,' Stella said, and they left their husbands out in the dark yard finishing the last of the champagne.

In her bedroom Stella rummaged through the closet. 'I've got so many clothes that I've gotten too big for; they might fit you – especially this one dress. I just love it, but not with these hips.'

She pulled out a crushed velvet dress with a low neckline. 'Try it on. Go on, Jenny, have something special to match that ring.'

124

With a weak protest, Jenny gave in, and found herself snuggling into the tight, short dress.

'I wasn't sure that you'd look good in black, but you look terrific,' Stella marvelled. 'Here,' she flung a pair of high-heeled shoes at her.

Jenny wobbled unsteadily on the high heels.

'Sit down,' and as she sat on the vanity bench, with a vengeance Stella tugged at her hair. 'Upsweep, that's what you need,' and she pinned and pinned until the curls were piled attractively on top of Jenny's head.

From the drawer she took out a pair of large rhinestone earrings. 'They're clip-ons. My damn ears grew back, the holes kept closing up, so this is easier.'

Jenny looked at the stranger in the mirror. Was this really her? She stared at the earrings. They were flashy, but kinda pretty.

'I know what you're thinking. I didn't steal 'em – I don't do that any more,' Stella confessed.

'I didn't accuse you.'

'Let's join the gentlemen now,' Stella said wickedly, as she painted Jenny's lips scarlet with a little brush. As the final touch, she aimed an atomizer at her and Jenny was surrounded by the musky scent of heavy perfume.

Back in the yard, the candles had flickered out and only a patch of light fell onto the grass from the kitchen window.

Jenny took the chair in the darkest shadow.

'What?' Bobby Lee said as he strained forward.

Stella laughed. 'I'll say what. What do you call it when a caterpillar turns into a butterfly?'

'Metamorphosis,' Jenny said in a strained voice.

The men smoked quietly for a few minutes. 'We better be going,' Bobby Lee said.

'So early? I thought maybe we could play us a little cards,' Rodney said regretfully.

'Maybe some other time. I'm driving out of state tomorrow. I got a run down to Tulsa,' Bobby Lee explained as he rose from the chair and stretched.

Stella handed Jenny the bag with her other clothes. They

hugged and then she and Rodney stood in the lighted doorway waving goodbye.

Bobby Lee drove in silence. Jenny could see by the set of his jaw that he was clenching his teeth together. She knew he was angry. Nervously, she chattered on and on about how lovely the party was, and when he parked she followed him up to the house walking unsteadily on the six-inch heels.

When they got inside she noticed that he didn't go to the den, and after a few minutes she heard him calling from upstairs.

'Jeannie, Jeannie! Come up here right now.'

She took off the shoes and walked barefoot up the thickly carpeted steps. With dread she opened the bedroom door, but no candles blazed. He was standing in the middle of the room clenching and unclenching his fists.

'Come here,' he ordered. She walked towards him on legs made of rubber.

Quick as lightning, his hand caught the dress and ripped it right down the middle. Then he pulled her towards the bathroom where she saw the tub filled with bubble bath.

He unhooked her bra, tore off her pants, and pushed her roughly into the water.

He knelt and pulled the pins out of her hair, and with the sponge, he rubbed her body briskly. 'The stink of it, just like the whores at all the truck stops, wantin' a quick fuck in a filthy bathroom. They all smell like this, Jeannie, just like this.'

The sponge pushed across her painted lips, and he turned the mirror towards her. 'Just look at yourself,' and she saw the lipstick smeared across her face and her eyes wild with fright.

'Off,' he commanded as he scrubbed her body, desperately trying to eradicate the scent of perfume and lipstick. He only liked the smell of innocent roses.

When he'd finished, he pulled her out of the tub, and she stood trembling on the bath mat. His smart, well-creased trousers were damp and streaked with soap. Almost gently now, he rubbed and patted her dry.

'That's better,' he said. 'Much better.'

Taking a fresh towel, he put it in the middle of the bed. 'Lie down,' he said. 'No, move over. I want your butt on that towel.'

She scooted, terrified, as she saw those eyes looking down at her from that hateful portrait.

'Don't move,' he commanded, and when he returned from the bathroom, she felt faint, for she saw the glint of his straight-edged razor.

Her eyes flew to the door. Should she try and run? But he caught her thought, went over to the door and she heard the finality of a click as he locked the door and took out the key.

He came over to her. 'Spread 'em!' – and she couldn't, so he moved her trembling legs, and she heard the swish of the can as he sprayed the shaving cream over her. He bit his lip in deep concentration and began shaving, up and down, sideways, wiping the cream on the towel.

He moved her reluctant legs, changed positions, but carefully, slowly, making sure he got every bit, he kept shaving. She closed her eyes, and the only sound was the scrape of the razor.

'There, that's better,' he said finally. She kept her eyes closed, as she felt him get off the bed. She heard the clatter of things from the bathroom, the soft sound of cloth as he removed his clothes. 'That's how little pussies should look,' he said, and the bed shook as he climbed in, knelt between her legs, and she heard his rough command.

'Look at him.'

She opened her eyes. His penis was erect, and on his knees he moved forward.

'I'm gonna fuck you, little girl,' and for a change he entered gently.

'Don't move,' he commanded, and he moved in and out of her, slowly. 'You're a good little girl, see how long Dickie can last when you're good.'

127

She closed her eyes, and the rhythm of his body increased. He withdrew. 'Tell him, tell him you want Big Dickie in there.'

Jenny gulped. 'I do,' she whispered.

'No, tell him.'

'I want Big Dickie in there,' she said softly.

'Okay. I'll give you some,' and he entered again; slowly he went in and out, and deep in her belly she felt it rise. She wanted to move with him.

'That's it, Baby Doll. If you want to, you can, back and forth. All little girls like to fuck once you teach 'em how.'

His words repulsed her; over and over he hissed them in her ear, but her body betrayed her and she felt some pleasure. She hated herself for the indignity of what he had done to her.

When he had finished he looked down at her. 'Your tits look bigger. Are you knocked up?'

She shook her head no. He rolled over, looked up at the portrait of his mother. 'She had real big teats,' he said. 'Painted 'em black with shoe polish so I'd stop sucking 'em. Can you imagine a mother like that – a real bitch!'

Jenny began counting back. It was almost eight weeks now – with alarm she realized Bobby Lee was right. She *was* knocked up.

'Are you hungry?' he asked.

'No.'

'I could run down and get you a dish of ice cream. Uh oh, I forgot. We're out of chocolate.'

CHAPTER 13

She did not have to face him in the morning. He had left early. Automatically she dressed, straightened the bedroom and went downstairs to do some chores, all without thinking. She made cereal and toast only to throw them away as her throat couldn't swallow. She went out into the beautiful fall morning to sit listlessly on the chair, staring at the clouds that drifted and changed direction in the brilliant blue sky.

In all her life she had never felt so alone. Her hand rested on her flat stomach. Was it possible? Out of those ugly encounters, was it possible that a life had been created and in this very minute was growing?

She yearned for the shabby bedroom with the map of Africa on the ceiling, and the innocence she had felt then. Mistakes could be so final. No, it would not do to call up Momma and cry her heart out; the Reverend, he believed marriage to be until death did us part. Even if this were not so, could she take a baby so fresh and new to breathe the stale air in the Mission and eyes to trace the world in tumbled bricks and graffiti walls? Maybe this would change him; Bobby Lee, someone's daddy, maybe this was the miracle she needed. Could a sweet, lovely baby erase the gutter language from his mind and replace it with love?

No, she wished him away, this child that grew, and her hand slowly rubbed the flat surface of her stomach and she knew without knowing how, that all her regrets and wishes would not erase him. No, she felt a connection. He lived.

From the empty house she heard the phone ringing. 'I won't answer it,' she thought. She imagined Stella, her voice excited, planning, sharing, cribs, curtains, toys, names tumbling off her tongue. No, she could not listen and pretend, when here under her hand a tiny being lived, her jailer who held the key that would keep her here in this beautiful prison without walls. She knew he was male. Stella said (it seemed so long ago), 'men – they're in charge, always have been, always will be.' She could not bear it, if it was a girl. No, she did not want anyone to suffer as she did.

Jenny closed her eyes. Pinpoints of colour swirled and dipped. The beads called to her, gave her shaking hands a purpose. She went up to the playroom, took them out, sorted the colours . . . and like an anaesthesia for the mind, she began designing the necklace. Outside falling leaves brushed against the window, and they inspired her. From the plasticene she moulded these leaves to be festooned with pearls. The work was good, it had the ability to stop the ticking of the clocks, and halt the fear running through her mind.

She worked fervently until shadows on the floor alerted her that it was time to go down and start the supper.

Like an actor from the Jekyll & Hyde movie, he came in, kissed her cheek and held out the carton – some sort of peace offering.

'I remembered, Dutch chocolate,' he said, as he put the ice cream in the freezer and stared through the screen looking out into the yard.

He showered while she set the table, and she heard from upstairs the vague sound of singing.

Across the table they sat, two strangers, and finally she could eat, her appetite matching his. She pretended and hoped that she was answering at the proper pauses as he told her of his day. Through the fog she heard that at the end of the week he was going on a long run, all the way to Denver. Her heart sang – *five days of freedom*. Sometimes these were won at a great price, as on his return there were

130

new indignities, but sometimes he returned with a guilty air and thankfully she was ignored.

He passed the kitchen counter. 'What's this – cookies?' He fingered the tray of baked leaves.

'No, it's clay. Last week Stella brought some beads over from the Mission and with Raylean doing the cleaning, I've got plenty of time, so I've been playing around making things.' She held her breath.

He poked at a leaf. 'It looks real.'

'Do you think so?' she responded, pretending she wanted his approval.

'Yeah.' From his pocket he removed a letter. 'It's from the library, addressed to you.' He held it up, not handing it to her. 'Bring me a beer and let's talk about it. Seems a lot has been going on that I don't know about.'

In the den, he drank his beer, watching her carefully. She was thankful that she had brought in her second cup of coffee; it gave her something to do. She sipped and replaced the cup in its saucer, then sipped again. It was an activity of sorts. For she couldn't bear the thought of sitting across from him with her hands folded obediently in her lap.

'Now what about these beads?'

'Well,' she began, 'someone donated boxes of jewelry parts to the Mission, and Momma saved 'em for me. She knew I always liked to make things. I liked art in school.'

He nodded. 'What about this?' He held up the offending letter.

'It's only an application for a library card.'

He flapped the letter back and forth against his knee. 'When did you go to the library?'

'One day when it was nice out. All the housework was done, so I walked up to the centre.'

'Are you sure you didn't drive up with Stella?'

'No, I walked.'

'You never mentioned it.'

'I guess it was when you were gone, so I forgot.'

'You forgot. And what else did you forget to tell me?'

'Nothing, Bobby Lee. I just had some time, before.' She stopped. 'I always went to the library before. I like to read.'

'I guess there's no harm in that. But I don't want you riding around in that car with Stella.'

'I'm not. She hardly has any free time. She'll have less now with the baby and all.'

'The baby?'

'Yes, she's pregnant.'

'Well, well, good ole Rodney. I guess that will tie her down a little, keep her out of trouble. I never could figure out why he bought her that car.'

Jenny waited as he finished his beer.

'The library has a lot of books on crafts and design. I'd like to borrow some of them,' she said quietly.

'Yeah, that's right. I remember Stella saying you were kinda artistic.'

Jenny drained her cup, it seemed to clatter as she replaced it in the saucer. Nervously she went on: 'There's a craft shop next door to the library. They have all kinds of things.'

He laughed. 'But you don't have any money.'

She looked down into her lap.

'Well, well, Baby Doll, maybe I could start giving you a little allowance. Would that make you happy?'

Surprised, she nodded yes.

'But if I do, I don't want you buying that disgusting lipstick, nor do I want you stinking of perfume.'

'No, I wouldn't do that,' she answered him. She smoothed her skirt tightly around her knees.

'Why do girls always do that?'

'What?'

'You know, pull their skirts so tight around their knees. I gotta right to look up there if I want to.'

Jenny gulped. It was beginning. Something awful was beginning.

He gestured with his hands. 'Open.'

She looked around wildly. 'Here – now?'

'Sure, why not? Open,' he commanded.

132

She felt her legs trembling and felt a tic in her left cheek begin its dance. Impatient now he shouted, 'Open!'

Slowly her knees drifted apart.

His face wore a slight smile.

'You're wearing pink pants.' He leaned his head back further on the couch. 'When Georgia and I walked to school on rainy days I made her walk over the puddles, so I could see her pants reflected in the water. She wore pink panties a lot.' His smile deepened with the memory of his sister, where love and hate bloomed side by side.

'Take them off.'

Jenny sat there, her legs still trembling nervously, fear coming alive in the pit of her stomach.

'I said take them off – now!'

She stood up, held the arm of the chair and removed her underwear. They dropped on the floor in a tangled blur of pink.

'Now sit down the way you were before.'

She did.

Minutes ticked by. The soft sound of the TV expounded on the virtues of laundry soap as he looked, cocking his head from side to side.

'I like that,' he pronounced. 'We got a new rule around this house. From now on you don't wear panties when I'm home, and when you sit, you sit just like that so I can look any time I want to. I'm your husband; I've got rights.'

It was on that evening that she found the ability to do it – to transport herself away. Later on, the psychiatrist told her it was a form of self-hypnosis, a need-created skill that permitted her to survive the years of that abusive marriage, and even to live through the night which was to come – the night that Melanie died.

She didn't know if it was fifteen or even thirty minutes later, but the hall clock chiming eight o'clock released her.

'Ball game's on. Turn the channel,' he ordered.

Thankfully, she got up and changed the channel, picked up the empty beer bottle, her cup, and somehow she smiled at him and said, 'Dishes,' and she was free in the kitchen crying over the sink as she rinsed the dirty plates and stacked them carefully in the dishwasher.

She took the tray of leaves up to the playroom and arranged them in a pattern. She lost herself in thoughts of the work at hand, selecting, rejecting, until she was satisfied with the clusters of pearls fixed in bunches between the leaves, the necklace in perfect symmetry as the leaves graduated smaller and smaller toward the back.

She threaded the cord through the holes, not knowing the length she wanted. She went to the mirror and held the finished product up to her throat. The tangles of her hair prevented a clear view, so with a rubber band she secured her hair into a careless ponytail. Now she saw the necklace clearly. It was perfect. She took pleasure in the beauty she had created. She sat down to finish it; it needed a clasp.

At first she didn't hear him, but with that instinct she had developed she felt his eyes and looked up to see him leaning in the doorway, a rapt look upon his face. She could not know the pleasure he felt looking about the toy-filled room, and her sitting at the tiny table, her project spread upon it. She must have looked like a small child playing a favourite game.

He nodded towards her knees, and she let her legs drift apart.

Satisfied, he said, 'Goodnight, Baby Doll.' At the sight of his retreating back she said silently over and over, *'Thank you, God. Thank You.'*

In the morning on the kitchen table he had left it, the library application, and next to it a generous stack of bills, her allowance.

With disgust she realized she had become like a wild animal, her spirit broken; she could not run out of the cage even with the door wide open, for she had nowhere to run to. She took the bills and sat down looking through the craft catalogue. She had found something, however, a life-line that would help her to survive.

Suddenly, the nausea overcame her. She barely made it

to the sink. It was true, she had kept pushing it out of her consciousness, but now she had to face it. She was pregnant.

What would happen now? Could the marriage get better? Could it get worse? She had no idea how he felt about children. In all this time Bobby Lee had only once mentioned his daughter, the day she had found the blue plastic bow. He had said it was probably Tammy's.

CHAPTER 14

The books and the jewelry transformed her life. They created a wall behind which she could retreat from the other part of her life. Fortunately, just lately, Bobby Lee had been getting more and more long-distance runs, and to her surprise one day while looking for paper to draw on, she found two very curious things.

The first was his bank book, hidden inside an old magazine in the prim living room that they never used. She stared at the numbers; her husband was rich. Methodically entered in regular sequence, he had saved over twenty thousand dollars.

She couldn't believe it; a daydream started vividly in her mind. If only she had a small portion of it, she could run away, find a house somewhere, have the baby in peace. Visions of getting her high-school diploma by test could be a real possibility. She could work, she had done lots of things at the Mission – it was all experience. But she needed money.

Sitting on her knees in that dim beautiful room her imagination ran wild . . . to the future when the baby was bigger. Maybe she could even go to art school?

She dreamed on and on, not realizing at first that someone was knocking. Carefully she replaced the book inside the magazine and answered the front door. She had forgotten it was the second Tuesday.

Raylean and Patsy waited impatiently on the porch.

'Oh, something's come up. I don't need you today,' she

137

said. But seeing the anger in the woman's face she hastily went on: 'Of course, it's not your fault, so I intend to pay just the same,' and Jenny went to the hall table and collected the envelope that Bobby Lee always left for her.

Suspiciously, Raylean took the envelope, looked her over, and her eyes stopped and rested on her tummy. It was too soon, but somehow she knew.

Jenny saw them go down the steps and she could hear Patsy whining, 'What about the ice cream?'

She began the search. She had no idea what she was looking for, but this was a house of secrets; of that she was certain. In the dining room, under a neatly folded pile of linen tablecloths, she found the album.

It was a curious record. In it were early pictures of Bobby Lee's mother, her smile wide and proud, and so young, attired in a magnificent wedding dress, her hands trailing an enormous bouquet of roses. Next to her stood a man in a tuxedo, but carefully the photo had been altered. Instead of a smiling male face, a round empty hole stared back at her, where a small pair of scissors had methodically snipped, leaving the groom a faceless nonentity.

Next came a series of happy baby pictures. There was his mother holding a curly dark-haired child, who clutched a rag doll. His sister, it must be Bobby Lee's sister – he had called her Georgia. Jenny stared at the tiny face and could find no family resemblance to Bobby Lee.

Then it began, page after page, pictures of the children – a happy or crying girl-child, and next to her a faceless small boy. Like the groom, the entire album had been altered *to remove the very existence of Bobby Lee*.

At the very back of the album, Jenny found a folded piece of paper. Scrawled across it in vivid red lipstick were the words *Bitch, Bitch, Bitch* repeated over and over.

Not knowing what to expect, with trembling hands Jenny unfolded the paper.

138

It was the last will and testament of Sylvia Antree, executed some five years ago. She had left the house, cash and a fortune in stocks and shares to Georgia. And to her son Bobby Lee, she had left the sum of one dollar.

How she must have hated him ... but why? Jenny slammed the album shut. Secrets – there were so many secrets in this house.

She cocked her head and listened, for faintly she heard it again, that sound of weeping. It was only the wind, or a lost kitten, she told herself – and yet it always seemed to come from upstairs. Despite the warm, sunny day, she shivered involuntarily.

'Silly, I'm being silly,' she whispered, but forced herself to go upstairs and investigate. In front of her bedroom door she paused, for the noise had grown softer now, but she was still certain that it had issued from the attic. Bobby Lee had mentioned bats so she armed herself with a small toy broom from the nursery and began to climb the narrow stairway. Halfway up she felt a sudden change: the air grew unnaturally still. She froze and listened but there was only silence now.

Jenny opened the attic door, dust motes danced in the stale air and a trapped wasp buzzed as it flung itself repeatedly against the window. She could feel it happening to her – that familiar lightness in her head, and when she looked towards the window SHE SAW THEM – arranged in a perfect heart of sunlight just as they had been bathed in moonlight on that fateful night in 1927.

The snowy-white satin coverlet was like a luxurious bed where they lay on three matching pillows – the beautiful woman flanked on each side by a small child, the curly blonde heads leaning lovingly inward towards hers. Such a tender scene ... until Jenny noticed the blood-red stains blooming on the magnificent cover. A large, dark-haired man had slumped forward, not touching their perfection; a small silver revolver gleamed in his open hand.

Time stood still. And then a searing pain shot through Jenny's head. She closed her eyes and when she finally opened them . . . her harrowing glimpse into the past was gone.

She sank to the dusty floor and leaned back against the trunk, trying to catch her breath. Everything seemed normal now; the old toys, tops, balls and forgotten dolls were sad, true, but only in an ordinary way. Her shaking hand sought the floor but instead came to rest on the doctor's kit. Reluctantly she looked towards the door; the long scratches on it took on a more sinister significance now.

Then the lightness in her head returned and she saw him – a small dark-haired boy – and she covered her ears as his voice released a horrible howl and his fists beat a frantic tattoo against the attic floor. Suddenly he turned to face her and she looked into the boy's startling blue eyes . . . *it was Bobby Lee*.

She squinted her eyes tightly shut, willing the vision to go away, and began praying frantically, her chanting drowning out the inhuman sounds. It seemed an eternity until she felt rather than heard the silence. *Afraid, she was so afraid!*

Fearfully, she opened her eyes at last. The attic looked the same as before, but it was different now, for she had seen too much of its abominable past. The evil that had taken place here, in this room . . . the walls . . . the floor . . . *the window* had all been witness to it, and now she knew THE HOUSE REMEMBERED.

The soft ping of summer rain began, playing a tune of sorts against the solitary heart-shaped window. The imprisoned wasp hurled itself on the glass one last time, then lay on its back on the floor, feebly twitching its tired legs. Jenny crawled to the door and made her way unsteadily downstairs, vowing never to enter that room again.

In the coolness of the kitchen she sipped water and counted the ticks of the clock, trying to control her panic. She remembered Bessie and her talk of a torn curtain, of glimpses into the future. But this time she had looked back.

She felt a small movement in her stomach and knew the

child lived. She needed to talk to someone – not about what had happened, for she didn't understand it herself; no one would.

Stella – she would feel safe if she could talk to Stella. She ran down and dialled her sister's number.

'I'm pregnant, too,' she blurted out.

'Oh, that's wonderful. How far along?'

'I think about two months.'

'Well, go to my doctor, she's marvellous. It's really a husband and wife together in practice, but you'll love her. She's so gentle and she'll answer all your questions.'

Jenny took down the doctor's name and number and knew she couldn't go yet. It wasn't grown out and it would be too embarrassing to explain the shaved area.

'Pick a day so we can go shopping together. We need to buy all sorts of stuff. Oh gosh, it's gonna be fun,' Stella gushed. Maws begun knitting booties already and she doesn't even know about you.'

'I don't want to tell her yet.'

'Why not?'

'I don't want her to worry. I'm only sixteen.'

'She had me when she was seventeen,' Stella reminded her.

'Thursday would be good,' Jenny said, changing the subject while she mentally counted the allowance Bobby Lee had left her.

'No, I can't do Thursday. Rodney's mother is coming over. She's a bit of a nuisance. Being a widow she's always hinting around to Rodney how much help she could be if she lived with us. I swear she's got her eye on my extra bedroom. She's a dear sweet soul, but no thanks. We like it just the way we are. We treasure our privacy.'

Jenny realized it then. She had almost reached out to Stella with some vague notion that maybe her sister could help. Maybe there was some way to escape the terrible trap in which she found herself. But no, Stella had her own life now.

'You're pretty quiet, baby sister,' Stella commented.

'Aren't you happy about it? You're the one who always loved babies.'

'Of course I am. I'm thrilled,' Jenny lied.

'That Rodney, he's really something. Sez I look so beautiful now. A lotta people say that a woman's extra pretty when she's pregnant. I guess I feel that it's true, do you?'

'I guess.'

'What you been doing, now that the garden doesn't need tending?'

'Well, I've done a lot with the stuff Momma saved me. I've made a couple of necklaces, some earrings. It's been fun.'

'I can't wait to see them. Why, I get compliments every time I wear those earrings you made me, I took them to the jewellers, got clips put on.'

'Good, they looked pretty on you as best as I can remember. Our wedding day was a bit of a blur.'

'Yeah, I feel goose-pimply every time I think about it. Bobby Lee falling in love with you just like that, and all the while I was worried about him being older and all. I thought he'd try taking advantage of you, but instead he married you and gave you a wonderful house and that marvellous ring. Shows how wrong a person can be.'

A lump came up in Jenny's throat. She was sure she was going to cry, so she said hastily, 'Someone's knocking. It must be Raylean.'

'And I forgot, a cleaning lady to boot. Yes, it certainly shows how wrong a person can be,' Stella repeated.

Jenny hung up the phone, laid her head on the table and cried. Somewhere in the back of her mind she had sensed that extra room, and desperation had made her hope.

In some unspecified way she had thought that Stella could help her. She was her big sister, she had always looked after Jenny – but with a surge of temporary hatred, Jenny acknowledged that it was Stella who had gotten her into this trap to begin with.

She imagined sitting in art class. This fall she would have

been a senior. She had always been hungry to learn, to create. She gave up that dream, wiped her eyes and went upstairs in the house full of shadows and secrets, laid out the beads and tried to forget herself in the creation of beauty.

Over the months she had borrowed most of the books on designers from the library. The 1940s had so many women designers, and Jenny felt an unashamed pride in perfect strangers. She read avidly of Coco Chanel, an orphan who became a respected world figure in *haute couture*. She studied her jewelry, so classic, so permanent. Closer to home, she read of Miriam Haskell, whose jewelry designs were so elegant, burnished gold and tiny seed pearls fashioned into brooches of magnificent splendour. The names reeled in her mind – Hattie Carnegie, brooches of whimsy, Nettie Rosenstein, jewelry of every description and style.

The books created such a hunger in her, that she saved and promised herself an excursion. She would take a trip to downtown St Louis, and devote one full day to going into the best stores, to look at this jewelry. She wanted to see it, feel it in her hands. She couldn't even tell Stella, for she would never understand. And when Jenny finally did this, it changed her life for ever. 'It allowed her to dream.

'*Some day*,' she promised herself, '*I will create marvellous pieces like this*,' and this dreaming helped her bear the reality of her life on the other side of the wall.

CHAPTER 15

Bobby Lee found nothing in her pregnancy that he thought was beautiful. Her body repulsed him now, but in this there was no escape from his twisted sexuality. It only allowed them to sink further and deeper into depravity. They always did this, the bitches. He should have known better. They always changed, Bobby Lee thought bitterly. He loved the buds, but he could not bear the full-blown flower.

Jenny saw herself as she saw him, as two different people. Her other self was the person who could pull down the shade and be somewhere else successfully until pain brought her back to reality.

The rule of no pants infuriated him now. 'I don't like looking at that bush. Put 'em on.'

Gratefully, she obeyed. In the bedroom, his order to have her disrobe was painful, as she stood there before him and he berated her ugliness.

'Look at that. Your tits are like cantaloupes, so big and ugly, and that stomach of yours is so goddamn swollen, how do you expect me to get hard. It's your fault Dickie's so soft. Your fault!' And with this he grabbed her hair and flung her down in front of him. 'Kiss it,' he ordered. She clenched her teeth together, sure she couldn't do it.

'Go on!' He pulled her towards him.

She felt the baby turn. She knew it was this unknown being who enabled her to comply. Her lips reached out; tentatively she touched it.

145

'That's better.' He lay back. 'Now, put it in your mouth, suck it, coax it. It'll get hard, you'll see.'

She felt vomit in her throat as she did as she was told.

'You bitch – that's not it. You're not doing it right.' Suddenly he flung her away, and strode out of the room, furious.

Jenny reached for her gown, and climbed into bed. It was only a minute or so until he returned.

'What the hell are you doing? Get out of that bed.'

She stood up, and he whipped the gown over her head. He sat in the chair facing the mirror and began smearing chocolate ice cream on himself.

'Now, Baby Doll, come and get it.' Rudely he tugged her hair as he pulled her towards him. 'It's your favourite, chocolate. Lick it all up like a good girl.' She saw his eyes, glinting in the mirror as he watched.

She began, and in her mind's eye she started designing a pair of beautiful emerald earrings, until she was immersed totally in the fantasy of her work. He stopped abruptly.

'Good, now you've got him nice and hard.' He pulled her up, forced her over the side of the bed. She felt his finger, cold and wet. She could hardly breathe, for the pressure on her bulging stomach was painful. Then he plunged in, a scream escaped her and she bit the cover until it was over.

'That's how it's gonna be from now on. I'm gonna fuck you in the ass, and you're gonna suck Dickie. It's your fault for gettin' so ugly. No sirree, Dickie don't wanna go in any big pussy. No sirree, that's how it's gonna be. You'll learn to love it, too.'

It was that night she began dreaming of the garden shears, the same dream awake or asleep.

Bobby Lee's dreams were different. He dreamed of little girls, in various towns, and over the years there had been many. They were all different girls – but they were all the same. They were all Georgia.

Arrested in time, he had to keep her – *her love, her touch*

– for she had been the only warm thing in his small life. He sought her over and over again.

His fruitless search at times made him reckless. Pictures swam dizzily together in his head – tight curls kneeling down before him, smooth little hands, satin-pink tongues. His fingers ached; denied.

He dreamed his dreams. In the coolness of the Denver Mall, he saw her, a blonde girl of about ten, leaning over to tie her shoe. He saw the pale pink of her pants. He felt her essence even now – *Georgia* – and like a hunter seeking prey he followed, slowly looking through the crowd for her blonde curls.

He found her turning away from the counter holding a chocolate ice-cream cone.

He bought a paper and sat on the ledge opposite her at the fountain. Above the top of the Denver *Post*, he watched her small pink tongue licking greedily at the melting cone. He crossed his legs to hide his erection, and remembered other towns, other places with small wonderful girls just like this one. Curious, for they were always Georgia. She licked, she jiggled an impatient foot, and ignoring her mother's cross words, she sat forgetful now of her dress, which rode high above her knees – small pink knees which were not held closely enough together.

Intense now, he stared at that secret place. Clearly he remembered: *she told him to look, she told him to touch.* 'Oh!' he heard her exclamation of dismay as she looked down at her spoiled dress. This was his signal. He rose and went quickly to her side, holding out the peace offering of his clean white handkerchief.

He felt it slipping out of control, but always she said the same thing: '*Do it, Bobby Lee. Do it here.*' So he reached down, and pretending to mop up the ugly brown stains in her lap, he touched and caressed the soft mound of her.

Intending to thank him, she looked up, and seeing his red sweating face, instead jumped off her chair and ran quickly into the crowd. Regretfully he watched the pink bow disappear.

In his ears she chants, saying it over and over; '*It wasn't me, Mamma, it was Bobby Lee. It wasn't me, Mamma, it was Bobby Lee.*'

Betrayal is the colour of attics and then it begins, the silent howling in his throat and the phantom ache in both of his fists from their futile pounding on the floor.

He'd had one at home once – no, twice – a . . . Georgia, *but she's gone now, and left Mamma in her place.*

CHAPTER 16

Zachary was born on a beautiful spring day. Jenny named him after a hero in a forgotten book she had read a long time ago. She didn't expect to feel this tremendous well of love, not when half of him belonged to a man she had come to despise.

She no longer prayed for Bobby Lee to love her; it was obvious he did not and never would. But this small helpless bundle she held to her breast would be love enough. Stella and Momma said he looked like her, and she hoped with all her heart that he did.

At home in the den, Bobby Lee brought in the bassinet and for the first few weeks Jenny slept on the sofa downstairs, as she wasn't allowed to climb the stairs.

It was wonderful, just the baby and her. And it was heaven when Bobby Lee was out of town. She could pretend he didn't exist.

She didn't like feeding the baby when he was present, for he would stare and watch them and make obscene remarks.

'It must feel good, all that sucking on your titties.'

She didn't answer.

'I asked you a question. You like that sucking?'

Jenny nodded yes.

'Does it make that big pussy hot?'

'No. Bobby Lee, it's a natural thing feeding a baby. It's the best thing for 'em; it's satisfying.'

'Satisfying,' he mocked. 'You mean hot. It's making you hot, I can tell.'

She ignored him. Finally he came over and sat on the couch next to her, and looked at his son vigorously sucking.

His hand reached out and roughly caressed her other breast. He leaned down and began sucking. She looked at the back of his sleek head and felt a surge of overwhelming hate. His fingers slid up her arm and one finger forced her lips open, and his fingers probed her mouth, caressing her tongue.

After a time he lifted the still-nursing child and put him in the bassinet screaming with hunger.

He went down to the vacated place and proceeded to suck, alternating between each of her full breasts. Then he stood up, unzipped his pants, and forced his erect penis into her mouth. With the screaming infant in her ears, she tried as she had never tried before, and it was over soon.

'You liked it, too,' he gloated. 'All that sucking got you hot, Baby Doll.'

She went upstairs, she simply had to shower, and ignored the baby, who was still screaming fifteen minutes later when she came back down.

She called the doctor in the morning, told her that her milk had dried up, and asked for instructions on which baby formula to buy. Jenny's mind whirled constantly. What could she do? Where could she go? But sunning Zack on the wide lawn always dampened her revolt; he had a nice crib, new clothes, the right formula, vitamins, toys . . . she couldn't take him to some dingy place where strangers minded him and she could only earn a bare living. No, her body was the sacrifice, the trade-out until some future time, when she could see a way out.

She day dreamed of a large truck and brakes squealing on a wet pavement, the sound of a crash, loud and terrible, and she could see Bobby Lee's face smashed and still through the shattered windshield.

The dream satisfied and scared her, and when that one wasn't good enough she dreamed of the garden shears. Her hate for him and love for her child bloomed side by side in her being. Zachary grew sturdy and fat and one day he said it: 'Mama.' She thought her heart would break with happiness. She knew without a doubt she would lay down her life for him, let alone her body.

It was the day Stella brought her daughter, Penny, over to visit, that the idea came. After vigorous play they took the children up to the nursery.

Jenny showed Stella the jewelry. Her creations had mounted over the long months and she now had forty finished pieces.

'These are simply beautiful,' Stella said sincerely as she threw necklace after necklace over her head. She tried on all the earrings. 'You should sell them,' she urged. 'Why, shops would buy these, they're so unique.'

'Do you really think someone would buy them?'

'Yes, I do. I'll be your first customer. I'd like to buy this pair.'

'Don't be silly, they're yours.'

'No, Jenny, I want to buy them. Wait – I just thought of something. My neighbour does ceramics. She's going to be in a craft show. It's in a week or so, and you could be in it, too. Women will love this stuff. You'll sell it easily, I'm sure.'

'But I don't know anything about how you do it or anything.'

'I'll find out. Oh, it'll be fun. I'll help you. I'll look after Zachary for you, too.'

Stella got the details, and when she called and told Jenny the date it just slipped out. 'Oh good, that Saturday Bobby Lee will be out of town.'

'Something's wrong, isn't it?'

'Yes, it is, but I really can't talk about it.'

'It's that sex thing, isn't it? It never worked out.'

'That's right. I guess it's me – I just don't like it.'

'A lot of women seem to feel like that. At least, when we get talking over coffee, and sex-talk comes around, some of the girls say they just lie there thinking about something else. I feel so lucky that Rodney and I are good together. I enjoy loving him.'

151

'That's good,' Jenny said, and she really meant it. But she couldn't imagine anyone enjoying Bobby Lee's version of love, and each time she had accepted the way it was, it changed; it became worse.

'It's your fault, dammit,' he'd scream at her. 'Dickie won't get hard,' and his eyes glinted ominously as a fresh idea came into his mind. Always seeking for that magic thing that would make Dickie hard.

'When I was gone last week, who'd you fuck? Was it the delivery man?'

'No,' she retorted indignantly. 'I wouldn't do anything like that.'

'Sure you would. That pussy's not had any dick for a long, long time. Who'd you fuck?'

'Bobby Lee – I didn't. I wouldn't. I couldn't do anything like that.'

'I don't think you understand,' and his fingers closed tight around her throat. 'Tell me about it. I wanna know all the details. Tell me a story, Baby Doll, tell me your dreams. Tell me all about that fucking and sucking you've been doing.'

This was total madness. She felt faint from the pressure of his fingers on her throat.

'Go on. The story could begin like this. "When I was walking around the house without my panties, I got so hot that I played with my pussy, and the mailman looked in the screen door and saw me, so he took his dick out and came on in."' He paused and he was breathing real hard. 'Go on, tell it.'

'Tell what?' she whispered.

'The story. I just gave you a good beginning, now tell it.' He shook her for emphasis.

'What should I say?'

'You know, start the story like I told you.'

'I can't,' she protested. 'I can't say stuff like that.'

'Sure you can, you've got to. It's your goddamn fault Dickie won't get hard no more. Tell it,' he shouted, and Jenny heard the baby in the next room begin to cry.

152

'It was hot yesterday, so I walked around without my pants.'

'Was your pussy red hot?'

The baby's squeals increased.

'Yes, Bobby Lee, it was.'

'It was what? Say it.'

'My pussy was real hot—' She felt him harden against her leg, and heard the zing of his zipper as he took it out.

'How big was it?' he asked in a breathless voice.

'What?'

'His dick. How big was it?'

'Real big.'

The sounds from the baby's room were almost deafening. So in a rush, she did it, what he wanted her to do. She told the make-believe story, and as she spoke he parted her legs, entered, and it was over quickly.

She gathered her clothes.

'Don't spoil 'em. You can't go running up there every time he cries.'

She left, fed the baby, burped him, and quickly he slipped back into sleep.

She went into the other bathroom and stared at herself in the mirror. 'I hate you,' she said to the image in the glass, and with that she began throwing up.

CHAPTER 17

It was the night before Bobby Lee was to drive to Denver, and the ball game was on, that she had the courage to do it – a small revenge. She had to do something, for she was beginning to be frightened of her violent thoughts.

Zachary was restless and fitful, so she had to run up and down the stairs several times to make sure he was still asleep.

Bobby Lee had reinstated the no panties rule, and as she went back and forth getting his beer and popcorn, with each errand he flung up her skirt. 'You gotta big ass, Baby Doll,' he jeered, and on his last request she really didn't know exactly what made her do it, but she peed in his glass, poured part of it away and filled up the rest with his favourite beer.

Sitting across from him, legs spread wide, this time she didn't care, for she was busy planning his future menus: snot in his stew, shit in his roast beef, piss in his beer, pubic hair in his Coke. She watched as he downed the glass and wiped his mouth on his sleeve.

The hatred, hard as a rock, lay heavy in her chest. Whatever he was gonna do, let him do it, she thought. Who cared? For tomorrow he'd be gone, and she could dream of wrecks on the highway and the garden shears. She tried desperately to call up a vision; like a Siren she called and lulled, but a genuine sight eluded her. At least he was out of town frequently now. She thanked God for that, and hoped with all of her heart that his schedule would not change, unaware that these out-of-town runs were at his own request. Now that his little bud Jeannie had flowered, Bobby Lee had to seek his Georgia elsewhere. In nameless towns he'd find one, then start out again to find another.

She closed her eyes and searched. No genuine vision came.

It might have been something in her face, or the stillness of her stare, for in an unguarded moment, he saw it clearly. He hesitated, then said softly, 'I think the baby's crying.'

His words released her. Upstairs there was silence, so she went out to the porch and looked at the darkness, felt a fierce madness, gathered it up and climbed the stairs to the silent bedroom to wait.

Later she felt him on the bed. He sighed and turned away from her and soon she heard the sound of regular breathing, even and measured as the tick of a clock. But she knew that like her, he did not sleep, and she wondered if he guessed what she thought about on quiet, dark nights.

In the morning he was gone, and when she went to straighten the bedspread, her toe stubbed against it.

The metal was harsh and real; she trembled as she slid it out. The shears, she had *really* brought them up! It was all beginning to blur – her thoughts, her daydreams, reality itself. She knew she was walking a thin line. '*Dear God, for Zachary's sake, don't let me, please don't let me do anything. Let my disgusting retributions be enough.*'

In the yard, in the sunshine with her son toddling across the green chasing the cat, she dug a hole and buried the shears. But in her daydreams they still existed, ominous and threatening, an instrument of revenge.

That day she strived for normality. They played ball on the lawn, had a picnic lunch, she sang lullabies at nap-time, and sat in the rocker and watched as her son slept.

Evening was quiet time. She lay on the couch, observing Zachary in his serious game, cars weaving in and out of obstacles, and the hum of his pretend language.

Later, Stella called full of enthusiasm. It was all arranged – the table covers for the fair, the borrowed jewelry props.

'You'll do great, baby sister, you'll see,' and Jenny tried to borrow her excitement and make it her own.

The day of the craft show dawned, a perfect autumn jewel, cool and clear, leaves rustling and drifting slowly in front of their car as it moved along the highway.

The trunk was packed carefully, and the children secured on Jenny's lap chattered happily to each other. Stella drove effortlessly, and when Jenny complimented her on her skill, she offered to teach her.

'I'll come out some morning. The road by your house is great – scarcely any traffic. Why, Jenny, I could teach you in just a couple of days. It's easy, honest.'

When they pulled up to the square where the craft fair was being held, Jenny caught the excitement at last.

Tables lined the pavement, and all manner of crafts were displayed here – ceramics, quilts, needlepoint, artwork, and so on. To their surprise, they saw no jewelry.

Securing the babies, a tight squeeze in one buggy, they found their allotted table. Stella had done well. She had brought a lovely soft velvet cloth in midnight black, and had managed to borrow some earring and necklace stands from a jeweler with whom she was friendly.

They took turns arranging and rearranging the table until Stella finally said, 'I'll amuse the children while you finish it off. After all, you're the artist.'

It came naturally, the skill, placing earrings here, then a draped necklace to match, the colours grouped together in a tasteful manner. Before the table was finished, a well-dressed woman paused, gently fingered a piece or two then asked, 'How much for these?' She held up an intricate pair of pearl and crystal earrings which resembled those that Jenny had designed for Stella's wedding.

Jenny was surprised and flattered by the woman's interest, but before she could make up a price, Stella stepped forward. 'Those are ten dollars,' she said casually.

Jenny almost gasped but gave a nervous cough instead, for all the supplies together had cost less than that.

'Fine, I'll take them. Do you have a box? It's a gift.'

'No, but I have some lovely paper and ribbon,' Stella offered, placing the earrings on a piece of vibrant pink tissue. She wrapped them carefully and finished it off with a handsome bow.

When the woman was out of sight, Jenny squeezed Stella in a big hug. 'My gosh, the supplies didn't even cost that much!'

'Your things are beautiful and hand-made. You shouldn't sell your talent too cheap,' Stella lectured. 'Now, let's do a price list.' She grabbed a notepad and they decided between them what to charge. Carefully Jenny wrote descriptions and prices for each piece.

The morning went swiftly and two more pieces of jewelry were sold before the man came to the table.

He made Jenny nervous, standing there examining each piece, carefully turning them over, seeming to weigh them in his open palm. From the pocket of his well-tailored suit he took out a jeweler's eye, and with practised care he scrutinized a piece or two at close range. Eventually he leaned forward and met her eye, looking Jenny over as thoroughly as he had done the jewelry.

'Did you make these?'

'Yes,' she answered quickly, and regretted that it sounded so curt.

'They're very well done,' and he continued holding a large brooch.

'Thank you.'

Stella hovered, but when Penny began to cry, she rocked the pushchair and moved away, leaving Jenny on her own.

'It reminds me of work by an artist in New York called Miriam Haskell.'

'Oh, I read about her,' Jenny said, 'and saw some of her designs – but I didn't copy any of them.'

He laughed. 'I didn't mean that you had. I simply meant that you seem to have a similar talent.'

There was that word again. Miss Dunn in art class had said that.

The man reached into his breast pocket and took out a

silver card case. He offered one to her. 'Here's my card. I'm Paul Winthrop, a buyer from Enchanting Jewels.'

Jenny took the gold laminated card and read the same information he had just imparted. Below his name two addresses were listed, one in New York, one in Rhode Island.

'I'd like to buy them,' he said.

'Which pieces?' Shyly she handed him the price list, all the while wishing Stella were here instead of rocking the babies.

'All of them,' he said, and from the same pocket he took out a small notepad and began writing down numbers as he slid each piece along after recording its price.

'Stella,' she called out, and her sister returned, still rocking the stroller from side to side as the children were now busy tugging at the string of two balloons that bobbed in the air.

Stella looked him over, but he did not glance up as he continued recording and counting the pieces.

'It's five hundred total.'

Jenny gulped and nodded at the unbelievable number.

'But naturally it's wholesale. Ten per cent is normal, so shall we say four hundred and fifty dollars?' He glanced from Stella to Jenny, and held out his hand toward Stella. 'I'm Paul Winthrop from Enchanting Jewels, New York.'

Stella reached forward and shook his hand. He then offered his hand to Jenny and she followed suit.

'You ladies do beautiful work.'

'No,' Stella corrected, 'my sister is the artist. I'm Stella Miller and she's Jeanne Antree.'

'Pleased to meet you both. It seems we can do some business.'

'Jenny,' she said.

'I'm sorry.'

'I'm Jenny Antree, not Jeanne.' He nodded, not understanding the change.

'Well, can we wrap it up, and then I'd like to talk to you, Jenny, about our company.' He reached for a cheque book. 'Is it Jeanne or Jenny Antree?'

Stella could always think on her feet. 'No, please make it out to me, Stella Miller. I do work as her manager.'

Mr Winthrop looked towards Jenny for permission then proceeded to write the cheque. He glanced at his watch. 'Fifteen minutes be enough time for you to wrap it?'

'That will be fine,' they said in unison.

They took turns, carefully wrapping each piece in tissue.

'Can you believe it?' Stella said jubilantly. 'God, it's wonderful. I'll cash the cheque for you.'

Jenny was grateful for this, her sister's care in not asking why Bobby Lee and she were so distant that they had to keep secrets from each other.

One small fat hand suddenly let go and the red balloon was free at last; it sailed happily up into the brilliant autumn sky, followed by Zachary's heartbroken wail.

'That's okay, baby,' Jenny cooed. 'Momma will buy you another one. Two or three even.'

Finished at last, they packed the jewelry into the cheap shopping bag, the only thing at hand.

'Ugh, that bag's so tacky,' Stella grimaced, 'and he's so elegant, to use your word.'

He returned, asked for a simple receipt for the company records, then invited Jenny to have a Coke so they could talk.

Stella nodded. 'Go on – I'll take care of this,' and Jenny left her folding the table covers and hushing two crying toddlers, as Penny's balloon had now joined Zachary's up in the autumn sky.

They walked to the refreshment stand and sat at a picnic table where Paul Winthrop told her all about Enchanting Jewels.

'We're always on the lookout for designers with fresh ideas. What's your background? Which art school did you attend?'

If she had been Stella, some name would have rolled off her tongue easily. Instead, she said, 'Only high school art.'

'It doesn't matter, the company often uses freelance designers. Do you have any more finished pieces?'

Regretfully Jenny shook her head. 'No.' But some instinct made her tell him about her sketches.

'Finished sketches? We need minute detail for them to be of use.'

'Yes, I often draw pieces that I don't have the right supplies to make and I don't really know how to make the moulds,' she admitted.

'Well, Jenny, that's okay.' Again he reached for another card. 'Send them to me at my office, that's the New York address. We always work a season or two ahead. Right now we're producing our next year's fall line.' He took out the makeshift receipt. 'Good, good, I've got your address. I'll send along a packet of information on the company, guidelines, things that will help you work for us, and if you get another collection together, send it along on spec.'

He saw her confusion and explained. 'If you send a collection, it's on speculation. If we like it, we'll forward a cheque. If we can't use it, we'll return it promptly and reimburse you for the postage. But designs carefully drawn are always considered.'

They shook hands, and Jenny watched him walk away, not sure if this was real or one of her many daydreams.

It was three months later before she finally had a notepad filled with designs with which she was completely satisfied. Four hundred and fifty dollars were hidden in the playroom, and this secret cache of money made her feel safe. If necessary, she could pick up Zachary and run away, but it was almost as if Bobby Lee sensed this, for his behaviour would suddenly be okay and it was with great happiness that she saw the toys Bobby Lee brought home from each trip for Zachary, to be wrapped ready for Christmas. He loved his son, he must do.

He further surprised her by bringing home an enormous Christmas tree that touched the ceiling, and she felt so happy, as cheerfully they decorated it with Zachary dancing with excitement around them, babbling the words, 'Santa – Santa coming.'

Bobby Lee even agreed to have Christmas dinner at Stella's, and Jenny felt awkward about it, as they never invited anyone to their house.

Again as if reading her mind, he suggested they invite the family for a New Year's Eve party.

Surprised and pleased, Stella and Addie accepted. It was agreed Stella would bring them all in her car as the Reverend's old truck was unreliable in the winter. The day dawned picture-book perfect. The snow had stopped and covered the ground in a blanket of pristine white, so that the house and grounds looked like something out of a storybook as well. The fir-trees at the rear held clumps of snow, the holly bushes gleamed with red berries, and even the large pin oaks selfishly held their brown leaves till spring.

Raylean had been hired for two days and the house fairly shone. The wood floors gleamed, the vases were clean and bright, the rugs vacuumed to perfection.

Bobby Lee brought in logs and lit fires in two fireplaces, the one in the living room and in the dining room where they were to eat their festive dinner. Bobby Lee even bought a new cover for the sofa in the den, and the turkey was roasting fragrantly in the oven when the guests arrived.

Jenny had given Addie permission to bring Scotty, the little boy living with them at the Mission, for his mother was ill and Addie thought this outing would be such a treat for the boy.

Jenny proudly showed her mother the house as she walked gingerly through each room, as if she were in a museum.

'It's beautiful, Jenny, simply beautiful,' and she gave her daughter a hug. 'I know about the bars. Stella explained you're so far out and by yourself when Bobby Lee's gone, it's safer. I'm so happy for you.' And she held her a bit apart, studying Jenny's face, trying to solve some sort of mystery she saw there.

The young men, Rodney and Bobby Lee, had taken the children outside, and from the kitchen window, the others could see them taking turns sledding down the gentle hills, later building a crooked snowman. Occasionally a child came in the back door, for only a moment, to blow on its cold hands then put on the damp mittens again, anxious to return to the white wonderland.

The Reverend and Addie were left in front of the TV, mesmerized, drinking hot tea, while Stella and Jenny set the table and tended to the simmering pots.

In the buffet, Stella reached for one of the linen tablecloths. Her hand touched the album. 'Pictures?' she asked.

'No,' Jenny said abruptly. 'It's something of Bobby Lee's. It's private.'

Stella frowned and pushed the album further back under the cloths.

They set the table, and it was beautiful, with white linen, gleaming china, and a vase full of red roses which Bobby Lee had bought. In the corner of the dining room they set up the card-table and small chairs for the children, Zachary, Penny, and Scotty.

Jenny's heart went out to Scotty, this boy with the pinched white face and patched jeans. His image was a vivid reminder of her former poverty. She never wanted her son to look so sad and needy. She made a mental note to herself to pack up a small bag of toys that he could take back with him to the Mission.

To please Addie they had placed the Reverend at the head of the table opposite Bobby Lee. This honour went to his head, and the brief blessing they hoped he would bestow turned into a mini-sermon, until Addie tactfully leaned over and squeezed his hand. He looked up, as if remembering it was dinner, said a hasty 'Amen' and began filling his plate.

Small fights at the little table forced Stella and Jenny

intermittently to get up, settle the kids, and return to their delicious dinner.

The turkey and dressing were succulent, the corn on the cob dripped with butter and the asparagus was covered with melted cheese. Jenny looked over at Stella and smiled, remembering how she always wanted asparagus and later discovered that she didn't even like it. The candied yams were perfect, coated with syrup, and they had made the cornbread from scratch. The salad was crisp lettuce with cherry tomatoes and cucumber, and it seemed everyone at the table wanted a different dressing.

Bobby Lee ate heartily and the men complimented the women outrageously on the dinner.

Jenny glanced up at her husband, so handsome, so neat in his plaid shirt and corduroy trousers. For a moment she almost forgot, in her happiness blanking out how her life really was. After pumpkin pie smothered in whipped cream and coffee, they cleared the table, and began a four-handed game of canasta.

Looking fearfully at the cards, for the Reverend was sure it was some sort of Devil's game, he took himself off to the den to snooze in front of the TV.

The children had been sent up to the nursery, and occasionally one of them tottered down in tears with a small complaint.

Addie reigned in the fabulous kitchen, happy with the work of wrapping leftovers and doing the dishes by hand, as she was afraid to touch the dishwasher.

As midnight approached, Bobby Lee got out the fireworks. 'Bought them in the Ozarks,' he said, and he put on his jacket, cleared a space in the yard, placed the tubes in some cans, and after dressing the sleepy children warmly, gave each a pot and spoon and told them they too could welcome in the New Year.

Shivering on the porch, they all waited happily for the church bells to ring in 1957.

The first peal of the bells sent the children running wildly through the snow banging their pots.

Bobby Lee lit the Roman candles and they soared skyward; showers of red and purple lit the sky and reflected down on the silvery snow. Again and again came the boom of the fireworks and the magic of brilliant colour filled the sky.

Three small children, falling in the snow, eyes wide with excitement, welcomed in the New Year.

'Happy New Year,' Rodney said as he kissed Stella, then turned to Jenny and placed a warm kiss on her lips.

They all hugged Addie and wished her the same. Jenny even kissed the Reverend on his cheek, and Bobby Lee, shaking snow from his shoes, came onto the porch.

'Happy New Year, Baby Doll,' and for the first time in a very long time she felt a gentle kiss.

Inside, he opened the champagne. They toasted each other and the brand New Year; even the Reverend lifted his empty glass.

As Stella gathered the belongings together, Jenny remembered and went upstairs to bag a few toys for Scotty. When she got to the nursery, she saw it scattered about the room – the money. Playing, they had unearthed her secret cache beneath the toy chest.

Behind her she heard Scotty say, 'We was playing store.'

'That's okay.' She hushed him and quickly put a few unwanted toys into a brown paper bag.

At the door, they all kissed, promised each other they would get together soon, and then Scotty thanked Jenny for the toys. Zachary, already asleep on the couch, didn't know she was giving away some of his old things.

Waving to them, the successful night was almost over, they were almost gone ... when Scotty broke away from Addie's grasp and ran back up the steps.

'I'm sorry. I wasn't stealing, really. I just forgot.' In his hand he held out a hundred-dollar bill.

'That's all right, Sonny,' Bobby Lee said as he stooped down level with the child, patted his cheek and took the bill from the boy's outstretched hand.

They watched the winking of the tail-lights getting

smaller and he closed the door, fastened the chain and said evenly, 'We're gonna have to talk about this,' as he waved the bill in front of her face.

Jenny turned out the lights and followed him up the stairs as he carried their sleeping son. Bobby Lee laid the boy down on the bed, took off his shoes, covered him with the blanket, turned to Jenny and said, 'What's this all about?'

'Sssh,' she said as she closed the door to Zack's room. He slept in the room next to their bedroom. 'I'll explain.'

Jenny walked to the nursery pretending to be worried about the mess. She picked up a toy and put it in the toy chest. With dismay she saw her sketchbook flung carelessly on the floor.

He followed her into the room. 'Stop,' he commanded. 'I'm talking to you. What's this all about?' He tugged at her shoulder, pulling her up from the floor.

Nervously Jenny sat on one of Zack's little chairs. 'You know those beads,' she began.

'What beads?'

'Those beads and jewelry parts Momma gave me.'

He nodded.

'Well, I was always playing around with them, making jewelry. I ended up making a lot of pieces – necklaces, earrings, bracelets.'

His face was bland, expressionless, so she had the courage to go on.

'Stella knew about a craft fair. She thought I could sell them—'

'Stella, Stella, Stella!' he yelled, his voice rising in anger. 'Always gettin' you into trouble, that bitch sister of yours.'

'No, Bobby Lee,' she pleaded. 'Stella was right. People *did* buy my jewelry and a man from New York, he bought it all, all I had left.'

'A man from New York?'

'Yeah, he's with a big jewelry firm, he bought it.' Hurriedly she went to the cache of money and held it out to him. 'Here. He paid four hundred and fifty dollars.'

'Are you nuts!' he said as he looked at the money in

166

disbelief. 'Why were you hiding it? Planning on running away, were you?'

Her face betrayed her. 'No. I was saving it for more supplies. Why, he even told me they buy designs.' She reached for the sketchpad, and held it towards him like a peace offering.

He took the book and flipped through the pages. His face gathered up into a puzzled frown.

'He said they buy designs from freelance artists,' she repeated.

'Artists?' he spat at her. 'An eighteen-year-old high school dropout like you an artist? Don't be ridiculous.'

'Honest, Bobby Lee, he said that.'

He whirled the pages and began laughing hysterically. From the other room she heard Zachary begin to cry. She tried walking past him.

'You can't go running to him every time he cries.' He left the room and she heard the click as he locked Zachary in. When he returned, his face was a mask of fury.

He still held the sketchpad. 'Artist my ass,' he sneered savagely, and he tore the first page.

She forgot herself and lunged at him, pulling at the book. 'Please, Bobby Lee. Please don't tear it!'

He started again with the wild laughter and strips of paper landed at her feet. Hopelessly, she fell to her knees gathering up the pieces, stupidly trying to fit them together, the confetti of her dreams.

Finished, he flung up her skirt, tore her pants off. 'That's it – just like a doggy,' and he entered and began thrashing into her. Pain on every level assailed her; the sound of her son screaming and pounding on the locked door, the strips of dreams around her, and him punishing her from behind.

She had waited too long; she should have gone when she had the chance. Now the money was his.

Successful again, he had pushed her back into her cage, locked the door and swallowed the key.

167

CHAPTER 18

The odd circumstances happened all at once. The portrait of Mrs Antree slid off the bedroom wall, and the glass shattered into a hundred pieces. The shards tore into the picture, and like a well-used dartboard, marred the face beyond redemption.

Zachary began having trouble going to sleep. Jenny felt sure it was due to his recent birthday excitement. He insisted on taking all of his new toys to bed with him, and trucks and cars lay around him like offerings to a newly turned three-year-old.

'I have to stay awake until they stop crying,' was his explanation to his mother.

'Who?' Jenny asked, puzzled.

'The children, the ones in the attic who cry.'

Goose flesh rose on Jenny's neck, and spread quickly to her arms.

'There are no children in the attic,' she told him emphatically.

'I heard them, Momma, lots of times.'

She scooped his precious flannel-clad body against her breast. 'No, no, Zachary, it's the wind. Sometimes it blows and chases around corners and makes funny noises.'

'It sounds like kids,' he insisted.

'I know, but the wind plays tricks sometimes. Remember that time the wind snatched the kite that Daddy flew for you? That naughty ole wind took that pretty kite way, way up and kept it for himself.'

'Somebody should spank the wind if he's bad.'

'Yeah, honey, somebody should. Now go to sleep.'

Jenny herself had trouble falling asleep that night, and thought she was dreaming early in the morning when she heard the terrible pounding on the door.

Out of the window she saw the small van in the driveway. Grabbing her gown she answered the door just as the man was turning away.

'Telegram,' he said, handing out the yellow envelope to her.

With shaking fingers, she signed for it, took it into the kitchen and laid the ominous envelope on the table while she made a pot of coffee to calm herself.

She reached for the knowledge, but nothing came to her. Had it really happened, a smashed truck on a lonely curved highway?

Finally tearing the envelope open she read the troubling message:

> *Bobby Lee,*
> *There's been a car wreck. Wanda's dead, the funeral was Friday. I can't keep Tammy, I'm too old and I'm poorly. I'm sending her by train. She'll arrive Tuesday at 2 p.m. I have pinned your name to her coat.*
> Mrs Nettie Green

Jenny read the message over and over. She was coming here; Bobby Lee's child was coming here. Jenny had no idea how old she was or anything at all about her.

There was nowhere she could call him, for he was on the road somewhere. With a start she realized that today was Tuesday already. The child would soon be here. Feverishly, she called Stella.

'Of course I'll pick you up,' her sister said. 'It'll be fun for the kids, seeing all the trains.' Then she paused. 'It's awful. I wonder how old she was?'

'I don't know,' Jenny replied. 'He never mentioned Wanda, or Tammy either.'

'Funny, but that puts you in a spot, not knowing anything and to have this dumped in your lap.'

'I know, and I can't even call Bobby Lee. He's somewhere in Florida.'

'Well, we gotta pick her up. We can't just leave the kid hanging around Union Station with a name pinned to her coat.'

They spotted her immediately, a small red-headed girl of about seven with the large sign pinned firmly to her shabby brown coat. *Tammy Lee Antree.*

Jenny left Stella behind her holding onto Penny and Zachary's hands, while she carried Heather, Stella's new baby, in her arms. Jenny went up to the girl, stooped down to her level and said, 'Hi, Tammy. I'm Jenny. I've come to get you.'

The thin, white freckled face looked up, and the large blue eyes assessed her.

'No, I was sent to my daddy.'

'It's okay. I'm your daddy's wife. He's not here right now, he's off driving his big truck, so I came to get you instead.'

The girl looked behind Jenny and saw Stella holding the two small children by the hand.

'Who's that?' she asked.

'Well, that lady is your Aunt Stella, the little girl is your cousin Penny, the baby is Heather, and he—' she pulled Zachary forward '—he's your little brother.'

'I don't have a brother,' she said defiantly.

'You didn't know it till now, but Tammy, he is your brother, truly he is.'

Zachary stepped forward. 'Did you ride on that big train?' he asked, his voice breathless with excitement.

'Yes, I did,' she answered proudly.

'Gee, I never rode on a train.'

'Maybe 'cause you're too little,' she answered, and at first she pulled away, but he kept reaching, so finally she let him take her sweating hand.

171

Jenny unpinned the sign, then savagely crumpled it up and threw it in the nearest waste can.

On the ride home, Zack and Penny chattered, but Tammy remained silent, and when Jenny looked back, she saw her blankly watching the passing scenery.

When they pulled up to the house, her sad pinched face looked up and said, 'I remember it, this house. Momma said it was a hell-hole. Or maybe even a jail with all those ugly bars on all the windows.'

Shocked, Jenny said, 'Why, Tammy, whatever made you say that? It's a lovely house.'

'No, it isn't!' she screamed. 'My Momma was right. She said it, now she's in heaven with God and I want to go there,' and tears flowed as she sobbed. Jenny reached down and smoothed her hair, and picked her up, while Stella struggled with the others and bravely Zack and Penny dragged the battered suitcase up the stairs.

After taking off their coats and making cocoa and sandwiches, they managed to settle the children. Heather had fallen asleep and they put her on the couch secured with pillows, while Zack took the others up to the nursery. Tammy had finally begun to calm down. Stella and Jenny had barely sat down with a cup of coffee, when Zack came back down, crying.

'She said the Boogie Man is up there,' he sobbed.

'Who said that?' Jenny questioned.

'My new sister, she said it. I'm scared.'

'There, there.' She took his hand and walked him back up, took out the new crayons, and art pads, and in a minute she had them all happily drawing pictures.

'It's gonna be hard,' Stella commented. 'After all, the child's grieving. How old is she?'

'She said she's seven.'

'In the long run, it could be nice for Zack,' Stella said.

'Yes,' Jenny agreed, and she kept silent, hoping if she didn't utter it, it wouldn't be true. It was over three months since she'd last had a period.

'When's Bobby Lee gettin' back?'

172

'Not till Saturday or Sunday.'

'Well, you'll have a couple of days to get her settled. Men aren't too patient with difficult children.'

'I know.' Jenny was very apprehensive about Bobby Lee's reaction to having his daughter dumped on him after all this time. But Jenny had had no choice; she couldn't possibly have left her standing at the station.

The first problem came at bed-time. Tammy refused to sleep in the trundle bed in the nursery.

'No, I'm scared in there,' she pleaded.

'Okay.' Jenny calmed her. 'Okay, we'll make you a nice room here,' and she opened the door to the plain room next to her own bedroom. 'We'll put up some nice pictures, and you can get some favourite toys.'

'I want my doll now,' she cried, and they opened the tattered suitcase, and she pulled out the Raggedy Ann. Her finger smoothed over the toy and she sought comfort in her old companion. In the suitcase Jenny also found a tattered flannel nightgown, decided the child could skip the bath for tonight, and tucked her in under the covers.

'Where's he sleep?' she asked, pointing toward Zack.

'Like you, he doesn't want to sleep in the nursery, either, so he has the room on the other side of my bedroom.'

'Leave the light on,' she pleaded.

'Yes, we can do that, and I'll leave the door open. How's that?'

She nodded, and a thumb crept up to her mouth.

'Only babies do that,' Zack said.

Jenny shushed him.

Tammy woke once that night. Jenny held her, rocked her gently and hummed songs that the words were forgotten to a long time ago.

'I want my momma,' the child sobbed.

'I know,' Jenny said, 'but your momma wouldn't want you to be sad. God needs her.'

'I need her more,' Tammy cried. 'I hate God.'

Jenny patted her back and let her sob out her grief. After

173

a time her crying ceased and she caught her breath in great gulps.

'I'll take care of you,' Jenny promised.

Her tearstained face studied her. 'You're not her, you're not my momma.'

'No, but I am your friend,' and Jenny searched for something else to say to comfort her, 'and you still have your daddy. He loves you,' she said, while remaining unconvinced, for in all the years she had been married to Bobby Lee, she couldn't remember him ever sending his daughter a letter or a present.

'He does?' she questioned. 'My daddy loves me?'

'Yes, he does.'

'I don't remember him,' she said sadly. 'I don't remember him at all. I used to have his picture, but Momma tore it up.'

'Well, you won't need his picture any more. He'll be home in four days.'

In those four days Tammy adjusted remarkably well. Jenny's heart almost broke as she watched her taking care of Zachary. 'Watch those steps. Be careful,' she warned as she tagged after Zack, assigning herself the task of his caretaker.

Jenny went through Tammy's few articles of clothing, washed and mended what she could, and resolved to ask Bobby Lee for money because the child needed so much.

As Jenny watched the two of them playing in the yard, she studied Tammy but could see nothing of Bobby Lee in this child. She was small-boned with reddish-blonde hair. Her narrow face was sprinkled with freckles, her eyes, like his, were blue, but a different shade, and shape. For the first time she wondered what Wanda had been like and whether Bobby Lee had treated Wanda in the same cruel way that he treated her. From the kitchen drawer she took out the small record book and studied the notations. In the last two years, the incidents of abuse had become less frequent. To survive, to bear it, she had started the record book. Each time Bobby Lee had forced himself upon her she recorded it in code. It helped her. She could see in black and white columns how many perfect days she had bought for her son, bought and paid for with the submission of her body.

Last year it was only thirty-six times, less than ten per cent.

She looked out at the little girl running in the sunshine. Would her coming make life better or worse?

Nervously, Jenny waited for Saturday. Sometimes he returned from the trips anxious to rain indignities upon her, and other times, sheepish and nice, he barely noticed her.

His quick step and his whistle made her think that this time it would be okay. Under his arm he carried a large Woolworth bag. Something for Zack. That was one area of her life about which she felt lucky. He was good to Zack, always buying him a little present here and there, always telling him, 'We guys gotta stick together,' and somewhere down deep she believed he did love his son.

Her face, her transparent face, always alerted him.

'What's wrong?' he said.

'Coffee's fresh,' Jenny stalled. 'Sit down. I'll tell you all about it,' and she told him what had happened.

'Damn that ole bitch, just like her daughter. That ole lady knew what she was doing, puttin' that kid on a train like some goddamn package. You shouldn't have got her.'

'I couldn't just let her stand there in the train station, Bobby Lee. I didn't know where to call you. I didn't know what to do,' Jenny finished lamely.

He went to the door and watched Tammy and Zack running through the leaves, their high-pitched voices caught by the wind.

'It's okay with me, I don't mind,' Jenny said. She watched his face that was tight with anger. 'It might be good for Zack. He likes her, she's real careful with him.' It was her way of pleading for the child.

'That ole bitch – like mother, like daughter,' he spat.

'It'll be okay, Bobby Lee, you'll see. After all, she is your daughter.'

He turned to her, the anger now redirected. 'Oh, is she? How in the hell do you know? That Wanda was fucking everything that wore pants. Just like you, Baby Doll, she loved prick. Whose kid am I supposed to be supporting here?'

She heard the click of the bolt as he locked the door. 'Since you're such an authority on everything, lend me your expertise on this.' He unzipped his pants, his organ limp but beginning to stir as he spoke. 'Who'd you fuck today?'

She pressed her lips together tightly.

'Go on, tell me. Sent them out to play so you could get it on, didn't you, Baby Doll?'

He reached under her skirt. 'Forgot to put your pants on.' His fingers probed. 'I must have just missed him. Did he go out the back door? Where's your panties, Baby Doll?'

'I knew you were coming home today,' she whispered. 'You said . . .'

'Wanted to be ready for me and Dickie, did you?'

'You said, you told me—' she barely whispered.

'Any cunt that anxious don't get any,' and he pushed her to her knees.

'The children, what if they come to the door?' she pleaded, but already he was forcing it forward.

When he had finished, she got out the book, entered the date and the letter 'F' for fellatio.

She started supper and when she heard them laughing at the back door she pulled herself together and even managed to smile.

'Your daddy's home,' she said brightly. Tammy cautiously followed Zack into the den where Zack had already leapt onto Bobby Lee's lap and was giving him hugs and kisses.

'What'd you bring me?' Zack asked.

'Why should I bring you anything? Have you been a good boy?'

'Yes,' Zack insisted and began looking around for the

sign of a present. He spied the big bag and jumped off Bobby Lee's lap and began ripping it open.

'Oh boy!' he yelled as he pulled out a large truck.

'It's just like the one Daddy drives,' Bobby Lee said, and he turned his attention to Tammy standing quietly in the doorway. He studied her carefully, then said, 'Haven't you got a kiss for your daddy?'

Shyly, she stepped forward and gave him a quick peck on his cheek.

Jenny felt grateful. Again, her sacrifice, her pain, had bought happiness for this child.

'Let me look at you. It's been a long time. Why, you're a little beauty,' he lied, hating that look of Wanda almost standing before him.

Tammy blushed, but Jenny could see that she was pleased.

He rummaged through his pockets, and found a pack of gum which he offered her. 'I didn't know you were here, or I would have bought you a present, too.'

'That's okay,' she said, reaching for the gum.

'Next time,' he promised, and winked at her. 'Welcome home, Tammy.'

On impulse, Tammy grabbed his neck and planted a genuine kiss.

Later, at bed-time, she told Jenny, 'He's not like Momma said, he's nice. Momma lied to me. Is that why God took her?'

'No, honey, God don't take you for lying. We just don't know why He takes some people. Maybe He just needed a wonderful, beautiful person like Wanda.'

'I needed her too,' Tammy said sadly, and she clutched her doll and her thumb slid up to her mouth.

Jenny thought she'd worry about that later. The girl was far too old to be sucking her thumb, but for now she had to come to terms with death.

Later, in the night when Jenny heard her crying, he almost stopped her. 'You can't cater to this kind of behaviour,' Bobby Lee snapped.

'Please, let me go to her,' she begged. 'She's still dreaming about her mother.'

He released the restraining grip on her wrist.

'We're not gonna make a habit of this,' he warned.

'I know, Bobby Lee, I know. She just needs a little time.'

Sometimes she heard her before he woke, and she would slip in to hold the child, to reassure her, until her bad dreams left and she could sleep again.

It was ideal. Zack and Tammy drew closely together. Even the difference in age didn't seem to matter. Her nature gave her a purpose; she had a little brother, and she thrived on the knowledge that she could take care of something.

'Oh, Stella, it's perfect,' Jenny said. 'They're so good together.'

'That's nice to hear, for Penny is jealous as hell of the baby. It's certainly not perfect here. I can't wait for her to feel protective towards Heather.'

And often their telephone calls would have to end quickly, for the baby's screams over Penny's teasing demanded Stella's immediate attention.

Tammy's favourite occupation was the crayons and art board. For hours she would draw trains and cars and animals to amuse Zachary.

'Why, that's beautiful,' Jenny said, as she picked up a paper. 'That's a wonderful picture of an elephant.'

'I remembered it from the time my Momma took me to the zoo.'

'It's a very, very, good picture,' Jenny complimented her. Idly, she took up a crayon and found herself sketching a flower.

'That's a rose,' Tammy said proudly.

'Why, yes it is,' she answered, and realized how good it felt to be drawing again.

'You draw real good,' Tammy said. Jenny looked down at the sketch; the little girl was right.

'I used to draw a lot, a long time ago,' she said sadly, knowing she wasn't talking to Tammy at all but to herself.

'Did you draw tigers and giraffes and stuff like that?'

'No, I used to draw jewelry.'

'Why'd you do that?'

'Because after I'd drawn a piece of jewelry, I'd try to make it – necklaces, earrings, things like that.'

'I want one, please,' Tammy begged. 'Make me a pretty necklace. I'd wear it all the time, I promise.'

'Well, Tammy, if I still have the beads and stuff, I'll try.' Jenny went to the closet, moved the toys and found the box still there.

'Oh, goody, goody.' Tammy hopped around the room. 'See, Zachary, she's gonna make me one. You don't need any jewelry, you're a boy.'

'Trains, trains, draw me a train, a long one,' he pleaded, following his mother around the room and waving a blank sheet of paper at her.

Jenny took the box of supplies down to the kitchen. She trembled as she remembered him tearing her sketches to bits; since then she hadn't dared to dream, but now the beads running through her fingers called to her again. She yearned to create.

She felt a small pulse in her stomach and looked up at the calendar. It was almost four months now. She had tried her best to ignore it, reassured by the lack of morning sickness, telling herself the missed periods were due to nerves. But now, holding her hand on her tummy, she knew for sure.

'*I don't want you, I can't have you – not now, no, no!*' she panicked, and was deeply ashamed of her thoughts.

Over the years with Bobby Lee, Jenny had mastered the art of putting that which was unpleasant far away, and so now she ignored it and busied herself with Tammy. They shopped for new clothes and she sent for her school report to be forwarded, but in the end Jenny didn't enrol her, for there were only two weeks left until the long summer holidays.

CHAPTER 19

It was a glorious summer, one of sun-dappled days and twilight sunsets, with Tammy and Zack running over the lawns catching fireflies.

There were picnics and drive-in movies, and to surprise them, Bobby Lee rented a cabin at Lake of the Ozarks. Jenny could almost forget the dark urges that lived within him, and she pretended to herself that those things hadn't really happened, but inwardly she knew they were ticking away like a time bomb inside him, and could explode at any moment.

At the cabin she was grateful for her husband's energy, for he taught the children to fish, and they adored the boat; he would row them out to the middle of the deep lake and stop and drift, letting them drag their tiny nets along, enjoying their surprise at the number of small fish they caught.

'Come on, us guys have gotta stick together,' was Bobby Lee's frequent comment as Zack followed him off into the woods to glimpse a sight of a deer, or some other creature.

Bobby Lee loved his son; that small, thin body never tempted him. He never felt the blind force of anger towards him, no. Zack was the buddy he'd never had, for his mother always drove them away, the friends he should or could have had as a child. He would have sacrificed his best marbles, his baseball cards – *anything* – to have had one of his own kind as a friend, but it never happened. Still, at least he had him now, his friend, his pal, this small child who filled his need.

Tammy was happy to stay behind at Jenny's side, setting the table or doing the dishes. Once or twice she forgot and called her Momma, and her face looked pained.

'You can call me Jenny or Aunt Jenny if you like,' Jenny suggested.

'I haven't forgot her, honest,' Tammy said earnestly.

'I know you haven't. You'll always remember your mother. I know you loved her and I'm sure she loved you very much.'

'That's right,' and she would skip off into the woods, forgetting to be guilty for being so happy.

After the vacation, back at the house, Stella and Jenny planned an outing to the Mission, then they started visiting almost weekly.

It became a ritual for Zack to select a toy to donate each time they visited; on that particular morning the decision took longer than usual as he couldn't decide between a red car and a set of blocks.

'I already picked my toy,' Tammy said proudly, holding up the de-luxe set of crayons.

'Those are your favourites, honey. You don't have to give your best things. We meant toys or things you might be tired of,' Jenny explained.

'No, I want to give these. They will make somebody happy,' she said.

In the car driving to the Mission with the children in the back seat bickering over a toy, Stella finally asked Jenny: 'When are you gonna announce it?'

'Oh Stella, I don't want this baby. It's just not right. With Tammy and Zack, everything's good, even with Bobby Lee, everything's okay there, too.'

'I know, but when the baby's here you'll feel different,' Stella said firmly, as if saying it would make it so.

'I'm not so sure,' she answered.

'Sure you will, babies are so little and helpless, they just melt your heart. You'll love it, you'll see,' Stella promised. 'How far along are you anyway?'

'I think almost five months.'

'What'd the doctor say?'

'I haven't been.'

Stella stopped at the light and turned to face her sister. 'Why not?'

'I don't know, I just can't face it,' Jenny said helplessly, and inside she was crying out to tell someone how trapped she felt. Somewhere inside there was always a vague hope that when Zack was older – it always ended like that – *when Zack was older* – but now, with this new life beginning again, the jaws of her desperate marriage were slammed tightly shut again.

When they got to the Mission, Addie looked at her youngest daughter, hugged her tight and said, 'Congratulations.' Jenny was surprised, for she didn't think she was that big, but somehow other women always knew.

Tammy curtsied to Addie and asked if she could call her Grandma.

'Sure, honey. I'd be proud,' Addie said, and kissed the top of her shiny red hair.

'I got one Grandma already, but she doesn't want me,' Tammy said sadly.

'Never mind, I want you.'

Later, when they noticed Tammy drawing on the paper bags, Addie smiled. 'That could be your daughter, Jenny, always wantin' to pretty up the world.'

'She's quite an artist,' Jenny bragged, and felt as proud of Tammy as if she were her own.

Scotty joined them, and again Jenny felt a pang of sadness as she saw the small dishevelled boy. Zack proudly held out the red car. 'It's for you,' he said, and instantly regretted his generosity. 'I get to play with it sometimes though,' he stipulated, and the children went out into the yard where the adults were sure much fighting over the car would eventually break out.

'How's his mother doing?' Jenny asked.

'Not very well,' Addie said sadly. 'The Reverend said she just can't seem to welcome Jesus into her heart. He tried to get her baptized and all, but she always changes her mind, sneaks out drinking and comes back saying she's real sorry. It happens over and over again—' Addie stopped short as Thelma came into the kitchen.

She nodded to everyone and with a shaking hand, reached for the coffee pot.

'Hello, Thelma,' Jenny said.

The woman nodded and sat down, staring into her cup, her hands clasped firmly around it to still her trembling. It was this sight, this kitchen, this place, that permitted Jenny to bear Bobby Lee's cruelty for Zack's sake.

On the ride home Stella and she discussed Thelma.

'It's a shame, she's so young,' Stella said. 'I like a drink now and then, but it must be terrible being an alcoholic.'

'Does Maw think she's an alcoholic?'

'Yeah, the Reverend thinks so too, and he oughta know. And they even suspect she might be doing drugs.'

'Drugs? God, how awful. It's such a shame about Scotty. I know Maw tries to keep him clean and stuff, but she's got so much to do without being a mother to him.'

They both nodded and enjoyed the ride home: the children were happy and tired.

It was that night when Bobby Lee finally realized Jenny was expecting, and it was that night which revived Tammy's nightmares.

Jenny was sure the children were both asleep, when he started on her again. Sitting in the den, with the TV blaring, after getting his second beer, he looked at her like he was seeing her for the first time.

'Damn, those tits of yours are big,' he spat.

Jenny drew her blouse tight around her and with her arms she tried vainly to cover her chest.

'No, don't do that – let me see.' She let her arms drop to her sides. Just like a goddamn cow – can you say "moo"?'

She clenched her teeth together. His insults did not hurt her any more, they just created anger, red and terrible,

184

running through her mind. She did not see the room any more, just shears sharp and shiny in her hands.

'Come here,' he yelled, and then he slid his hands up and down her body. 'That's quite a tum tum,' he said. 'Ugly sucker full of stretch marks and veins. Shit!' he exclaimed, recoiling. 'There's a fucking bun in the oven.'

Jenny stood rigid as a stone as his hands squeezed and pinched at her belly.

'How far along are you?' he asked, his voice quiet and menacing.

'I'm not sure,' she replied.

'What happened to that goddamn diaphragm I got you?'

There was no point in saying he was so sporadic that she never had time to put it in.

'Cow, goddamn cow, why'd you have to ruin it? I can't bear to look at you. You're disgusting.'

In her mind the shears clicked, then she heard sobbing and whirled around to see Tammy on the bottom step looking over the bannister. She had heard it all.

'Tammy,' Jenny said.

'Oh no, you don't,' Bobby Lee spat at her. 'I'll take care of this.' He stood up; his face shifted. Smiling at her, he walked over and took his daughter's hand. 'Having bad dreams, honey?' he said, and gently he led her up the steps.

Jenny straightened the room, did the dishes, and when he came back down, he seemed to have forgotten all about it. Despite her enormous relief, she barely slept that night. Tight and rigid she lay alongside him and her mind was busy trying to find an explanation, something she could tell Tammy about what she had heard, but the little girl never asked.

The first day of school arrived and Tammy, bright as a penny, filled Jenny with pride. She hadn't anticipated how much Zachary would miss her, however. They left her in the second grade room and Jenny was pleased to see that the teacher, Miss Conners, was young and eager. She was sure Tammy would do well.

As they left, she had to struggle with Zachary, for he

cried and pleaded to stay at school. Her promise that he
would soon be going to nursery school did not pacify him,
and at home he followed her around from room to room.
Jenny was grateful when Raylean arrived and she could
send Patsy and Zack up to the playroom so she could have a
few minutes to herself.

When Jenny finally went to the doctor she was scolded for
waiting so long, and the doctor expressed concern that this
child seemed so small.

Where the summer had been peaceful and happy, the fall
was disruptive and full of irritations. Zack had become
whiny and difficult, and Tammy, instead of being pleased
and fulfilled at school as Jenny had expected, was sullen
and hard to handle.

She did not discuss any of it with Bobby Lee, for she did
not want Tammy to be subjected to any harsh discipline of
his. She felt that would only make things worse. So Jenny
suffered in silence and her legs ached all the time. Her
stomach bulged, but this baby was quiet. She did not feel
the constant tumble and turn she had experienced with
Zachary.

Stella was her sounding board. The telephone – her
lifeline – helped her to cope.

When she mentioned Tammy's strange behaviour, Stella
calmed her and pointed out that her adjustment had
seemed too quick, too smooth. After all, losing her mother
at that young age was very traumatic.

When Jenny tried talking to Tammy about the baby, she
seemed totally uninterested. 'I hope she's a girl,' was her
only comment, and Jenny was disappointed for Tammy
was now mean and spiteful even to Zack, who adored her.
She ignored her behaviour until one day passing the
nursery door she heard Tammy telling Zack, 'You're not
my friend any more. My friends are Jane and Betty at
school.'

'Why, Tammy? Why can't I be your friend? I love you,'
Zack pleaded.

'No, my friends are all girls, I told you,' she said.

'I'm your friend. I'm your very best friend,' Zack said, ignoring what she had said.

'No, you're a boy. Only girls can be my best friends,' she repeated.

'Why?' Zack demanded.

With that she took the band of his trousers, pulled it out and pointed down. 'There, that makes you a boy, and that's why you're not my friend.'

He stared dumbly into his trousers and began to cry.

'I wanna be a girl,' he sobbed. 'I wanna be a girl too so we're friends again.'

'You can't, unless I get the scissors and cut it off.'

'No! no!' he screamed in terror, running out of the room into the hall, and bumping roughly into his mother. Her stomach pained, a sharp knife running through her.

It was nothing like the normal Tammy – those words, so cruel, *so familiar*, the scissors, *her shears*. Jenny lost control and swooped into the room, grabbing Tammy roughly by the arm.

'What a terrible thing to say to him. You apologize this minute and tell him you didn't mean it.'

Tammy looked up at her defiantly. Tears were shimmering in her eyes, but she held them back.

'I won't,' she said, 'and you're not my friend either,' she accused.

'Go to your room, and stay there,' Jenny ordered.

She took Zack down to the kitchen, made him cocoa and gave him some cookies, and began telling him about Hallowe'en, how it was coming very soon. The distraction worked, for he began wondering if he should be a bunny or a cat, or maybe even Batman.

Jenny tried leaving Tammy alone; sometimes she tried talking to her, but the little girl was closed and distant, so she went back to ignoring the behaviour, hoping it was a passing phase that would work itself out.

Jenny worried about the arrangements with the new baby coming. With Zack she had slept downstairs, but that would be impossible now. She couldn't leave Tammy and Zack upstairs alone, especially when Bobby Lee was out of town.

Her temper was short with both of the children; her legs hurt all the time, and running up and down the stairs made her so tired she couldn't wait for bed-time, when they were asleep. To add to the problems, Miss Conners sent a note asking her to come up to the school and see her about Tammy.

That day she dressed in her best maternity suit. It hung loose. She was nowhere near as big as she had been with Zack. Jenny confronted the mirror and came face to face with how bad she really looked. Her hair was long and scraggly. Bobby Lee forbade haircuts; he claimed women should be feminine, and that meant long hair. In desperation, she pinned it up, but her face remained sallow and grey-looking so she took out the forbidden lipstick, touched up her lips, and even put a dab on her cheeks, rubbing it in, trying to give herself some colour. That was the best she could do.

Taking Zack's hand she started off down the road. Zack was on his best behaviour as he knew they were going to visit the school. He was jittery with excitement. The walk to the centre, which had always been so pleasant, was now filled with pain, as every step made Jenny's legs ache worse than ever.

Miss Conners ushered them into the empty morning kindergarten room. Like someone who was wonderful with children, quickly she settled Zack over on the other side of the room by a toy closet and gave him permission to play with whatever he liked.

She sat opposite Jenny, both on tiny infants' chairs, then seeing how awkward this was for her, she apologized and brought forward the larger teacher's chair.

'We're very worried about Tammy,' the young woman began. 'She's quiet and uncooperative in all her classes. I understand her mother died very recently.'

'Yes, Tammy came to us earlier this year. There was still

188

a week or so to go of school, but my husband and I decided it might be best to wait for the fall term.'

Miss Conners nodded. 'Can you tell me anything about how she got on this summer, anything at all that might help us? For instance, how does she get along with you?'

Jenny twisted her hands nervously in her lap. She wanted to be as clear as possible while explaining something she couldn't really explain at all.

'At first everything was fine,' she said. 'Given the circumstances, she seemed to adjust very well.' She looked nervously toward Zack. 'She really was good with him.' Zack was happily stacking blocks. 'It was remarkable,' she went on, her voice softening. 'She seemed to love him right from the first. It was so sweet – she was so protective of him, so patient. She adored him.'

Miss Conners nodded. 'And how did she feel about you?'

'We got along fine in the beginning. I explained to her that I didn't want to, nor could I, take the place of her mother, but that I would be her friend.'

The teacher nodded, listening attentively.

'But then something changed – I don't know exactly what or when. Now she accuses me of not being her friend.'

'About her grief: was she able to cry and get it out?'

'Oh, yes. In the beginning she often woke at night crying, and I would go in and comfort her. She has a special doll which she'd cuddle while sucking her thumb. I worried about the thumb-sucking, but felt I shouldn't correct it at this time, so I never did.'

'I see. I think you did right to ignore it. How about now? Are there still incidents of crying at night?'

'No, not really. After a couple of months my husband felt I was coddling her, so he would go in and quiet her.'

'Your husband – how does she feel about him?'

'Fine. I think they're fine. She's the child from his first marriage and he hadn't seen much of her until her mother died and she came to us.'

'Are they close?'

Jenny looked over at Zack, and tried to answer truthfully. 'He's much better with my son. Tammy seemed to prefer me. That is, she did until lately, and I can't honestly tell you why that's changed.'

'About discipline: how is that handled?' Miss Conners was studying Jenny's face closely.

'Oh, she's never spanked, if that's what you mean. There was no reason to do anything like that. Only once, very recently, when she was sent to her room for scaring Zack.' He looked up when his name was mentioned and then his attention went back to building his tower.

The sound of blocks tumbling was a brief respite, and calmly Miss Conners said, 'That's okay, Zachary. I bet you can build it up again, maybe even higher.'

'Yes, I can. I'll do it,' he announced.

'Scaring Zack?' Miss Conners pursued, not forgetting for a moment where they had left off.

'Yes, that's what's so puzzling. As I said, they got along so well. They had the happiest of summers, but now she seems angry with him as well.'

'Angry, not sad?' Miss Conners questioned.

'Yes, that's the feeling I get. She seems angry all the time.' It dawned on Jenny for the first time that that was really how Tammy had become. Not sad, not grieving – but very angry.

'Do you think your husband could come in? It might be helpful to speak to him.'

'He travels a lot,' Jenny answered lamely.

'But surely he could find an hour to spare?' Miss Conners's voice turned a bit sharp.

'Yes, of course. I'll ask him.'

'Let me know when it's convenient, and I'll fix my schedule to suit him.'

Reluctantly Zack left his towers of blocks, and they accompanied Miss Conners to the classroom, where Tammy was going to be excused early.

'What are you doing here?' Tammy asked, her voice mean.

'We wanted to meet Miss Conners and see your school. I think we'll have time for ice cream,' Jenny said, hoping the bribe would soften her.

Silently, they walked to the sweetshop. 'I think I want chocolate,' Zachary mused.

'I hate chocolate,' Tammy stated in a low voice.

'Well, then, choose whatever you want,' Jenny said calmly.

'Candy apples, candy apples,' Zachary chanted. 'I want candy apples too,' and he reached up on the counter trying to secure one.

'You can't have both,' Jenny said. 'Decide which.'

'Candy apple,' Zack said.

'I don't want any,' Tammy said, her face set in a tight mask.

'I'll get one for you for later,' Jenny said briskly, and ordered two.

Walking down the road Zack babbled about being in school.

'That wasn't really school. I bet you were in kindergarten,' Tammy said.

'Yes, I was, and I built a tower real tall,' he bragged, indicating with his hands.

Walking ahead of her Jenny heard Tammy say to Zack, 'I hope nobody saw her.'

'Saw who?'

'Your momma. She's not my momma, she's a cow with big tits.'

Jenny caught up with them. 'Tammy, shut your mouth. Where did you learn those nasty words?'

She looked at Jenny, her face red with anger. 'He said it – he called you a cow with great big tits.'

'You shouldn't eavesdrop on people.'

'What's eavesdrop?' she questioned.

'Listening to other people's conversation.'

'I heard it all. I didn't mean to. I just came down for a drink of water, and it's your fault you sent him up there. I hate you.' She ran ahead crying.

191

Jenny ignored the situation and tried to interest them in the forthcoming Hallowe'en.

Zachary had decided to be a cat, 'a big black one like one of our own cats', and Jenny busied herself making his costume.

'Have you decided what you want to be, Tammy?'

'No.'

'How about a fairy godmother with a wand and a crown? That would be really beautiful,' she coaxed, knowing how the child loved pretty things.

'There ain't no real fairy godmothers.'

'No, Tammy, there aren't, but it might be fun to dress up like one.'

'I wish there were,' Tammy said wistfully, and Jenny didn't ask again, but she bought the satin fabric and began making the costume.

When the children were in the yard playing, Jenny brought up the subject of school to Bobby Lee.

'Miss Conners wondered when you could come and talk to her about Tammy.'

'Is she having trouble in school?' He dropped the newspaper.

'Yes, they're worried about her. I went the other day; they asked me a lot of questions.'

'What sort of questions?'

'You know, was she grieving, was she misbehaving at home, that kind of thing.'

'Well, *is* she giving you trouble?' he questioned, watching Jenny's face closely to assess the answer.

With an effort she looked back at him, hoping he believed her. 'Not exactly trouble, Bobby Lee. It's just I think she's really missing her mother.'

'What does that mean? Is she giving you sass? I'll spank her bare butt for her if she is.'

'Oh no, don't do that, please. It's nothing. What should I tell the school?'

'Tell them to go to hell. I don't need to go talk to those busybody teachers. I can handle my own kids,' he snarled, and when Tammy walked by the hall, he shouted, 'Come here.' She walked into the room, her eyes pleading with Jenny to help her.

'It's okay, Bobby Lee,' Jenny urged.

'What have you been telling those damn teachers? It's time we had a talk, little lady.' Roughly he grabbed her arm and yanked her up the stairs.

Jenny stood at the back door, watching Zack play. She wanted to cover her ears, for she thought she would hear Tammy's crying, but she heard nothing, just the ticking of the clocks.

Next day at breakfast Tammy wouldn't eat.

'Come on, honey, you gotta eat or you'll make yourself sick.'

'I hope I do get sick and die so I can be with my momma. You're not my momma. You're not even my friend. You let him.'

'I'm sorry if he spanked you,' Jenny said, and she truly meant it.

'You're not sorry, you let him do that, you let him,' and she ran from the room crying.

Jenny didn't know how to explain it to the child, that she had no right to interfere. Bobby Lee was her father, he wouldn't have let her help anyway.

Jenny kept holding out the promise of a fun day. Hallowe'en was coming and there'd be dressing up, having fun. Maybe it would help?

Bobby Lee was out of town and things did seem to settle down a bit.

With great excitement Zack dressed in his catsuit, and he ran around the house meowing, scaring the daylights out of the real cats.

Reluctantly, Tammy put on the beautiful gown, and standing before the mirror Jenny could see she was beginning to feel the excitement of Hallowe'en, too.

'I'm pretty, aren't I?' Tammy questioned.

'Yes, you are, honey.'

'I bet nobody else has got a costume this good.'

'Nobody,' Jenny agreed. 'Do you have a joke or are you gonna sing a song?'

'Zack's gonna do a joke. It's not a very good one, and I'm gonna sing "Ole MacDonald Had a Farm".'

'That's great. I bet you'll get lots of candy.' Jenny fluffed out their 'trick or treat' bags.

'We better get going,' she said, and hands linked they started off down the road. The first house they passed was Raylean's. Her light was on, and Jenny stood in the road and watched the children go up onto the porch.

She heard Tammy's lusty song, and Zachary tried joining in with her.

They walked farther and farther, as houses were not very near.

Their bags grew heavy with apples and candy and after an hour or so, porch-lights were switched off and the trio started back. The children were anxious to get home and look through their treat bags.

The phone was ringing as they entered the hall. It was Stella.

'Check the kids' stuff, Jenny. I just heard on the news that some nut's been putting razor blades in the apples and candy.'

'Razor blades? How awful! Who would do such a thing?'

'God only knows,' Stella said. 'What's the world coming to?'

'I better go. I can see they already dumped their bags out.' Jenny hung up and quickly went into the den. 'Let me look at your goodies, to be sure it's clean and all.'

They watched as she sorted through the candy bars and apples, carefully looking at each piece.

'Okay. How about some cocoa?' They went into the kitchen where again they spread out their loot, and Zachary pronounced that they would have candy probably till Christmas.

'Don't eat too much, now, or you'll get a tummy ache,' Jenny warned.

'We won't,' they chorused, while stuffing their mouths full of chocolate.

'Can I sleep in it?' Tammy begged.

'Sleep in what?'

'The dress. I never want to take it off, it's so beautiful.'

'Well, just for tonight,' Jenny agreed.

'I don't want to sleep in my costume,' Zack said. 'It itches.'

Both children went to bed peaceful and happy, and Jenny hoped that the worst of it with Tammy was over.

CHAPTER 20

The school called twice, asking when Mr Antree could come in. Jenny gave the same excuse both times: her husband was out of town, she'd let them know as soon as she could.

They finally sent a form asking parental permission for Tammy to talk to the school psychologist. Jenny planned on forging Bobby Lee's signature, for she knew he'd never agree, but before she had the chance to do so, he found the form, hidden in a kitchen drawer.

'What the hell's this?' he demanded, holding up the offending paper.

'I was going to show it to you. They need your consent.'

'They got a nerve. None of my kids is crazy. No sir, I don't want Tammy talkin' to any head doctors. She's fine just the way she is.'

'She is better,' Jenny agreed. 'Ever since Hallowe'en she seems a lot happier. Why, all the time she keeps dressing up in that satin dress I made for her.'

'You tell those bastards to go to hell. My kids ain't crazy.'

'Okay. I'll tell them you won't give your permission.'

'That's right, you tell 'em,' and he slumped into his chair, drinking beer after beer, seemingly lost deep in thought. 'No, on second thoughts, don't say anything. Just ignore it!'

Weeks went by and Jenny ignored two more notes, until finally someone from Child Welfare telephoned.

'Mrs Antree? Clinton School have informed us that your daughter, Tammy Antree, was recommended to see the school psychologist. They are concerned because they haven't yet received your written permission.'

'My husband's out of town,' Jenny hedged.

'Well, in that case I'm sure you could sign.'

'I'm not her natural mother, only her step-mother. Her mother died last spring and I think that's part of the problem – her grieving.'

'Oh. In that case ... I'm not sure what to do in this situation, either. When is your husband expected back?'

'Next Friday.'

'I'll mark the file, and get back to you.'

'That's fine,' Jenny said, and hung up. She was worried. Bobby Lee seemed so against it, yet he'd just have to go along with it. She was beginning to feel awfully funny, as if they were hiding something. She hoped the school didn't think she was beating the child or mistreating Tammy in some way.

She didn't want to ruin the weekend, so she only told Bobby Lee about the call on the Sunday night.

'What'd you tell them?' he questioned.

'I said I'd talk to you about it. Do you want to sign the paper and Tammy can take it to school tomorrow?'

He didn't answer, and when she brought in the form and a pen, it just lay on the table before him, ignored.

Monday morning at breakfast Bobby Lee announced, 'You better stay home today, Tammy. You're looking peaked,' and he reached over and felt her head.

'Oh goody,' Zachary said. 'Can we play store?'

Tammy looked from Bobby Lee to Jenny with a puzzled look on her face. 'I feel fine.'

'Don't argue with me,' he yelled.

'But Daddy,' she protested, 'today is Show and Tell. I wanted to take my costume to school.'

'I said don't argue with me.' He stood up and quickly his hand shot out; he slapped her hard across the face, and he turned and left the room.

The imprint of his hand blushed red on her cheek, and she gulped, trying to hold back her tears.

'I'm so sorry,' Jenny whispered. 'You didn't deserve that.'

'She must have,' Zack said. 'She must have been real bad. Daddy never hits me.'

'Oh shut up, and I *won't* play store with you, either.' Tammy ran upstairs crying to her room.

Before Bobby Lee left for work he said, 'You keep her in the house, you hear?'

Jenny nodded, not understanding at all what was wrong.

It went on all week, him telling Tammy she looked peaked, and warning Jenny to keep her in the house. The baby turned and Jenny felt nauseous with worry. Every day the school called and she lied, saying Tammy was ill.

Friday dawned and Bobby Lee came home cheerful as could be.

'What we need is a little fun around here. I've got a real surprise. We're going to the lake; I rented the same cabin again.' He looked toward Jenny, smiling.

'Going to the lake? But it's so cold now.'

'Oh come on, spoilsport, it'll be fun. Remember that big fireplace? We'll roast some wieners and marshmallows, maybe even take the kids on a hayride if we can find one.'

Jenny touched her swollen stomach. She felt so tired, so awful. Her legs ached. The prospect of being in the draughty cabin and sleeping on the hard bunk-beds was a nightmare.

'Are you sure it's a good idea to go at this time of year? Why, with the baby and all—' she said feebly, knowing she wouldn't win.

'Baby's not due for two more weeks,' he said, grabbing Zack and tossing him in the air. 'What do you say, Tiger? Wanna go to the lake?'

'Yeah, Daddy, yeah,' and Zack squealed with delight as Bobby Lee tossed him in the air.

On the ride his festive mood persisted as he pointed out the beautiful leaves to the children. 'Lookit there, all red as fire.' The scenery en route to the Ozarks was beautiful in a sad winter way; the grey sky only made the turning leaves seem more brilliant.

In the small town they stopped for groceries and gas. Bobby Lee was generous with the children, for they had picked out lots of candy and cookies. He laughed, 'Greedy little guys, aren't you?' but he paid for it all.

'Going up to the cabin?' the man asked.

'Yep,' Bobby Lee answered.

'Funny time of the year. They're never rented at this season. Better buy some firewood, I reckon. It gets right cold up there with the wind coming off the lake.' And the man looked at them with a puzzled expression, noticing Jenny's bulging tummy.

'It's a free country,' Bobby Lee snapped angrily.

'I didn't mean nothing,' the old man said. 'I just meant nobody comes this time of year.'

Bobby Lee plopped the bills on the counter and slammed the door loudly as they left.

It was just as Jenny had feared. The cabin was cold and dirty. But cheerfully, Bobby Lee started the fire, and the kids seemed to be enjoying the adventure. After bundling up, they went outdoors to see if they could spy any wildlife.

'There's bound to be owls around here,' Bobby Lee said as they walked through the woods with the leaves crunching underfoot.

The lake was still; not a ripple showed, and it seemed like a dark mirror. Jenny shivered with an unknown premonition as she heard the first hoot of an owl.

'See, I told you guys. Let's try to find him,' Bobby Lee said, and walked off into the dark woods, as Jenny remained at the edge of the lake staring at the still water.

She was miserable and cold and slept badly on the hard bunk, but the children were enjoying themselves and it was pointless to complain. They only had one more day.

Sunday dawned, a grey, gloomy day. Stormclouds hovered, and Jenny warned the kids to stay close to the cabin.

They whooped and hollered as they searched for fossils,

and Zachary brought every rock to show her, announcing importantly that it was a fossil.

She began to prepare an easy supper, cheeseburgers and beans. She'd let them roast marshmallows for dessert. It had worked out after all, the two days in the cabin. While she'd been secretly miserable, the children seemed to have had a marvellous time.

The hamburgers sizzled and Jenny hoped the others weren't too far away, for supper was almost ready. While they were gone she had packed their things, hoping they could start back before dark.

She took the pot over to the sink where the soap suds had dissolved and the grey water appeared like a blank school slate.

She looked down and it rose up from the bottom of the murky water. A face, Tammy's face, her blue eyes wild with fear. The red curls bloomed around her head like a terrible crown, and her mouth, open in a terrified 'O', worked frantically like the mouth of a dying fish. Then bubbles came to the surface and burst.

The vision was real – too real.

'*Noooo!*' Jenny screamed, as she ran to the door to see Zack standing there crying.

'What's wrong? Where's Tammy?' she demanded breathlessly.

'He wouldn't let me go with them,' he said between sobs. 'Daddy wouldn't let me go.'

She grabbed his shoulders and shook him roughly. 'Where did they go?' Surprised at her roughness, Zack cried harder.

'It's okay, Mommy's sorry. Now tell me, where did they go?'

'They went out on the boat and Daddy wouldn't let me go with them.'

She picked him up, ignoring the pain in her full belly, and ran to the edge of the lake.

In the dimness of the grey day she saw nothing, only the waves whipping up in the wind, and she felt the first drop of

A. N. Steinberg

cold rain. She peered at the horizon, but could not spot the boat; the lake had so many coves and inlets that it could be anywhere.

The premonition was real – it was soaking into her as surely as the rain. Finally she saw it, the boat, but it wasn't right. She couldn't see them. Finally it dawned on her why; it was capsized.

Zack felt her terror, and began a slow wail. The sound of his cry echoing on the lake set her off and she began screaming, 'Help, help!' but there was no one to hear her.

'We gotta run, Zack, run fast.'

'Carry me, Mommy,' he begged.

'I can't carry you. Just do as I say,' and they ran, falling and stumbling in the now blinding rain for the mile and a half it took them to reach the store.

The shade was pulled firmly down, but she pounded and screamed until a light went on, and finally the old man opened the door.

Inside, she tried to tell him, and finally he called the sheriff. Two cars came eventually, and someone put a blanket around them. Zack was quiet now; he was thoroughly cried out. Jenny felt the blackness reach out to her.

Hours or minutes later, she couldn't tell which, they were herded into an ambulance and driven quickly the fifty miles to the nearest town.

He swam strongly in the dark, cold water but in his right leg was the beginning of a cramp. It was so close, the shore, so close. He had no idea if she could swim, but even if she could it was too rough and too far, for he had capsized the boat in the very middle of the lake. He was sure he had struck her firmly with the oar. It was her fault entirely. Like that bitch of a mother she had a big mouth – she'd tell, he knew it. There was no other way.

He reached the shore, pulled himself out, and lay in the mud, shivering with cold. The rain pelted him and in the distance he heard the wail of an ambulance. He dragged

202

himself around and tried vainly searching the lake for movement, but there was none, only the surge of the waves beneath the torrents of rain.

'Little bitch,' he thought. All of them were the same, guarding it, keeping him away from it. Not Georgia – *no, she tempted, she lured* – but then like all of the cunts, she blamed him. No, she only had to kneel by her bed and pray while he had to face all the demons in the attic.

When she awoke in the hospital bed, Jenny felt rippling pains. At first she thought she was in labour, but the pains subsided.

'My son – where is my son?' she screamed.

'He's okay,' the nurse assured her. 'He's having a great time. All the nurses are taking turns amusing him.'

'My husband, my daughter – are they okay?'

'Calm yourself, Mrs Antree. Everything's under control,' the nurse said, ignoring her question.

Jenny swallowed the pill she was given and felt drowsy again. From a distance she heard male voices. 'Stupid city slicker going out on the lake on a day like this. Stupid fucking shit.'

She felt herself drifting away. Much, much later she awoke to sunlight and Stella sitting on the end of her bed.

'What's happened to Bobby Lee and Tammy?' she cried anxiously.

'Bobby Lee's all right, he's in the next room. They kept him in for observation as he swallowed a lot of water.'

'Tammy?'

Stella's eyes went down to her lap. 'They haven't found her,' she said quietly.

'Haven't found her? You mean she's in the lake?'

Stella nodded. 'Bobby Lee's so upset that they didn't put on their life jackets. He blames himself. He's been crying like a baby and they've had to keep him sedated. He keeps saying over and over that they stayed out too long. The storm scared Tammy; she stood up, that's what capsized the boat.'

'Where's Zachary?'

'He's fine. Maw's got him outside.'

Jenny struggled to sit up. She glanced out the window at the bright autumn sunshine. How quickly the world could change ... and she shivered thinking of Tammy in that dark, silent lake, her face just like the one she had seen in the kitchen sink.

It was two days before they found the body. Zachary was inconsolable. He wanted to go back to the lake for Tammy. The funeral was closed casket, and Bobby Lee had to be held up, his grief was so severe.

Grandma Green came from Indiana. Her face at the graveside was set firm and she didn't shed a tear, but before she left she walked up to Bobby Lee and spat right in his face. Next she came up to Jenny. 'You're even worse than he is. You know, you evil bitch, *you know*!' Frozen by shock, Jenny felt the wetness as the old woman spat on her and turned away, crying hysterically.

That scene, that awful scene, had Jenny feeling so sick that she couldn't shake the feeling for days.

'Oh Stella, what did she mean, she hated me, she hated Bobby Lee?'

'You just have to try and forget it. People do and say strange things when they're half-crazy with grief.'

'I know in my heart I did the best I could for her,' Jenny said, with tears in her throat.

'I know you did.'

CHAPTER 21

Days went by in a grey numbness. Finally, Jenny tried to shake herself out of her lethargy for Zack's sake. Pushing herself into some sort of action, she gathered up all of Tammy's clothes and toys to give them to the Mission. Zachary pulled out the Raggedy Ann from the pile. 'I want it,' he pleaded.

'Boys don't have dolls,' Bobby Lee criticized.

'I'm keeping it for her, in case she comes back from heaven,' he said, and clutched it firmly to his chest.

'She's not coming back,' Jenny told him over and over.

'Maybe she is,' Zack argued. 'I remember what she said – she said she didn't want to go.'

The hair on the back of Jenny's neck stood up. 'Where didn't she want to go?' she asked him.

'She didn't wanna go on that boat to heaven.'

Jenny sat down clumsily on the floor and gathered her son to her. 'Zachary, you can't keep hoping that Tammy will come back. She's in heaven with her mommy now. She won't come back.'

He held the Raggedy Ann tightly. 'But I know she didn't want to go. She said so.'

Jenny's heart thudded in her chest with fear. 'Try to remember, honey. What exactly did she say?'

'I 'member like the alphabet. I know, I'm not too little to 'member things. She said, "I don't wanna go," but Daddy said it's her turn. Sometimes it's just us guys, but that time

205

he said, "Come on, Baby Doll, we'll have a boat-ride before dinner."'

'What? What did he say?'

'Daddy said, "Come on, Baby Doll, we'll have a boat-ride before dinner," and she said no, she didn't want a ride.'

'Before that, Zachary, what did Daddy say? Did he say "honey"?'

'No, I told you, Mommy. He said, "Come on, Baby Doll, we'll have a boat-ride before dinner."'

Jenny's head swam, she felt dizzy. 'Go on and play, Zachary. Go on.' The words 'Baby Doll' rang in her brain. He couldn't have said that. No, he couldn't have . . .

Bobby Lee stayed around the house. It was two full weeks before he went back to work. In that time he was quiet and nervous; he never spoke to Jenny except to order a beer or complain about dinner. He was animated only with Zack.

She was happy to have him out of the house when he eventually went back to work. The words *Baby Doll* came to her in the dark, and she did not let herself think of their possible significance.

Finally, two days after she was due, Jenny felt the first labour pains. Stella came and drove her to the hospital, and told her not to worry about Zack. Stella knew Bobby Lee was on the Denver run, so she stayed in the waiting room until Jenny's daughter was born: a tiny baby, not quite six pounds. When they placed her in Jenny's arms she felt only one emotion – pity. She could not even feed her, for her milk would not come.

Stella had explained the recent tragedy, so the doctor kept them in a full seven days.

When Bobby Lee came to take them home, Jenny had not even named her daughter. Quickly Stella rattled off a list, shoving a *Name Your Baby Daughter* book in front of her face. Jenny's finger stopped on the twentieth page and thus the baby was named Melanie.

'It's a sweet name,' Addie said. 'Cheerful, like. I'll bet she likes music.'

Jenny had the same arrangement she'd had when Zack was born; the bassinet was in the den with her, and she only had to walk to the kitchen to warm the baby's formula.

Stella kept Zack. 'He's having fun. He's no trouble, honest. It's good for him being around Penny and Heather,' and they both knew what she meant. For now, it softened his missing Tammy so much.

Jenny spent the days staring at the wall. She rarely got out of her nightgown. She held Melanie as little as possible. She could only look at her baby's tiny red face and burst out crying.

'I'm sorry,' she heard herself say over and over. She could not hum any lullabies – only the words, 'I'm sorry.' She did not know what she was apologizing for. Was it because she had given her life, or because she was a girl? Or for some other unknown reason? She wasn't sure.

Looking down into Melanie's small face, she was reminded of the doll. This baby was the same size, and her small unseeing eyes wandered, and she saw the same unfocused look as one eye shone white.

'No! No!' she screamed, and left the bassinet to go to the screen door, crying hysterically.

When she went back into the room, she ignored the weak, whimpering baby, covering her ears with her hands until she saw the small face relax into sleep.

She could only rouse herself to pretend to Stella on the phone, injecting a false brightness into her voice as she asked about Zachary.

'I'm fine. Everything's better,' she lied, only to hang up and stare at the clock, thinking how her life was ticking away and her new daughter's pain was only just beginning.

When he was home, Bobby Lee would come into the room, look at Jenny in disgust and say, 'You're gonna have to get yourself together,' but he never pressed it beyond that.

When it was Melanie's six week check-up the pediatrician

seemed worried. 'She hasn't gained much weight. Is she eating all right?'

'Not too well. She usually falls asleep before she finishes her bottle.'

He tapped his pen nervously. 'Is there some reason you're not breastfeeding her?'

'I don't have any milk.'

'Oh, I'm sorry. Now I remember Dr Cohen telling me you've suffered a recent tragedy. That can do it, but we've got to watch her. She's a little one, and we need to be on the lookout for failure to thrive.'

Jenny nodded.

He leaned back and studied her. 'How are you doing?'

'Better,' she said.

'Are you feeling depressed?'

'I guess so.'

'You really should see the other doctor. We've got medication that can help.'

'I'll do it real soon,' she said.

'You better; the medication can get you through it. For now you must take good care of this little one. Make sure she finishes her bottles. She needs to gain weight.'

'I will,' Jenny promised.

Jenny went for her own check-up. She was cleared to go up steps now, so Zachary was coming home, and she had a bottle of pills that were supposed to help her with the postpartum depression. Her energy level was at zero, and she was coming down with a cold, but she felt that she couldn't impose on Stella any longer. Her sister had been looking after Zack for almost eight weeks now.

Stella brought him over. He ran around the house like it was a new place. 'I 'member this,' 'I 'member this,' he commented, running from room to room. 'I wanna see her, I wanna see my new sister. Will she play store with me?'

'Not yet,' Jenny laughed. 'She's too little,' and he tiptoed up to the bassinet that had been taken upstairs, and with a chill Jenny had let Bobby Lee put it in Tammy's old room.

Zachary stared at the tiny sleeping baby. 'She's not a

sister yet,' he said solemnly, and in the tenderest of gestures he placed the tattered Raggedy Ann beside her. 'It's for girls,' he said and walked away to see what he remembered in the playroom.

Stella and Jenny left the children in the nursery and went down to the kitchen to have coffee.

'How you doing, little sister?'

Tears flooded Jenny's eyes. 'Not too good. I miss her so much. I keep thinking of her little body in that cold lake for all those days.'

'I know.' Stella's eyes brimmed. 'Well, at least she's with her Momma, if heaven really exists.'

Jenny nodded, agreeing with her.

'How's Bobby Lee taking it?' Stella asked.

'I don't know. I'm so caught up with myself I can hardly even think about the baby.'

'That's natural. You're depressed. A death like that, it's so damn sad. Did the doctor give you anything to help?'

'Yeah, she gave me some pills. I've been takin' 'em, and for Zachary's sake I gotta get myself going. I feel so old, Stella, and I'm only twenty-one. That's so sad, to feel like this and to think I'm only twenty-one.' Her tears flowed again.

Stella jumped up and patted her. 'Cry it out, honey, get it out. I can take Zachary back. I can keep him a little while longer.'

'No.' Jenny dried her eyes on the dish-towel. 'You've done so much already, and maybe having him here with me will help.'

'Okay, but you just holler if you change your mind,' she offered.

The children stood at the top of the stairs. 'Baby's crying,' Zachary said.

'Okay.' Jenny got the formula, warmed it up, and they went upstairs. Jenny sat in the rocker holding Melanie, who took only one ounce then fell back asleep.

'She looks good,' Stella commented. 'Does she cry much?'

'No, she seems too good,' Jenny said, and began touching her cheek to get her sucking again. 'She don't eat enough. The doctor said to keep trying. She hasn't gained much weight.'

They both watched as the tiny jaws resumed sucking.

'She seems tired of life already,' Jenny said sadly.

'Why, Jenny, shame on you, what a terrible thing to say! Damn you, take those pills. This isn't like you at all.'

'I know. Sorry, I just feel so down. Maybe Zack chattering around here will help.' Jenny burped the baby and put her back in the bassinet.

Stella looked around. 'Wasn't this Tammy's room?'

'Yes. I feel funny about it, but Bobby Lee just can't bear the baby being in our bedroom. I was scared of leaving her in with Zack. He might not understand how little and fragile she is, and the nursery is too far away. I'd never hear her cry.'

'I wasn't criticizing you. It was just a comment.'

Later they kissed, the children said goodbye, and Jenny stood in the doorway, waving.

The house felt so empty without Tammy, and Zachary began to mope around as well. So his return didn't have the desired effect at all. They each grieved privately.

Sadly, Jenny could hear Zack talking to himself in the nursery one day. His voice rose and fell as if in real conversation with someone.

Jenny had just finished feeding Melanie, when Zack came in with a sheet of art paper.

'I found this. Tammy must have forgot it. But it's so ugly, not like her other pictures.' He held it out to his mother. Jenny took the paper and she almost threw up. She gagged and put her hand over her mouth.

'I'm sorry, Mommy,' Zack comforted. Her eyes were riveted to the page and at last she knew exactly what it meant.

'Where'd you find this?' she asked.

'In the secret place that Tammy and I had.'

'Where is that?' Jenny asked, trying to keep her voice calm.

'Under the toy chest. It's a very secret place. You have to move it, then put it right back.'

Jenny's hands trembled like autumn leaves as she held the paper. Across the top of the sheet Tammy had written *I hat Daddy*. She had forgotten the e, as she didn't know how to spell *hate*.

The obscene picture told the story clearly. The first figure was a man standing up: a little girl knelt before him, sucking his penis. The next figure clearly showed the little girl, her legs spread wide, and Jenny ran to the bathroom and heaved.

Zachary stood in the doorway. 'I'm sorry, Mommy. I'm sorry you're sick,' and she heard an echo. She seemed to hear a voice saying, *'Come on, Baby Doll, we'll take a boatride before dinner.'*

CHAPTER 22

Jenny began to doubt her sanity, as she contemplated the pieces of the puzzle. They all fitted. On her frequent calls to the doctor, he prescribed more and more tranquillizers. Often she forgot how many she had taken, and mixed up anti-depressants with the tranquillizers. She thought back to days, nights past – all the times that Bobby Lee had been alone with Tammy. Yes, in her fuzzy reality she knew it. It was true, his insistence on settling her if she cried in the night. She looked at her son. *My God, had Bobby Lee touched him in that way?*

No, Zack clearly adored Bobby Lee. He often repeated, 'Us guys gotta stick together.'

She went to the drawer and pulled out the record book. So many days, so many weeks were clear: no secret marks of degradation. It had been a full three months since he had touched her.

In her mind she went over and over that day at the lake . . . the strangeness of the outing, the totally senseless boat-ride. A chill ran through her. No, it wasn't senseless at all: he must have carefully planned it. The school, the request for a psychologist that Jenny herself had stalled for him . . . No, she knew in her heart that what seemed unbelievable was true.

Bobby Lee had murdered his own daughter.

'What's that?' he said.

She jumped. She hadn't heard him come in.

'What in the hell are you doing sitting in the dark? Where's Zachary? And where's dinner?' he snapped.

He touched the switch and the kitchen was flooded with light. Seeing her with the small book, he reached over and took it out of her hand. His forehead creased as he looked at the senseless dates and initials.

'Goddamn, Jeanne, you're getting crazier by the minute. I'm going to have to have you committed.'

She rose and put the pans on the stove. Tuna casserole, that was easy.

She heard him go up the steps and soon there was the sound of Zachary's excited chatter. The drawing – thank God she had re-hidden it! Did it prove anything? She didn't know. If she told anyone what her life was like, would that prove anything? Again, she didn't know.

She left the kitchen and stood at the bottom of the stairs, listening. She could only hear a word or two, then silence. Her imagination ran wild. She rushed up the steps and threw open the door. Zachary was happily playing with his trains on the nursery floor. Then she saw Bobby Lee in Melanie's room, standing over the bassinet.

'You're a piss-poor mother,' he said contemptuously. 'Look at that, she spit up all over herself.'

Jenny snatched her up and turned away from him, laying her on the bed to change her soiled clothes. She could almost feel his eyes roaming over that small pink body. Melanie coughed.

'What's the matter with her?' he asked.

'A cold – we've all got colds. I'm taking Zack and her to the doctor in the morning.'

She changed the small sheet, and before she could settle her again, they both smelled it.

'Goddamnit, now you've burned the dinner, you dimwit! Here, I'll take her.'

'*No.*' The word burst from her as she laid the baby down gently in the bassinet.

He looked at her quietly, trying to get behind her cold

214

eyes, trying to fathom what she was thinking. That was when she knew she was in danger. He had killed once; he could do it again.

He walked over to the bassinet. With a calloused finger he traced the baby's velvet cheek.

'She's a little one, all right,' he said, as his eyes met hers, and they were sly and full of menace. 'Go on,' he yelled, 'before you burn the goddamn house down.'

She ran down to the kitchen. The pans were scorched, the burnt pasta all over the stove.

She heard them coming down the steps, and 'Goody, goody,' Zack's singsong phrase.

'We're going to get pizza,' Bobby Lee said. 'come on, partner, let's do it!' and they went out the door, hand in hand.

She waited until the car pulled away then ran for the phone. Somehow she'd tell Stella and she'd know what to do.

The phone was answered on the second ring. 'Hello,' a strange voice greeted her.

'I need to talk to Stella.'

'I'm sorry, she's not in. This is Pam. I'm babysitting for her.'

'Where is she? It's important.'

'I'm sorry, they went to the movies. They said they'd be home at ten-thirty. Is there any message?'

'No, no message,' and she hung up, frantic. She *had* to talk to someone. She rang the Mission.

Big Sam answered.

'This is Jenny, I have to talk to Maw.'

'She's in the service.'

'Sam, get her, please.' With shaking hands she opened the little bottle and took out a pill. She looked down. Which bottle did she open? The anti-depressants or the tranquillizers? She wasn't sure, for she had taken so many that day.

Jenny heard the hum of the music and finally her mother's impatient, 'Hello?'

'Maw, it's Jenny.'

'What is it? I was in the service.'

'I know, Maw.'

'Well?'

'I'm scared,' Jenny whispered.

'What? I can't hear you,' she said.

'Maw, he killed her. I know it now, he's crazy. Something's wrong with him'

'Who's crazy? No, honey, you're not crazy. Women get to feeling funny and bad after having a baby sometimes. It'll be okay. You'll see.'

The chorus rose. She could hear the mismatched voices singing. Addie hadn't understood.

'Okay, Maw, okay,' and she hung up the phone.

She looked down at the bottles in her shaking hands. Could she do it? Would it work? Dare she try and drug him? Noisily they came back in the house. The fragrant smell of pizza with pepperoni filled the room.

'Here, you two wait. I'll get the plates,' Bobby Lee offered.

She sank down in a chair and put Zack on her lap.

'Ow, Mom, you're holding me too tight,' he complained, and wiggled out of her grasp. 'Dad said I could stay up late and watch TV.'

'He did? That's nice.'

Silently, they munched the pizza, and Bobby Lee brought in Coke. They watched the small screen flickering in the dark room, and Jenny saw Zack lean back against the pillows, and soon he was fast asleep.

It was ten o'clock when the phone rang.

'Who could be calling this late?' he said. 'I'll get it,' and he went out into the hall. He returned, gave her a funny look and said, 'It was Stella. I told her you were watching TV.'

'That's okay. I would have talked to her.' She started to rise.

'Sit,' he ordered, like she was a disobedient dog. 'Seems someone called her earlier and the sitter said it was a woman sounding strange and excited. I told Stella it wasn't you – or was it?'

'No, I didn't call her.'

Jenny sat mute in the chair, staring at the flickering screen, wild plans running through her mind.

When he fell asleep, she could take them and leave, but how? Could she really carry the baby and Zack down the dark road? The nearest place was Raylean's, but she wouldn't help her. Morning, if only it came, she could go then. But suddenly he seemed to know something was wrong. She sat still as a statue, the medicine coursing through her veins.

'Bed-time,' he said, as he clicked off the set. He reached for Zack and slung their sleeping son over his shoulder.

'I've gotta get the baby's bottle,' Jenny said, and she headed for the kitchen.

Jenny tested the bottle and went upstairs to Melanie's room. She turned away from the baby as a coughing fit caught her. She'd have to go in later and rub Zack's chest with Vick's so he could sleep. In the morning they were scheduled to go to the pediatrician.

'That's it,' she thought. Stella was driving her. She'd tell her then and they'd never come back to this house, to this monster of a man who was her husband.

She held Melanie close and coaxed her with the bottle. She felt a distinct rattle in her tiny chest. Listlessly, the baby sucked, then slipped back into sleep.

'You gonna take all night in there?' she heard him yell.

'The doctor sez I gotta get her to eat more; she falls asleep before she finishes,' Jenny answered, not sure he could hear her.

She tickled Melanie's cheek, and slowly the tiny jaws moved. Then she saw his shadow fall across the floor. She looked up to see him standing naked in the doorway.

'Come on, Baby Doll. Your wifely duties are waitin' for you.' He took the baby out of her hands, and laid her gently in the bassinet. Then his hands shot out and grabbed her roughly by her hair and half-dragged her to the bedroom.

In that moment she was sure he was going to kill her.

She could do it, one more time, whatever he wanted, for in the morning, if she lived, she promised herself, it would all be over. But for now she had to convince him she was the same as she had always been.

'Take 'em off, I wanna see your body.'

Slowly, seductively, she removed her blouse and bra, undid her skirt and let it fall to the floor.

'I see you're not wearing panties,' he said, beginning to breathe hard.

'You told me not to,' she said, keeping her voice soft and pliant.

'Good, sometimes you're a good girl, Baby Doll.' His eyes flicked over her body. 'And sometimes you're not. Ugh, look at all those veins on that flabby tummy. Looks like one of my road maps,' he sneered. 'And those stretchmarks. God, they're ugly. Why'd you have to do it, ruin that smooth flesh?'

She looked down, subservient, a look he loved.

'And that bush, we're gonna have to keep it shaved. Remember when I shaved it, did you like that?'

'Oh yes, Bobby Lee, I did,' her voice breathless now with terror.

His hand reached out; under her breast he jiggled the flesh. 'Lookit them tits, nipples big and dark, almost purple. I liked them small and pink. I remember when they were. Why'd you do it, Baby Doll, let them get so ugly?'

'I'm sorry, Bobby Lee. I'm sorry.'

'You goddamn better be.'

She felt a nerve in her leg begin to tremble as she stood before him.

'What's it gonna be?' he said, as he reached down and touched his limp organ.

'Whatever you want,' she said meekly.

He turned her around, and now she could see herself in the three-way mirror. Was this person in the mirror really her?

His hands ran smoothly over her buttocks, and roughly

he pushed two fingers in. 'I'd put Dickie right in there, in that tight little asshole if only you'd get him hard,' he said.

She bit her lip to keep from crying out as he shoved his fingers in and out.

'Bend over,' he ordered, and he continued for what seemed an eternity. 'Talk to me, Baby Doll. Tell me about it.'

'*It's the last time*,' she promised herself, and she began the dialogue of filth that he loved.

'It's no use,' he hissed, and he pushed her forward so that she fell hard on her knees. 'It's your goddamn fault he won't get hard.'

She sat down on the floor to wait, wondering what he was going to do. She knew she had to satisfy him somehow, for she felt the danger close, breathing down her neck. Maybe he would resort to some new, unknown thrill. In the mirror she saw his hands angrily clenching and unclenching; fear inspired her and she turned, looked down at him, and licked her lips.

'Let me suck him, please, Bobby Lee, let me. I wanna kiss him, suck him and feel precious Dickie in my mouth.'

She crawled forward. She looked up at him. 'Please, Bobby Lee, let me.' She saw his look of total surprise. Dickie twitched.

'Well, if you're a real good little girl I might. Tell me again what you want to do to Dickie.' His voice was ragged.

She found that voice again and pleaded, said the gutter words with conviction and finally he held it out to her, his offering.

She took him in her mouth and tried as she had never tried before. The shears, the shiny hedge-shears, allowed her to do it, for under her closed eyelids she could see them shimmering and ominous; in her ears she could hear the smooth click of completion – and it made her voracious.

She heard him moan with pleasure. But then she heard something else – a small subtle sound, one she could not identify, but she knew it was misplaced in the night.

She stopped. It fell out of her mouth. She listened.

219

'What the hell—' and he pushed her head forward again. The hesitation had ruined it, all her work for nothing. She had to begin again, but now it was difficult, for her ears strained to hear. She heard only the ordinary night sounds and a dog barking somewhere in the distance.

'Goddamn you,' he muttered as he twisted his fingers savagely in her tangled hair.

Her knee touched something cold. She slid one hand under the bed and felt them, the shears. They were really there. She knew that some days she brought them up and hid them under the bed. It would be so easy, even now, with his head flung back, his eyes closed, imagining whatever his twisted brain saw. She felt the coolness of cloth, Tammy's Hallowe'en gown, for lately she had kept them wrapped up in the satin gown, a sort of imagined vengeance.

The madness whirled and her fingers caressed the blade. She saw it flapping on the floor, a dying eel! Her mind soared with happiness.

So real were they, the movies in her mind ... but the cough saved her. Zachary was coughing in the other room.

She felt his release and spat it into the Hallowe'en gown. She grabbed a robe.

'Thanks, Baby Doll, you were great. You're not getting older, you're getting better,' and he lay back across the bed, a smile of satisfaction on his face.

'It's Zack – he's coughing,' she explained.

Her head whirled. The pills, the hatred, the violent act that she had almost committed, raged through her being, and she felt strange, unlike herself. Almost staggering, she went to Zachary's room.

With Zack peacefully asleep again, she tiptoed softly to check on Melanie. She opened the door to her room. The pills dipped and whirled around within her. She was dreaming, of dolls, and dead babies and satin cloth ...

A recess. There was a pause of Time until It fled and she found herself looking down at her dirt-stained hands. It was important to remember something. Of course – the shears! She fetched them and, standing in front of the bathroom mirror, holding hunks of tangled curls, she heard the satisfying sound of the *snip!* as hair, great mounds of it, fell into the sink. Then back to bed . . . She had a purpose: she had to wait for the alarm clock to ring, *then she could begin screaming.*

It is a nightmare – Raylean in the hall, the sound of screams echoing, bouncing off the walls . . . *hers*. She can see the singer on the TV commercial shattering wine glasses, and her volume stretches, searching for the windowpanes, imagining her terror and rage can do that, and then she finds herself touching the glass in the window, surprised that it is still there.

She knows there is an empty bassinet, the covers not even wrinkled, then there are strangers in the house, policemen, dogs. Cameras flash, and she feels the pressure of her son holding tightly to her knees, his screams matching hers.

Someone takes him, and she feels empty. Through the throng she can see Bobby Lee, his eyes bewildered, and as he reaches out to her, something stops him, and he only holds himself shivering in the morning.

She sits and like a sleepwalker she answers their questions, her voice harsh and dull, for she is all screamed out. Satisfied, they go away. A woman sits with her, a stranger. She holds herself and rocks; in motion she seeks to fill the emptiness.

Later, through the crowd another woman comes and tries to comfort her. It is minutes before she knows her.

She tries forcing herself to know that face, that voice, that touch and then through the fog she finally knows. It's Stella.

Stella opens the bottles Jenny clutches in her hands, and offers her two small yellow pills. She sinks back against the pillows in the same valley where Zachary's head rested only last night, and finally it's done. Now she can find peace.

221

Even though there is the eerie sound of yipping dogs, and the clatter of the French doors being opened to the yard and the woods beyond . . . *and Jenny knows for certain that they are about to make a grim discovery.*

CHAPTER 23

That time was behind Jenny now – the rocks hurled through the window, the hate letters Stella burned for her, the telephone ringing at all hours of the night. Hoarse voices screaming: 'You knew, you filthy bitch, you knew!'

The newspapers that were hidden from her with Bobby Lee's handsome, smiling face splashed right across them. The twilight time of leaving that house, with a bagful of clothes, some toys, and the diamond ring – for that was all that really belonged to Jenny. Already Georgia was standing in the hall taking possession of her house, for Sylvia Antree had left everything to her.

Jenny spent weeks in the hospital unaware of the sensational trial going on around her.

'Nervous breakdown,' she heard Stella whispering to Maw, who stood alongside her tall, white bed.

It was over, all of it.

Jenny was told quietly that her husband had been sentenced to life for the murder of their daughter Melanie. Tammy's poor drowned body was exhumed from its small grave, but it could not be proven that the injury on her head was not from the boat. It turned out that Bobby Lee had convictions in two other states for child molestation.

Stella had arranged everything for her – the divorce, the sale of the ring, and a new apartment. And like a shadow Jenny went back out into the world.

The small apartment was in a nice part of town, above a flower shop and across the street from a lovely park. It was nine months since she had seen her son. He seemed to have grown much taller, and she hugged him until he cried out, 'Mommy, you're hurting me.'

'Oh, I'm sorry, so sorry. I never meant to hurt any of you.'

'Are you sure you can handle it, having Zack?' Stella asked, concerned.

'Oh Stella, yes, I need him so much.'

It was strange looking at her own signature now – Priest, Jennifer Priest. Legally it was easy with the divorce coming through. It was understandable that she wouldn't want to keep that notorious name.

'I told Zack he was killed on the highway. I didn't know what else to do,' Stella whispered.

Jenny nodded. It was okay, for to her he *was* dead. She hoped that maybe Bobby Lee Antree had never existed at all.

She never knew that the house had burned to the ground; for those who had thrown rocks and nasty notes had thrown oil-soaked rags as well, and now it was gone, all of it. Only a mound of bricks was left, a heap of twisted bars, and it was good . . . for the crying voices of children were finally still.

Sad memories slowly dimmed for Zachary. It was easier on him, being young. He was in school now, and had joined the Cub Scouts. Only occasionally would he look at Jenny wistfully and say, 'Please don't leave me and go to heaven. Please, Momma, don't.'

Jenny would hug him tight and promise, 'I won't. I won't leave you, ever.'

'No, Momma, say it – say you won't go to heaven,' and as an afterthought he'd add, 'If you have to, take me with you.' The deaths had left their mark on him.

Jenny was scared of herself because she dreamed of dead babies and drowned dolls, and she thought about it, how easy it would be to fill the cocoa cups with pills, lie down holding her beloved son in her arms, and for both of them to just drift away to a better place.

'Talk to me,' Stella would urge whenever she saw that faraway look on her sister's face. 'Please, baby sister, there's been so much pain already because you didn't.'

Jenny tried. 'How can people live with memories like mine?' she said.

'I don't really know. People smarter than me say that time is the only healer.'

'It's dimmer now, but it's not gone. Oh no, I can see it clearly, all of it, on dark nights.'

Stella grabbed her hands roughly. 'You still have him, he's a wonderful little boy. He needs you, he loves you.'

Jenny looked at her hands, sometimes when she looked she still saw dirt on them.

'I can't remember Zack's conception. It couldn't have been too bad then, but Melanie – I remember hers clearly. She was born of filthy lust and burning hatred. A child shouldn't come from that. She had such a brief, sad life. No one ever loved her, not even me,' Jenny said brokenly.

'I know, it's very hard to think of the way she died,' Stella said, her eyes filling up with tears.

'Oh no, Stella, please don't think that. His filth never touched Melanie. No, Stella, *he* didn't kill her.'

Stella blanched white and looked about the cheerful living room as if searching for intruders. She reached over and put her finger across Jenny's lips, the shock plain on her face. 'Jenny, promise me you'll never say that to anyone again *ever*. Swear it!'

'I swear,' Jenny promised, and Stella couldn't look at her.

Her breath coming fast now, she reached for her bag, her hand shaking. 'I've started smoking again, did I tell you?' she said, deliberately changing the subject.

'No,' and Jenny watched her sister fumble for a long cigarette; she tried three times before she could light it.

It was Zachary who saved his mother, who saved them both. He had been on a school trip to the fire station that day, and was filled with such excitement and happiness that Jenny decided to prolong his nice day. Instead of supper in the flat, she made peanut butter sandwiches, packed up some Kool Aid and chocolate cookies, and the pair of them went across the street to eat supper in the park.

By the small lake Jenny spread out the cloth. The sandwiches tasted delicious; they saved the crusts for the ducks, who in a mass of quacks came up to beg.

'I've decided, Momma,' Zack said importantly.

'Decided what?'

'When I grow up, I'm gonna be a fireman, and if your house, or Grandma's church, or anyone's house catches on fire, I'll put on my boots and my hat, get out my fire truck, ride real fast and put out the fire, just like that,' he said proudly.

'Well, good. I feel very safe knowing you'd do that.'

'Well, sometimes when I'm in bed I think about what I want to be. I thought maybe I'd be a dog doctor, or a train driver, but today I decided for sure; when I grow up I'm gonna be a fireman.'

'Sure you are, honey,' and she hugged him close.

It was so wrong of her. He treasured life, he dreamed about growing up – she had no right to *not* do the same. She was only twenty-two years old; there was a whole world before her. She had a life and right then she decided to live it.

'You know, Zachary, I made a decision just now. I'm going to be a designer that makes beautiful jewelry.'

'Can you have two jobs, being that thing you said and a mother?'

'Yes, I can have two jobs. I can do both,' Jenny said firmly.

'Oh.' His face wrinkled with thought. 'Could I be a fireman *and* a train driver?'

'Maybe,' and they gathered up the cloth, shook out the crumbs, and headed for home.

The next day Jenny bought a drawing board and art supplies and she decided to try and find a new life.

It started slowly. The paper remained blank; no ideas came to her mind. She gripped the pen until her fingers cramped. 'Maybe tomorrow,' she thought.

For some reason the next morning she decided to use the back stairway, as Zack and she started out to walk to school. She found it, lying on the last step – one perfect rose, morning dew still trembling on its petals.

'That's it! Zack, I've got it – a summer garden. My jewelry will be a summer garden.'

He looked at his mother, puzzled. 'Can you call one flower a garden?'

'No, honey, you can't. I mean my idea. I want to draw them – flowers, lots of different kinds, then I can call the series "A Summer Garden".'

'Okay, Momma, if you want to,' he beamed, sharing her happiness.

On the way home, Jenny used the outside staircase again. She saw where the wayward flower had come from. The industrial waste can was shut, but a fern and a bit of baby's breath were peeking out from under the lid.

Cautiously, she lifted the lid. Bits of flowers, some wilted, some still good, filled the can to overflowing. Her hands sifted through the clean debris.

'Did you find what you were looking for?'

'Oh, I'm sorry.' In her surprise the lid clanged shut. 'I didn't mean to steal your flowers, it's just that—' she couldn't finish for he was smiling and looked amused.

'You can't steal what's being thrown away.'

'No, I guess not,' and she held on to the precious pink rose. 'This one's still good. I need them for my artwork,' she finished awkwardly.

'It's my flower shop, we've been neighbours for a long time. It's only right we should introduce ourselves.' He thrust his hand out. 'I'm Philip Tremaine.'

She took the warm, firm hand he offered. 'I'm Jennifer Priest.' It felt different using the prettier name. From now on she decided she was Jennifer, not Jenny.

'The little boy, is that your son?'

'Yes, his name is Zachary. He just started first grade.'

He nodded and pulled a pack of cigarettes out of his pocket. 'Lousy habit,' he said as he lit one and blew out the smoke. 'I don't do it inside. It'd be bad for the flowers.' On second thoughts, he offered the pack to her.

'No, I don't smoke. My sister just started again, though,' and she felt stupid for saying it. Why would he care?

The phone ringing persistently in the shop behind him ended their conversation.

'My assistant just quit,' he laughed. 'She's getting married and that makes me busier than ever. I'm doing all her flowers.' With a curious gesture he tipped his hand toward his forehead, in a sort of mock salute. 'See ya.'

She went up the steps thinking what a nice man he seemed. No, she corrected herself, she didn't know a thing about him. He probably wasn't nice at all. If Bobby Lee had taught her one thing it was that people were not always what they seemed.

The rose in her hand – that was genuine, though; it hid nothing, and she began to draw.

She sketched the flower in several sizes. Enamel ... it would be exquisite in soft pink enamel, the heart of the rose darker. She imagined leaves and drew one tiny thorn. She worked furiously that day, and designed a brooch and a necklace set on a chain with one perfect rose that would rest on the hollow between the collar-bones. This flower did not lend itself to being a bracelet, and the earrings, she decided, would consist only of the leaves curling up over the ear. She was satisfied with the work. She drew it over and over, and as she changed colours, the flower took on fresh personalities. The red was vibrant, the yellow subdued but elegant, the pink innocent ... and she changed and designed it slightly smaller in scope.

When she looked up she was surprised at the time. She would almost be late for picking up Zack.

She knew there were crossing guards, and soon she would listen to his plea to walk to school alone, but for now she felt he was too trusting, too friendly, and she knew there were men out there who offered candy and Dutch chocolate ice cream.

She grabbed her purse, ran out the back door, and was only minutes late. He was standing by the gate. He seemed so little, and she felt love well up in her so strong it threatened to drown her.

'Hi, honey,' she called out, and he ran to meet her.

Addie kept calling her, wanting them to come out on the weekend. Stella, too, was always on the phone asking when she wanted to start driving lessons.

'Not right now,' she put her off, saying, 'I can't afford a car anyway.'

'How's your money holding out?' Stella asked. 'It's a shame we don't have a few more diamond rings to pawn.'

'Yeah, but it's not too bad,' she answered truthfully, feeling guilty about spending so much on art supplies.

'Don't be so darn stubborn,' Stella scolded. 'You'd qualify for relief and food stamps.'

'I don't want to apply for that. I'm thinking of looking for a job now that Zack's in school all day.'

The job was there right at her doorstep. Her conversations with Philip on the back stairs with the constant ringing of the phone prompted his offer.

'By the way, do you have any time? I really need help, someone to answer the phone, take orders, and maybe learn a little about flower arranging.'

Jenny started to refuse, then remembering the dwindling bank account said, 'I could only work part-time, the hours when Zack's in school.'

'That's fine, you're hired,' and Philip was smiling, holding his hand out.

She followed him into the flower shop. It was a place of wonder. Steel cones held bunches of flowers, and one wall consisted entirely of refrigerators, with every flower imaginable inside waiting to be turned into an arrangement of beauty. The tables held masses of ribbons, tape and wires and other, unfamiliar items.

He studied the look on her face. 'What's wrong?' he asked.

'It reminds me of funerals.'

'Oh no, only the gladiolus. The rest, they represent moments of joy in life – weddings, anniversaries, birthdays, proms, promotions, the birth of a child, the wonderful moment of falling in love . . .' He held up a lily. 'Easter, the celebration of Christ. Christmas – oh no, flowers are the language of love.'

The phone interrupted their conversation. He pointed to the pen and order pad. 'You answer with the shop name.'

She picked up the phone. 'Hello, Tremaine's Florist,' she managed to say.

Quickly, she wrote down the order, four corsages and a bridal bouquet and five boutonnières, with two special corsages for the bride and groom's mothers. She covered the receiver and asked Philip for a quote, as they were asking for a price. She told them the amount and quickly wrote down the requested colours, the date the flowers were needed and the address for delivery. She hung up feeling satisfied with herself.

'Hey, Girl Friday, that was good. You learn fast.'

The day went quickly as she watched Philip at work. His large slender hands loved those flowers, and for him they fell into place as things of beauty. Talent – she now knew what the word meant.

Each day she took home a perfect specimen of the flower that she wanted to work on, and soon she had four pieces designed in a series. She had used the rose, a lily, a daisy, and a pansy. The pansy was her favourite. It lent itself to more parts of a set, for it made lovely earrings, and a bracelet of links was possible.

As she stared at her work, Jenny began to hope that maybe it was good enough to offer – but would Paul Winthrop from Enchanting Jewels even remember her, a nervous girl at a craft fair from years ago? He *had* to, it was her dream.

She had done her homework. In each design that used stones, she was specific: this piece needed cabochons, this piece baguettes, that one baroque pearls. She had studied the borrowed jewelry books with care. She was satisfied and pleased with her work.

One day when she started to rush out and pick up Zachary from school, Philip hesitated, but he finally said what he was thinking. 'Are you sure it's a good idea, picking him up every day?'

'Of course,' Jenny snapped.

'I mean, you don't want his friends teasing him – "Momma's boy", all that sort of thing. I know it's none of my business, but I remember what embarrassed me when I was his age, and being called "Momma's boy" was the worst.'

Jenny stuttered with surprise. He was right, it was none of his business. 'But he's so little,' she said finally. 'He doesn't know about—' she wrung her hands. 'He's so friendly, I worry about—'

Philip walked over and took her nervous hands. 'I know what you worry about, Jennifer. I own the building, too. I saw your rental application from the realtor. I know – but you can't wrap your son up in cotton wool. You gotta let him grow.'

'You know?' she said, suddenly feeling dirty.

He nodded. 'It must have been the very worst thing that could ever happen to anyone, but you have Zack and you can't let that tragedy taint his whole life.'

She felt resentment well up in her, cold and brittle. He knew; all this time that they had been sliding into an easy friendship, he had known about her and Bobby Lee. The feeling of being a piece of dirt returned. 'I have to go, I'm late,' she said angrily.

On impulse she splurged and took a cab to the Mission instead of the bus.

Zachary happily played with Scotty in the weed-filled yard, as Jenny helped her mother in the kitchen. 'I can do this,' Addie urged. 'Go on, sit in on the service. It'll do you good.'

To pacify her she went in, took a back seat, and listened to the testimonies. There was so much pain in the world. This one cheated on her husband, that one had turned out his own child, this man stole from his employer. 'Open your heart to Jesus,' the Reverend screamed. 'Do it, come forward. Let Him in. Jesus loves you, yes, Jesus loves you,' he bellowed out in song, and the organ wheezed and he grabbed his guitar, and Jenny found herself crying and stumbling forward to the makeshift altar. She felt his worn hand on her head. 'God bless you, Sister, God bless you. Jesus loves you,' and from head to head his work-calloused hand comforted and promised salvation.

He looked upward. 'You're saved, saved by the hand of the Lord,' and again the organ wheezed and the voices blended and she found herself singing:

> *'The Devil is a sly ole fox.*
> *If I could catch Him I'd put Him in a box.*
> *Lock that box and throw away the key,*
> *And that would be the end of He.'*

She had done it, she had done just that!

CHAPTER 24

On Monday Philip reminded Jenny of the time. 'It's three-fifteen,' he said.

'I know,' and she continued filing the orders. He looked up from his work on the bench and started to say something else, changed his mind, and began whistling instead.

It was only a few minutes until they heard Zack's voice at the back door.

'I did it,' he said proudly. 'I minded the crossing guard and I didn't talk to any strangers.'

Jenny put the papers aside. 'Great,' she said. 'You were gettin' too big to be picked up by your Momma.'

'I thought so too,' Zack said, shifting from foot to foot.

'I'll be ready in a few minutes. I'll just finish up.'

Zack nodded and stood impatiently in the doorway.

Philip offered, 'Long as you gotta wait for your mother, you wanna earn some change? Floor's pretty dirty. It could do with a good sweepin'.'

'Yeah,' Zack answered eagerly. 'That okay, Mom?'

'Sure,' and she blessed Philip. He was so good with kids. No, he was so good with people.

She could hear their conversation.

'You like baseball?' Philip asked.

'Yeah, I can catch pretty good. I'm not so good at batting, but I'm gonna try out for Little League next term anyway.'

233

'Little League, huh? How'd you like to see the Cardinals play some time?'

'Ooh, I'd like that real good. I've got all their baseball cards, well almost, 'cept one. I don't have Stan Musial. You gotta trade six cards to get him,' Zack said.

'Six cards, that's a lot.'

Zack continued sweeping vigorously, almost too vigorously as dust rose up from his efforts. He proudly took the coin, and kept fingering it as they went upstairs to eat supper.

Jenny didn't know what she felt. In one way she was glad. Zack needed a male to talk to, but promises of baseball games, that was going too far. She didn't want promises that wouldn't be kept, nor did she want to go to a baseball game with Philip. It would be stretching their casual work relationship and friendship into something more personal.

Jenny made supper while Zack played on the kitchen floor, sorting out the baseball cards, calling out each player's name.

It became a ritual, Zack stopping by to sweep the floor, empty the trash or do some other little job that really needed doing.

It wasn't charity. Jenny couldn't ruin the pleasure they took in each other's company. They were easy with each other and one day she heard Zack say, 'I'm gonna be a fireman when I grow up. How come you got such a sissy job?'

Philip laughed, 'I guess 'cause I wasn't good enough to do what I really wanted. I wanted to be a baseball player.'

'You did?'

'Yep. I played for the minor leagues when I was a young man, but then sometimes you gotta settle for what you can do, and flowers are good. My job makes people happy, most of the time.' He held out a ceramic cradle that he was filling with tiny roses. 'See this? By tonight this will be on someone's night-stand and some lady will be real happy

234

because these flowers celebrate a very happy time in her life. It's in honour of her new baby.'

Zack's face frowned. 'Our baby didn't have nothing like that,' he said sadly.

Philip gulped, glanced over at Jenny, a silent apology in his eyes. The moment passed and Jenny forgave him. Life was going to be filled with times when the past would crowd in again, if only for a moment.

They started closing up the shop, and Philip smiled at Jenny and said, 'When are you going to invite me up to see the mysterious artwork?'

'You could see it now if you want to. Momma draws real good,' Zack offered.

Jenny couldn't help herself. 'You're not kidding me,' she quipped. 'You just want to see how your tenants are keeping the apartment.' She was amazed at her ability to joke with him so easily.

'That's true – landlords have their rights!' Philip teased back, as he followed them up the steps.

He studied her drawings carefully. 'They're good – no, they're better than good. What are they for?'

'I'll tell you, but first I wanna remember my manners. Would you like a soda, coffee or tea?'

'Coffee would be great,' and Jenny left them, Philip crouching on the floor admiring Zack's baseball cards while she went to the kitchen.

Over coffee, she explained about the fair, the sale to Enchanting Jewels and Paul's kind offer to look at sketches for collections or ideas.

'Of course, that was a long time ago. He probably wouldn't remember me or even look at freelance ideas any more.'

'Years ago? Why'd you wait so long?'

Jenny's eyes dropped with shame. No, she told herself, it was not her fault. She was the victim. She tried the truth, and it felt good.

'My husband wouldn't allow it. He was furious, in fact. He took the money from the sale, tore up all my sketches, and all I had left was dying dreams.' She was shaking with shock and amazement. She had never in her whole life told anyone anything that personal.

'That's too bad, but you have them back, those dreams. Dreams are hard to kill,' Philip said softly. Then: 'I'm getting hungry.' He clapped his hands together. 'Anyone feel like pizza with pepperoni?'

A cloud crossed Jenny's face.

'How about McDonald's? They give out free toys,' Zack said with enthusiasm.

Jenny smiled. 'Sounds good.'

That's how it began, their close friendship. Jenny knew he liked her, but she wasn't ready. She wasn't sure if she'd ever be ready, for now she was always searching behind the mask. People were not what they seemed, she knew that now. Something dark and secret lived behind each mask.

Slowly she learned about Philip. He was thirty-seven, his wife had died of leukaemia, he had a house in the suburbs, a dog named Pal, a mother who lived in California, and she knew he loved baseball and flowers and felt cheated that his wife had never given him a son.

Jenny wasn't fooled. You never get what you see; life had taught her that lesson well.

Philip helped her write the proposal to Enchanting Jewels. He advised on how she should present the portfolio, and after a call to New York, where Jenny was told yes, they still looked at freelance material, she sent it off by registered mail.

Waiting was hard. She spent her free time in craft shops; her mind buzzed with designs and ideas.

She bought some wonderful coloured African beads, cord and feathers. She felt bold, her hands flew as she did it, her real work, stringing necklaces, and when she went downstairs to the florist's shop she wore some of her creations. One day she put on a pair of peacock earrings and a matching necklace; on a plain white dress they looked stunning.

'Wow,' Philip whistled. 'As the new generation of hippies would say, "Far out". How about it, little lady? Can I take you out somewhere and show you off?'

'Sorry, I promised my mother I'd go out to the Mission tonight. I've some outgrown clothes of Zack's to put in the clothes giveaway. The people there need so much.'

'The Mission?' he questioned.

'Yes, I guess I never told you I grew up there. It's the really rough part of town, Hyde Park. My mother married this minister – my sister always called him "that crazy Reverend", but he means well. He does some real Christian work. Growing up we were dreadfully ashamed of him, but now I realize he's for real – he means it.' It was becoming a habit with Jennifer. She was able to talk, to stop hiding things. It felt wonderful.

'Sounds fun. Mind if I tag along?'

'If you really want to,' she said, 'but watch it. Momma will be pushing you in to see the service, and the Reverend will be coaxing you to be Saved.'

'I guess we all could use being Saved.'

Zack was positively ecstatic that Philip was going along. 'I'm gonna tell Scotty about you being a baseball player an' all.'

'Gonna tell him about my sissy job now?' Philip teased.

'Maybe,' Zack answered, but he knew it was a lie; he wouldn't dare mention a flower shop.

'Oh Philip, can we take some? Flowers, I mean.' And Jenny headed for the trash bin.

'You don't need to do that. We can donate some,' he offered.

'No, no, that would ruin it,' and she began telling him about the mason and pickle jars when she was little and how she wanted to make the Mission pretty, and Zack and she whooped and hollered with success every time they found a stalk or bloom that wasn't too wilted in the trash can.

It was good, her relationship with Philip. She could finally be herself. There was no pretence, he saw the real

237

person – but she couldn't trust yet. Jenny believed there were still closed doors she couldn't open.

The phone was ringing early the next morning. Zack was still eating his cereal, and Jenny was dressing.

'Hello?'

'Who is he?' It was Stella, her voice excited and happy. 'Maw told me all about him, described him and everything. She didn't know the right word, but I'm sure she meant "preppy". How 'bout those Chino pants, Izod shirt – she called it Forest Green – those shoes they wear up East, and Argyll socks. Jenny, tell me, where'd you meet him and when?'

'Stella, slow down. It's only the guy I work for, there's nothing to it. We're just friends. He's a widower and he's lonely.'

'You mean the florist? But you made him sound so old and boring.'

'He is old. He's thirty-seven.'

'That's not so old, and anyway Maw said he seemed to adore Zack.'

'Yeah, they get along great, they're baseball buddies.'

'Sounds like a match made in heaven.'

'Oh Stella, don't be so ridiculous. He feels sorry for us, that's all, but he is a friend, a real friend. I can be myself with him, and he knows all about me. I never knew it at first, but he owns the building. The realtor must have shown him my application, so he knew about us from the start. It's nice not to be hiding things.'

'Don't be too sure it's only pity. Maw seems to think he was real fond of you and Zack.'

'I guess he is, but he's gonna be mad if I'm late for work. I better go.'

'Did you hear from the jewelry place yet?'

'No, not yet.'

'What were those earrings you wore to the Mission? Momma liked 'em but she was worried the Reverend was gonna see 'em.'

'Oh, they're great big peacock feathers. I'm just messing around. It's fun making that kind of thing. You know, the hippie generation, it's fun.'

'Sounds like it.'

'Momma, I can't find my socks,' Zack called.

'I gotta go,' and they hung up.

That was the night she had given Zack permission to stay overnight at his friend's house. Around three-thirty Philip commented, 'Where's our number one boy? He's late.'

'He's not coming. He's spending the night at a friend's.'

'Then how about a movie and a proper dinner, at a restaurant where you don't get a free toy.'

'All right,' Jenny agreed. 'That sounds nice.'

The movie was a bit embarrassing, for it was an intense love story filled with kisses and innuendo. It was what Jenny had thought love was like, a long time ago before Bobby Lee. She felt extremely uncomfortable, but dinner was better and she settled down. The candlelight was kind to Philip. It hid the small lines around his eyes, and for the first time she realized he was nice-looking in a quiet way. His sandy-coloured hair, groomed and smooth, his jaw, square and strong, and his brown eyes, warm and honest . . . with a sudden twinge she realized how much she really liked him.

She pointed to the dish in front of her. 'My sister Stella when we were little at the Mission was always yearning for asparagus. She'd yap on and on, how she'd serve it every day when she was grown-up. Turns out she hates the stuff, can't even force it down.'

'Life's little injustices,' he said.

They ate, and drank the wine, and it was a very pleasant evening. Driving home, Philip even asked her permission to smoke.

'I don't mind.' Jenny was used to him standing on the back stoop of the store taking his break while the smoke drifted back into the store no matter which way the wind blew.

He walked her up the stairs. It was an awkward moment, and before she could thank him, she heard the phone ringing.

'Oh my God, Zack!' she panicked, fumbled with the door and grabbed the phone on the third ring. 'Hello?'

'Jennifer Priest,' she heard a male voice ask.

'Yes, speaking.' Her heart was thudding; visions of police and emergency rooms filled her head.

'It's Paul Winthrop, of Enchanting Jewels. I've been trying to reach you all day.'

'Oh yes, Mr Winthrop.'

'Paul, please. We received your sketches for a collection. They're very good.'

'Thank you,' she said, and waited, her heart still pounding.

'We'd like to talk to you about it.'

'Certainly.'

'Not on the phone, Jennifer. We thought you could come up to New York, take another day to hop up to Rhode Island, see the plant so you'd understand how jewelry is really made.'

'Yes, I could do that.' Her mind was racing. How? Zachary . . . school . . . work!

'We can send you the plane tickets for the fourth and we'd like you to stay on until the ninth. Hotels, tickets, all expenses paid, of course.'

'Yes, that would be fine,' she said, keeping her voice calm.

'Good, I'll have my secretary put the tickets and details in the mail first thing in the morning.'

'Thank you,' she said, and stood still, holding onto the buzzing phone.

Concern plain on his face, Philip took her shoulders and turned her to him. 'Jennifer, what is it?'

'That was New York, the man in New York. They want me to come up there; they liked my sketches.'

For just a minute she saw in those warm brown eyes of his dying dreams, then he caught himself. 'That's wonderful,'

240

he said, and pulled her to him in a warm hug. 'Simply wonderful.'

Jenny turned down Stella's kind offer to look after Zack. She couldn't let him miss that much school. She called an agency who sent a woman over who had impeccable references. She was perfect; she was grandmotherly and warm and had raised three sons herself. 'Don't worry, I know all their tricks,' and Jenny was sure she did.

'I can't work Thursday or Friday,' she told Philip. 'I need to shop. I can't show up in New York looking like a smalltown hick.' She worried about the money, but since she was working, it didn't disappear as quickly.

'That's fine, but don't go looking too conservative,' Philip warned. 'I like those new designs, bold and brassy. You know, those feather things you made.'

'Do you really think I should wear them?'

'Yes, they show how innovative you really are. Don't hide your light under a bushel, Jenny.'

'Okay, Philip, I'll do it.'

'And don't worry about Zack, either. That woman sounds good, and he can still come here after school.'

Jenny's skin crawled. The scent of flowers overwhelmed her; the dark corners of the room seemed sinister.

'*No!*' The word came out, loud and full of terror. 'No, he can't come here after school.'

'Whoah,' Philip said softly. He walked over to her desk. 'Jennifer, you simply can't spend the rest of your life thinking every man is a child-molester. Why, I care for Zack. He's crept into my heart like the son I never had. I am so hurt, I can't even tell you how much.' He dropped the arrangement he was working on and went out to smoke.

She came up behind him. 'Philip, I'm so sorry. I didn't mean— You have no idea how hard it is to live with my guilt. Tammy, the lake, the signs ... they were all there, and I didn't see them. I curse myself over and over for my stupidity.'

Philip turned and he was a blur, for his eyes were full of

tears and so were hers. Jenny went on: 'Letters – I got hate letters, notes thrown through the windows. I got scores of them, and they all said the same thing: "*You bitch, you filthy bitch, you knew.*"'

Jenny trembled, and her tears fell. 'And Philip, honest to God, I examined my heart and my soul, and I *didn't* know. I never knew about men like that. Looking back, the signs were all there. A smarter person might have recognized them, but as God is my witness *I didn't know*. I was very young.'

He patted her shoulder. 'It's all right, I understand,' but she felt he didn't really understand.

CHAPTER 25

Jennifer met with Paul and his two assistants in his office, and they went over and over her sketches. The questions and possibilities raged: should they do all enamels? Or maybe use some stones, at least on the flowers with stamens? Cost sheets and estimates on production flew back and forth.

Jennifer's title for the collection 'A Summer Garden' was going to be kept. Production was eventually scheduled for early spring the following year.

Maybe they could also bring out a cheaper line in plastics. What did she think? And Jennifer's answers were always listened to carefully. Sometimes her suggestions were taken up, sometimes not.

On the second day, they went out on the train to the plant in Rhode Island. It was a monster of a building, with lathes and metal stamping producing a cacophony of sound, and the smell of paint thick in the air. Jennifer was shown moulds, stampings, filings, and the department where hairnetted women carefully mounted each stone by hand; on the cheaper line, the stones were glued.

Jennifer's sketches were copied, and given to the department to make them into reality, and she felt the thrill of a lifetime when she saw the prepared stampings. Above the hallmark it read *Designs by Jennifer*.

Her dreams lived in a bit of metal but she would have to wait a year, a whole year, to see them, her designs, twinkling on soft velvet in department store windows.

Back in New York, Paul said, 'I've been remiss. We never discussed money,' but they both knew she would have paid him to see her dream become reality.

She almost gasped when she saw the contract; her fee was more than she would make at the flower shop in two years.

She signed the contract and was handed the cheque that started her dreaming of little houses for Zack and herself. The contract covered her prototypes for bead and feather jewelry as well. 'The inexpensive line, it'll be a winner,' Paul said. 'After all, the hippies are coming. No, the hippies are here.'

With business finished, Jennifer wandered around the big city. She shopped and bought presents for everyone. For Zack she chose an enormous fire truck with lights that flashed and a siren that really wailed; for Philip she got a silver lighter, on which she had his initials engraved; for Addie and Stella she bought wonderful silk blouses, and for the Reverend she purchased an antique Bible with an ivory cover. She bought dolls for Stella's girls and by then found she was really exhausted.

At the hotel she fell into her soft bed; her plane was due to leave at seven in the morning. She couldn't wait to tell everyone about her trip.

Drowsy, and in that place between wakefulness and sleep, from a great distance she heard the shrill ring of the phone.

'Hello,' she muttered sleepily.

'Jennifer, are you okay? You sound funny.' It was Philip.

'I'm fine, I was asleep.'

'I'm so sorry to wake you but there's been a small problem.'

'Problem?'

'Yes, Zachary was going to meet you at the airport, and he doesn't want to alarm you.'

'Alarm me how? What's wrong?'

There was silence, then it came out in a rush. 'He broke a finger playing ball.'

'Oh my God, when?'

'Today, this afternoon. I told him not to come after school while you were gone, but when he got hurt, he asked for me, so the school called me. He's been X-rayed, his finger's set and he's proud as hell.'

Fully awake now, Jennifer yelled into the phone, 'What's he got to be proud of?'

'His catch. The bases were loaded and he caught it – a fast ball. He won the ball game,' and she heard Philip laughing. 'It's great. He can't wait to see you. Make a big deal of it, Jenny, he's the hero of the team.'

'Men!' she thought, and as she hung up she felt something that really scared her. 'I love him, really love him,' she thought, and she couldn't imagine what to do about it, for she was still so frightened of those closed doors and the masks that people wore.

CHAPTER 26

At the airport, she saw Zack through the crowd, his small hand with its bandaged finger waving in the air.

'Mom! Mom!' Zachary called as he rushed forward. 'Look, I won the game!'

Jennifer stooped down and hugged him. 'Oh, what a brave boy I've got. Did it hurt much?'

'Yeah, Mom, it did, but it was Jeff. Best batter on their team. He hit a fast ball and I was a little scared and it hurt a lot, but I didn't drop it. No, I held onto the ball real tight, even when my fingers hurt.'

'I'm real proud of you, honey. You're quite a ball player. Does this mean you're not gonna be a fireman after all?'

Zack laughed and hugged her back and asked, 'Did you bring me a surprise?'

'I sure did.' Over his tousled head Jennifer saw Philip. 'Thanks for coming. I expected Stella.'

'She seemed a little busy, so I offered.' He picked up her suitcase and they threaded their way through the crowd to the parking lot.

Philip eased his way into the traffic and said, 'Don't keep us in suspense. What did they say?'

'Philip, it's like a dream. I can hardly believe it. They bought them – the whole series. They'll produce it next spring. They're even keeping the name "A Summer Garden Collection", and that's not the most exciting part yet—'

'What, Mom, what?' Zack piped up from the back seat.

'My name will be on each piece of jewelry right above their hallmark, and the promotion cards will say *Designs by Jennifer.*'

Philip looked towards her, smiling broadly, and behind them a horn tooted angrily as he swerved and moved over to the slow lane.

'That's just great,' he said, and his hand slid across the seat to squeeze hers.

'We're all doing good, aren't we?' Zack said.

Jennifer turned to look at her son. 'Yeah, honey, we really are, and when we stop I want you to tell me all about it, that special ball game.'

'Sure, Mom, but you don't understand it as good as Philip does.'

She looked out the window and saw strange surroundings, a small unfamiliar road. Philip saw her gaze.

'It's a surprise. I hope you're hungry.'

'Starved. That food on the plane was nothing to write home about it, and anyway I was too excited to eat.'

'Good.'

Shortly they turned into a gravel parking lot, and the sign told her they were at *Rose's Italian Restaurant & Beer Garden.*

'Looks fun and smells good,' Jennifer commented as they walked through the restaurant and out back to the garden that had red and white checked tablecloths, flickering candles and paper lanterns swaying in the breeze.

'It's nicer as it gets dark,' Philip promised.

It was a minute or two before she saw them gathered at a back table, Maw and the Reverend looking stiff and out of place, Stella holding up a wine glass in mock salute, and running around the tables kicking up dust were Heather and Penny, and even little Scotty was there.

This is quite a surprise,' Jennifer said.

'In your honour,' said Stella, and held the glass higher.

After hugs all around, she sat down, and they ordered large plates of Rosa's mouthwatering spaghetti, and Chianti for everyone but the Reverend, who ordered Coca Cola with the children.

Jennifer was the focus of attention. After telling everyone about Enchanting Jewels she tried describing New York, her hotel, the shops, the carriages in Central Park, the lights, the excitement of the city, and she finished by saying, 'It's fabulous, but I wouldn't want to live there. It's great to be home,' and it was.

When leaving, Stella apologized again. 'Sorry, Rodney had to work late. You'll have to tell it all again to him.'

In the parking lot, by the light of the cars, Jennifer handed out the presents. 'Open them at home,' she said, then realized she had nothing for Scotty. Philip, bless his heart, found an envelope in the glove compartment, and she sealed a dollar bill in it and handed it to the boy.

Happy, but exhausted, they drove home, and the quiet from the back seat told her Zachary was already asleep. Philip carried him up, put him in bed fully dressed, took off his shoes, and covered him.

'Coffee?' she asked.

'No thanks, it will just keep me awake.'

'Philip, that was so nice of you, fixing for me to share my triumph with the whole family.' She noticed a bit of ribbon still sticking out of his pocket. His present. 'Aren't you gonna open it?'

'Sure.' He retrieved the small package, untied the bow, and looked at the silver lighter. He moved toward the lamp to read the inscription: *To Philip, with love, Jennifer*. 'Thanks, it's very nice.'

'I guess I shouldn't encourage bad habits, but I always think of you out on the porch searching through your pockets for a match.'

'Well, now, I guess you won't see me out on the porch searching for my lighter.'

'What does that mean?' she asked.

'With your new career, I don't think you'll have time to work.'

'Oh. I think you misunderstood everything. They bought

the collection, but it's nothing regular. Sure, I can think of other designs, but they only buy things here and there from freelancers like me. I turned down the offer to be a staff designer. I couldn't live there, not in a big city like that, with Zack. Where could he find a baseball team to break his finger?'

He laughed. 'But you did it, you really did it. I 'm sure you're very happy and proud. And they offered you a job.'

'Yes, I am, and sure, I plan on thinking of designs and Paul promised me they would be considered, but as I said it's nothing regular. I couldn't move to New York, I wouldn't want to.'

'Well, then, so I've still got my Girl Friday?'

'You bet.'

He started to say something, and changed his mind. 'I better be going. It's late.'

She walked him to the door. 'See you in the morning,' she said.

'Are you sure you want to work tomorrow? You look exhausted.'

'I'll be fine.' And she stood in the doorway and watched until his car disappeared down the ribbon of road.

That was the first night she had it, the dream. It was such a lovely dream. They were in a sun-dappled, walled garden. It was a strange, beautiful place. Clematis climbed over the warm brick wall and ivy clung tightly to it. A path led to the flagstoned patio. She could hear a *thump, thump* – a repeated sound of rubber against stone, a curious sound. In the dream she turned to see Zachary throwing the ball again and again at the step, where it hit the point and returned to him. 'My turn, my turn,' the high voice chanted. Scotty. Scotty was here in her dream standing behind Zachary, waiting his turn.

But there, further back in the garden, Jennifer saw her. How happy she looked. It was Tammy, grown taller, her pinched face fuller, her beloved Raggedy Ann new and crisp. She was leaning over a buggy. Jennifer tiptoed to see who she was offering the doll to, and smiled in deep contentment, for it was Melanie, grown bigger, her arms now plump, waving as she smiled, clutching at the shadows of the leaves from the trees above her.

From an unknown window Jennifer heard strains of music, soft, symphonic, the voices of violins.

Something called to her, just behind the leaves of the clematis, and it seemed important for her to know. So she walked over, pushed aside the leaves, and read the words that were carved and worn into the stone: *World's End*.

Good, she thought, and went back to her chair, to give herself up to the pleasant afternoon and the sound of the wonderful music.

The shrill sound woke her. Confused, she reached for the clock, tipped over the water glass, and heard Zack crying in the other room.

'I bumped it,' he explained, holding up the hand with the broken finger.

'I'll fix it,' she promised. 'A bit of tape should do it.'

'*They're dead*,' she said to herself, and in her stomach she felt it – a wiggle, an unpleasant sensation of movement. She went to the bathroom and felt sick. She stood over the sink, and after a time it stopped.

The next day, Philip took one look at her. 'Hey, Jennifer, go right back up those stairs and into bed. I told you not to come in today; you look more than exhausted.'

'I'm okay. It's just that I spent the whole night dreaming.'

'Nightmares, huh?' And he tapped her shoulder gently.

She turned to look at him. 'No, it was a very pleasant dream. It's when I wake up that it gets bad.'

'How's that?'

Her mouth stayed shut but her lips worked. She must, she must talk.

'In the dream it was Tammy, my stepdaughter, and my baby Melanie. They were in the dream, but they were different. They were bigger, I guess just like they would have been if they had both lived.'

'I'm so sorry,' he said.

Jennifer shivered. 'I felt I recognized this place. I don't

251

know why I should; it was so foreign, but beautiful. I've never been anywhere like it.'

She leaned back in the chair. 'It was a garden, with high brick walls, and I just now remembered something. There was a wooden door in the back; it was overgrown and wild, but in a lovely way, and carved in the stone were the words *World's End*.'

Philip's face drained of colour. 'What?'

'The words said *World's End*.'

The ringing phone ended the conversation, and again her stomach turned and tossed like a live thing trying to get out. With a shaking hand, she wrote down the order and handed it to Philip, who didn't look like himself; he looked strange.

It started on a regular basis then. Jennifer had the dream at least once a week. The figures changed, they did different things, but the children were all there, even Scotty. She thought his presence was the most curious thing of all.

'I had a good doctor that I talked to when Camilla died. I think he could help you. Call him and make an appointment,' Philip urged.

'I'll think about it,' she said, but she knew she wouldn't.

'He's not real expensive; he has impressive credentials. For a psychiatrist he has the reputation of being the best. Maybe medication could help.'

'Oh no, I wouldn't take anything. I took so many things when Melanie was born. They said I was suffering from depression, but I didn't like the way those pills made me feel. My thoughts were crazy, I did things—' she stopped and stared down at her hands. For a moment they looked dirty and she rubbed them on her skirt.

'Well, at least think about it, Jennifer. Talking it out might prove useful, and if it's the money you're worried about, I could help.'

'That's very generous, Philip, but no, thank you. I have the funds from the collection. I was paid a great deal of money – in fact, I was thinking about buying a little house.

252

AN EYE FOR AN EAR

The flat is nice, but I thought maybe a house with a yard, then Zack could have some pets. He does seem to get lonely. I don't know if I'd qualify for a loan, but I thought I might try, something like my sister's place. It wasn't real expensive.'

'I know a perfect house for you.'

'You do? Where, how much?' she asked.

'I'll take you out there after we close. It'll still be light.'

'All right,' and she went back to filing the paid bills.

'Hot dogs and root beer, please,' Zack ordered.

'That kinda food, all kids love it,' and Philip pulled up to the root beer stand. After stuffing themselves on hot dogs, Zachary ordered a hot fudge sundae.

'You're gonna have a tummy ache,' Jennifer warned.

'No, I'm not,' and he wolfed down the sundae.

Philip turned down a small exclusive lane, peppered with large oak trees on either side. Spread far apart, luxurious ranch houses settled comfortably on the earth, evergreen shrubs hugging their foundations.

'Philip, this isn't fair,' she objected.

'It's your house, ain't it?' Zack guessed, reaching for the handle of his door.

Jennifer was angry, but followed them into the house. Picture windows let in the lovely surroundings, and in the back yard a black dog leaped up towards the windows, greeting his owner with a chorus of barking.

'Gee, that's a nice dog,' Zack said.

'You like him?' Philip opened the door and the Labrador sprang in, jumping happily up at his master's immaculately pressed trousers.

Then, turning to Zack, the dog wagged his tail and began licking the little boy's face.

'Gee, his tongue's so rough. It feels funny, but nice.' Zack hugged the animal's willing neck.

Over the huddled mass of boy and dog Philip gazed at Jennifer with a look she had never seen before.

'His name's Pal, and he's been waiting for you all his life, Zack.'

253

'He has? Gee, I didn't know that. Does he do any tricks?'

'Yeah, he's great at fetch.' Philip picked up a ball and threw it out the door.

'Watch the pool, it's all covered.' And they found themselves staring at each other across the room.

'This isn't fair, not fair at all,' she whispered.

'Marry me, Jennifer,' he said. 'Like that dog, I've been waiting for you, too.'

'I can't, Philip. Oh, I wish I could, really I do.'

He came over and took her hand and they went outside and sat in the swingseat, watching Zack running back and forth and playing with the dog.

He ran up to them breathless. 'He did it. I told him to sit, and he did it. Tell me again about this dog, please, Philip.'

'There's not much to tell. His name s Pal, you know that. He does a few tricks, he's loyal—'

'No – the other part about me and him.'

Jennifer's eyes filled with tears.

'You know – that part that you said.'

'Oh. I said "this dog's been waiting for you all his life".'

'I'm glad,' and Zack started again hugging the furry neck. 'I had some cats once, but they ran off,' he said.

'Oh, cats can be like that sometimes. They're lookin' for the place that they came from. Cats love places, not people, but dogs, they love you. They'd go anywhere with you. It doesn't matter to them if you live in a palace or a cave, they love you; they love people.'

Zack nodded as if it were important to remember this wisdom.

'Tell me one more time,' he begged.

Philip reached over and touched his tousled head. 'I said "this dog's been waiting for you all his life."'

Zack nodded. 'I been waitin' for him, too. I just didn't know it.' And he ran off throwing the ball again.

'This isn't like you, Philip, it's so cruel. I never knew you could be cruel.'

'It's not meant to be cruel, Jennifer. I do believe the saying

254

goes "all's fair in love and war". I've loved you for a long time now. I want you to marry me, make me happy, give me this precious child for a son, complete my lonely life, give me something to live for.'

'I can't! Truly, I wish I could.'

'Oh, I don't want you to misunderstand this. I want nothing from you that I don't already have. I want your friendship, your companionship, your respect, your liking, and maybe your platonic love.'

'Platonic?'

'Yes. I don't expect anything else. I can't even begin to imagine what you've been through. I can only guess what you think of men. I've glimpsed that from all your suspicions. This proposal does not contain anything physical.'

She looked out over the trees and the purple shades of night already falling.

'It's like what happened before,' she said in a strangled voice. 'I sacrificed myself for a wide lawn and a big house, because I had nowhere else to go. Later, it was for Zack.'

'Oh no, you insult me,' Philip said, his lips curling with disgust. 'Do I seem like *him*? In my voice do you hear me bartering for your body?'

'No, but I still don't think I can,' she said.

'It wouldn't be much different from our friendship now, except it would be different for him. I'd want to adopt Zachary, give him my name.'

They both looked out over the yard, and they heard the rustling of the fallen leaves as boy and dog rolled around happily on the ground.

'This is such a sad house,' Philip said softly. 'I would welcome crayon on the doorframes, muddy footprints on the waxed kitchen floor.'

Jennifer smiled.

'I never told you about her, did I?'

'No.'

'I loved her very much. I met her in London right after the war. I was in the Army, coming back from Germany, and I went out to Kew Gardens. I wanted to see the greenhouses, for I'd heard they had a couple of strains of orchids that were rare.

'She was a volunteer there, and as the British would say, I chatted her up. Seemed she loved the flowers as much as I did. I spent some time there in London. It was a happy time. People glorying in life again; the shortages didn't even bother them. The British are such a brave people. Everyone was happy, reckless, impulsive, and in three weeks I married her. I loved her, but that was another place, another time. It has nothing to do with my love for you now.'

He paused and caught his breath and went on. 'We spent our honeymoon in a cottage that she owned by the sea,' again he paused, and she couldn't see his face. 'There was a record player by the window. We had only one record that still played – the others had warped in that closed-up house – and we played it over and over. It was Debussy's 'La Mer'. Even now if I try I can hear the violins.'

He moved closer to her. 'Jennifer, outside there's a walled garden with a door in the back, and under the clematis in the stone is the cottage's name, *World's End*.'

She caught her breath. It wasn't possible. It was the tear in the curtain, she had seen it.

'I still own that cottage. Some day if you like we can go there and you can see – it's written in the stone there, just like you dreamed. You *must* marry me. Don't you understand? Somehow we're connected.'

She went into his open arms and felt the comfort of his beating heart. Yes, she loved him, but she wasn't sure if she could ever love him in other ways. She didn't even know what ways there were.

'If you like we can sell this house and get another.'

'I don't know, I'm not sure. I'm so mixed up, Philip. Give me time, I need to think.'

She thought about it as Philip said, 'You get what you see.' He listed his faults. 'I smoke too much, I'm a slob. I leave my socks on the bathroom floor, I snore, you can't even talk to me when there's a ball game on. If ever I'm lucky enough to catch a fish, I bring it back from the trip and insist on eating it for dinner. I also insist on wearing my old raincoat with the rips, and I always get roaring drunk on Christmas and New Year's and I usually make a fool of myself, for I'm a crying drunk. There are no skeletons in the closet. I don't pull panties off clothes-lines to sniff and I feel I'm not weird in any respect.'

When he finished his list, she wondered if she could describe herself in the same way. She thought not.

They were married before Christmas. Stella and Addie were so pleased.

'I always knew reading those dictionaries would get you somewhere. He's real class, a gentleman through and through. You deserve him,' Stella said.

Maw was more reserved. 'Do you know him, Jenny. Really know him?'

'Yeah, Momma, I'm a lot older now, a lot wiser.' But she knew her mother was thinking it was shades of yesterday – an older man, a good job, a beautiful house.

Addie kept her worries to herself, however, and instead said a silent prayer: 'Please this time let this daughter walk with God.' It bothered her that each man named her different, first Jeannie, now Jennifer. She had named her Jenny.

Life changed. At first Zack was nervous, a new school, making new friends, but the house, the dog, having a real full-time dad made a difference. He adored Philip.

Jennifer learned to drive. They bought a secondhand car, and she had freedom. Philip hired a girl and she only worked with him two days a week.

'You know you don't have to. We can afford help.'

'No, I like working with you, just you, me, and the flowers. You taught me that they stand for happy times. I'm glad. I always thought of funerals.' And she truly enjoyed those days working with her new husband.

One day he mentioned it. 'You know, Jennifer, if you want

257

you could do adult education. I thought you always wanted to study art and design.'

'I do. Maybe later,' and she held it like a promise of something great for the future.

They had the tickets for New York. Philip wanted to go, so they could walk down Fifth Avenue and see them in the window – *Designs by Jennifer*. She couldn't wait. Paul informed her that the line would be out in about a month.

'You know, all of New York seemed like that,' she said.

'Like what?'

'It seemed full of people's dreams. It throbbed with excitement and misery.' She remembered thinking that it was a place where dreams came true, and dreams died. There was no middle ground; it was all or nothing.

'Yours came true, and I'm so glad. I want you just like you are, not an appendage of me, but yourself. We're equal. It's our house, our shop, our money—'

'The money,' she said, remembering. 'It's in the savings account. I haven't changed the name yet.'

'Do what you want with it. Buy trinkets or bon-bons, throw it away at the races, buy closets full of clothes, keep it there for Zack's college. Do anything you want.'

'No,' she corrected him. 'That's not what you just said. If it's mine, then it's yours, too.'

'Well, that's right, if it's mine, too, I think we should leave it for Zack's college.'

'I agree, let's leave it there.'

Philip kept his word. He never hinted at, or pressed for any intimacy. Now they even slept in the same bed, but it never went beyond kisses, hugs, lying close to each other. Jennifer knew what this cost him, for sometimes he'd get up, go out on the patio in his shorts covered by the battered raincoat and smoke until the wee hours of the morning. Oh, she wanted him, sometimes her desire she thought must have been as strong as his, but she didn't know what to do. She couldn't bear it if it was ugly.

One night after hours on the patio, he returned. She could hear the splash of water as he brushed his teeth. It was better to pretend to be asleep. How could she comfort him? So unfair, she was being so unfair.

She felt his body next to hers, as he got back into bed. She felt the softness of kisses on the back of her neck. A shiver ran through her. She wanted to feel his lips, his body next to hers. Slowly she unbuttoned the gown and turned to him, moving closer. She sought his lips. He kissed her back, a reserved, gentle kiss. ''Night, Jennifer.' She found his hand and brought it up to her breast, like velvet his touch, and soon his tongue warm and wet, kissing, sucking gently, his hands moving over the planes of her body measuring his love.

'Yes,' she whispered. 'Yes.' Still he caressed, treasured her flesh; his kisses trailed down, she felt the gentle probe of his tongue as he traced her belly button – down, further down, his kisses tracing. He laid his head against her, and on her knee she felt the beat of his heart.

'Jennifer?' she heard his whisper; it was a question.

'Yes,' she repeated. Permission given, she felt his lips there. Gently he coaxed, and she felt there was nothing dirty in his act. His tongue gave such exquisite pleasure, and when she couldn't contain it, she let it out, a sigh, a moan, and then she felt him lower himself upon her body, and like a flower ready to receive him, she opened and felt joy. This was love, this was two people celebrating the wonder of their bodies. It was good. On that night they were truly married.

She was excited about the New York trip. Everything was wonderful, but then she had the dream again.

She woke up in a cold sweat.

'What is it? Are you all right?' Philip sat up, rubbing the sleep out of his eyes.

'The dream, I had the dream again, but it was different. All the time it was happening I knew it was a dream.'

'Wait.' He got up and fetched her a glass of water and left the room. He was away so long she began to feel worried. She couldn't imagine where he had gone.

'They were in the basement,' he explained, and sat on the

edge of the bed, his fingers rustling through the box of pictures. 'Here.' He held it out to her.

Jennifer looked at the photograph. It was the garden in her dreams, the exact same garden.

Again he pressed a group of photographs into her hand. They were of the same place taken from different angles. One picture showed partially the word *Wor - -* while on the other she could clearly see the word *End*.

'What does it mean?' she asked.

'I don't know – could it be some kind of precognition? We were getting close to each other, so it must have been thoughts or images you were picking up from me.'

'But Tammy and Melanie; they're always there with me. Stranger yet, Scotty's there, too.'

'Please, Jennifer, let me make the appointment with Dr Thornton. Dreams speak to us in images, in symbols. It could help, and it certainly couldn't hurt. Do it for Zack and me, honey. You really need to talk about this and put the past to rest.'

She clutched her stomach. It was beginning, that awful crawling feeling. She always experienced this sensation when she'd had the dream of Melanie.

'Promise you'll call him in the morning.'

'I promise,' and they turned out the light.

She lay there in the dark and felt sick, for she could almost see them, a mass of wriggling green snakes, for that was what it felt like. It was this dream she couldn't talk about. It ran on and on, like the other movies in her mind. This dream did not shudder or miss a frame . . .

Always her hands winding and winding the cloth, the moon, the dance of fireflies and the feel of dew on her bare feet. Clearly she found again the sensation of digging in the cold earth, digging and digging a hole big enough to bury an unloved child.

In her sleep her throat worked, as it relived her inhuman howl, and the snip of the shears, cutting curls, cutting brown curls to fall softly in the bathroom sink.

CHAPTER 27

On Jennifer's first visit to the psychiatrist, she felt she wasn't going to be comfortable talking to him. Dr Thornton was young, about thirty-five, and he wore a grey shantung suit tailored to perfection. His tie, small commas of deeper grey and white, lay against his broadcloth shirt, not daring to move a fraction either way. This man's tie would not dare to misbehave. He was totally in control.

She could not see his shoes, but was sure they would be soft expensive Italian leather. It was difficult looking at his manicured fingers held in a tent. A pretentious pose, she felt – learned from the movies.

She was wrong, for he helped her. His directness could not be sidestepped.

'You're having nightmares,' he stated, his competent hands parting, preparing to jot down notes.

'I'm not sure they're nightmares.'

'Please take your time. If not nightmares, what are you referring to?'

'Well . . .' she hesitated. 'It goes back a long time. I had a very bad fall when I was a child. I was only seven when it began.'

'Uh huh. Go on.'

'After that, from time to time I had visions – no, that sounds wrong. I would see things in my mind that would really happen later.'

'In dreams?'

'Not always. Sometimes when I was awake – just a flash,

a picture of something. A lot of times they were innocent, inconsequential sort of things.'

'Are you saying that you experienced precognition?'

'I guess that's what I mean, but other times they were warnings – pointless warnings, for I could never avoid what it was I saw.'

'For instance,' Dr Thornton prompted, leaning forward, his interest piqued.

'I dreamed the house that I eventually lived in with my first husband. I dreamed of that house for years before I went there.'

'Go on.'

'It wasn't an error, for the house had one very distinct feature. It had a heart-shaped window in the attic.' She sighed, took a deep breath and tried to explain. 'In my recurring dream it was a place of terror. I always found myself being chased by dark, menacing shadows.'

'What was your reaction when you first recognized the house?'

'Utter terror. I cried hysterically. My fear was so intense I even wet myself,' she admitted.

'How did you cope after the initial shock?'

She tried to think back. 'Mostly I tried to ignore it, but often I could hear sounds – eerie, sad sounds that seemed to come directly from the attic.' She paused. 'My son even heard them and he was only three. It was the sound of weeping children.' Jenny thought about mentioning the terrible vision she had seen in the attic, but decided against it.

'I recall reading about the house. It had a dark history before your tragedy, and eventually it was destroyed by fire, was it not?'

'Yes, it was. I didn't know about it at the time, though. I was hospitalized and everyone made sure I didn't read the papers.'

'How long did your recovery take?'

'Months. Almost seven months.'

'Were you in therapy at that time?'

'No, Doctor, not like this. I was on medication.'

'So now your dreams have returned?'

'Yes. The first dream is a total recollection of the night my daughter died, and the other is really a very pleasant dream, until I awake.'

'Can you tell me about it?'

'My children and a child I know are all in this place, there in a very beautiful garden. I've now found out that this garden really exists. It's in the south of England at a cottage my husband owns.'

'You've seen a picture of it?'

'No. I mean I have now, but I had this dream, of the same garden, before I saw the photographs.'

'What disturbs you about the dream?'

'When I wake up it brings back my grief, for two of the children in the dream are dead.'

'Your children?'

Jennifer nodded yes, surprised that she could talk to him. 'The girl Tammy was my stepdaughter, and the infant was my daughter Melanie.'

'What happens in the dream?'

'Nothing, really. The children are playing, music drifts out through the window; it's the same music my husband said he used to listen to on an old record-player when he was there in 1945. I feel very happy, but the children are different; they've grown, I imagine to the same degree that they would have if they had both lived.'

'Do you feel guilty that you could have saved them somehow?'

'I feel guilty, but I know I couldn't have saved them.'

'Tell me, I already have a scant background from your husband, but please try to tell me in your own words what happened.'

'To Tammy – to Melanie?'

'Both.'

Jennifer took a deep breath. She didn't know where to begin, or if she could tell it all.

'When Tammy's mother died, she was sent to us, like an

unwanted package. Her name was pinned onto her coat and she was put on a train.'

'Did you resent this?'

'Oh no, she was more than welcome. She was a sad little girl. I could see how scared she was, but it worked out fine. I mean at first, she adored my little boy, Zack. She played nicely with him and watched over him. No, there were no problems in the beginning. She seemed to like me, too. We were both interested in art. It gave us a starting point.'

'How did your husband treat her?'

'Ignored her mostly, except he was real mean to her if she cried at night, especially if he was—' she stopped and felt her face burn.

'If you were involved in sex.'

Jennifer shook her head. 'Yes. Actually, that's not totally accurate. Sometimes he used to let me go comfort her at night because I knew how much she missed her mother, and if we weren't . . .' she paused, 'he'd let me go to her.'

'When did that change?'

'It was one night.' She gulped and knew she had to go on. 'It was one night he had me undressed; we were downstairs in the den. He was furious with me. He said my breasts were too big. I was expecting at the time.'

'He didn't call them breasts, did he?'

'No.'

'What did he call them?'

'Gutter language, you know.'

'Yes, Jennifer, I know, but it's important for you to say it, to get the poison out. I understand you suffered his abusive treatment for many years in silence.'

'He said my tits were too big,' she whispered, 'that he hated my nipples. He said he liked them little and pink, the way they used to be before the children.'

She heard the pen scratching on the paper.

'Then what did he do or say?'

'He called me a cow, made appropriate noises – and I'm not sure but I think that was the night he kept pinching my stomach, and telling me my stretchmarks looked like his road map. I can't remember exactly, but he made fun of my body. I was seven months pregnant.'

Surprised, she felt tears running down her cheeks. It was good to get them out, those ugly words. She went on.

'I looked up and saw her, Tammy. She was on the bottom step looking through the bannister. She heard it all, or most of what he said.'

'Uh huh,' he nodded.

'Bobby Lee changed tactics then. I pulled my dress around me to cover myself, and calling her honey or some other endearment, he grabbed her by the hand and took her back upstairs to her room.'

'What did you do then?'

'I went to the kitchen and washed the supper dishes. I remember I dropped a plate. It belonged to a valuable set. I was so nervous wondering what he was going to do when he came back downstairs.'

'What did he do?'

'Nothing. It was just like it had never happened, like he'd forgotten all about it.'

'Didn't you find that strange?'

'No, I never thought about it. He was always very volatile and moody. He could switch in and out of anger so fast you never knew what was coming next.'

'How'd you feel when he came down and didn't bother you?'

'Grateful. I was grateful that this one night I could go to bed and he wouldn't be bothering or teasing or hurting me in that cruel way of his.'

'Grateful . . . Had you ever thought about that word? Were you grateful that he had been satisfied and now he wouldn't be bothering you?'

'Oh no, Dr Thornton! I must have been stupid, but no, nothing like that even came into my mind. He was so unpredictable, I told you. His moods could change fast as lightning.'

There was a silence heavy between them. 'You've got to

believe me,' she went on painfully. 'I never knew, but when I look back that's when it must have started. Tammy became so hateful to Zack and me; she said I wasn't her friend any more, but school was starting and I thought maybe she was nervous about that. She began waking up and crying in her sleep. Bobby Lee was impatient with disobedient children. He said I was too soft with her, and that she needed discipline. He said that he would go to her room. He wouldn't allow me to do so any more.'

He nodded.

'He was her father. I knew he was being harsh and impatient, but there was nothing I could do. I had no idea of what was going on. I was very young.'

'Did he beat you?'

'No, not really. He pulled my hair once or twice, put his hands around my neck, but no, in the sense that women talk about violence he didn't do that. He gave me no black eyes or broken bones, but it *was* abuse. He totally controlled me, and there was no one I could tell. It was all so filthy, so ugly – no, I couldn't tell anyone about that. I felt ashamed, and somehow I thought it must be my fault.'

'He controlled you through degradation?'

'Yes. I never really understood it. I'd never read about this kind of thing in any book or magazine. I'd never heard anyone ever speak of it, you know, on the radio on those programmes, where they talk about abuse, so I thought it must be me. It had to be my fault that he did those things to me.'

'Oh! Sexual abuse is a category, true enough, but you're right, no one ever talks about sexual abuse in the confines of marriage. No, Jennifer, that subject's still locked up in the closet. It's taboo.'

He finished his notes.

'Please, go on,' he urged.

'Things got worse. Tammy was doing badly in school. I went to see her teacher; she asked if Bobby Lee could come in for a talk, but he got furious when I asked him. He cursed and raved and was livid when they sent a permission slip to be signed for Tammy to see a psychiatrist. I was gonna forge his name, but he found it, the note, before I could do it.

'That week he kept telling me to keep her out of school, as he said she looked sick. My legs ached all the time. My baby was almost due and I was so tired that I could barely keep the children clothed and fed. That's why I was so surprised when he decided we should go to the lake that weekend. It was almost winter. I protested, but any time I disagreed with him he just got ugly and took it out on the children. That's where it happened: he drowned her.'

Again Jennifer felt them, hot tears running down her cheeks. She searched for a Kleenex in her purse, and across the desk he handed her one.

'I feel so guilty. If only I had signed that note and sent it back before he found it.'

'"If only",' Dr Thornton echoed. 'The two most futile words in the English language, and guilt deserved or undeserved is the most destructive emotion known to man.'

He caught up with his notes.

'I saw her face, but like I said, those visions or glimpses into the future or whatever they were – they were useless, for I could never stop whatever was going to happen. I saw Tammy's face in the dishwater of the sink. I saw her very clearly drowning in that awful lake, but there was absolutely nothing I could do to save her.'

Jennifer groaned in grief; she put her hands up to her face to stop the tears glittering in her eyes from falling.

'We've covered a lot of ground today. I'm glad you changed your mind,' Dr Thornton said.

'About what?'

'I could tell you were sure we wouldn't be able to talk, and Jennifer, we're doing fine.'

Jennifer left his office feeling better, but the dreams persisted, and always on the following day she had them – the pains running through her stomach.

She was relieved when Paul called from New York and told her they were behind schedule; the Collection wouldn't be launched now until late in May.

They cancelled the New York trip and life went on smoothly, except for the days following the dreams.

It was one Friday night. Philip had arranged a sitter for Zack, and they were both dressing. They were going to a play and dinner. Just the two of them for a special evening.

The phone rang, and Jennifer heard Maw on the phone in hysterics. 'She's dead, oh Jenny, she's dead with the needle still sticking out of her arm.'

'Who, Momma?'

'Thelma. I just found her about a half hour ago. The ambulance already took her, but they said she's gone, overdose.'

'Oh, how terrible, Maw. She was so young!'

'The Reverend's acting real funny, crying and all in the chapel. He can't stand it that he feels like he failed her. On and off she was doing good.'

'How's Scotty taking it?'

'Why, he's sitting out on that ole picnic table, but that child can't seem to cry. He's all worried that she wasn't baptized. Reverend tried to have her do it, but she always changed her mind at the last minute.'

'I'm sure it doesn't matter, Maw.'

'Don't say that. The Reverend thinks it's very important, going to Jesus, and Jenny,' she whispered down the phone, 'it weren't no accident. She left a note.'

'Aw Mom, I'm so sorry to hear that.'

'Jenny, I know it's not right. She shouldn't be bothering you, she barely knew you.'

'Bothering me, how?'

'In the note she said it real legal-like, she said she was givin' him to you.'

'What do you mean? Giving me what?'

'Scotty. She gave you Scotty.'

'Oh, my God.' Philip saw Jennifer's face and took the phone.

Maw repeated it. 'Philip, I just told Jenny that Thelma's dead from an overdose and in her note she gave Scotty to Jenny.'

'We'll call you back,' he said, and hung up and turned Jennifer to face him.

'I know you're a generous, loving person, Jennifer, but it's a big responsibility. Do you have room in your heart for that little boy? It would be more your job than mine.' She nodded yes and they started for the car.

Again Jennifer was going to get a dead mother's child. It was *déjà vu*. It scared her.

It would be hard, for he was a street child, and far too old for his years, but she couldn't leave him there for the welfare workers to shuffle from place to place.

'He's really a lot like us,' Philip said quietly. 'He knows about loss.'

A feeling of panic overwhelmed her. 'Oh Philip, what if something happens to him? He could get hit by a car, he could fall off his bike, he could get a terrible disease. I'm scared.'

'Everybody's scared that's in charge of young lives. We'll do the best we can, Jennifer. We do it for Zack now.'

Jennifer in her best black crêpe dress, with her pearls, and Philip in his suit and tie, drove down to the ghetto to bring back a second son.

'He was in my dream,' she said.

'I know. Maybe precognition does exist,' Philip said gently.

CHAPTER 28

Taking Zack aside, they tried to explain about Scotty.

'He's going to be your brother. Philip has filed all the papers, and just like you his last name will be Tremaine,' Jennifer said. 'Would you like that?'

'Okay.' But she could see by the set of his jaw that something was bothering him.

'Zack, I lived at the Mission when I was little. We were very poor. People at the Mission *are* poor. They don't have nice stores where they can sell flowers and make money to buy nice houses, or cars, or new clothes or toys like we've got. I want you to be very kind to Scotty. He's very sad right now, as his mother died.'

'Everybody's always dying,' he said sadly.

'It does seem like it, but I want you to be happy about this. You'll have a real brother, and Philip and I are going to be his parents. Do you understand?'

'I had a sister once – no, I had two, but they left,' he said.

Jennifer hugged her son. 'I want you to be very unselfish. You must share your toys. We're buying a bed for Scotty just like yours, and his room will be right next door to you.'

'His bed could be in my room. It could fit.'

'We'll see about that,' and she kissed him hard. 'I love you, Zachary Tremaine.'

'I love you back, Momma.'

Jennifer's therapy continued. Philip was right: emotionally she felt so much stronger. She was finally able to talk

271

about the feelings she had about everyone wearing a mask and hiding dreadful secrets. Now she knew for certain that men could be kind and loving.

Their closeness continued and she finally understood what Stella had meant. She loved Philip's touch, his lovemaking, and she knew what a gentle man she had married, when finally one day she could undress in front of him, even in the light, and he said that wonderful thing to her.

'You're beautiful, all of you,' and in his eyes she felt this could be true. Her stomach was flat now, her breasts still firm and full, and once he traced a small stretchmark on her tummy.

'Oh, don't look so close,' she warned. 'I didn't want you to notice.'

'Notice what? They're beautiful too, all those lines. They have value. You made a great trade.'

'Trade?' she questioned.

'Yeah, you traded those wonderful stretchmarks for Zachary. You clever woman, you got the best of the bargain.'

She loved him dearly. She loved his mind, she loved the way he looked at life and love, and she thanked God for him.

Sometimes they talked about it, the cottage with the garden.

'Maybe this summer we could take the boys and see it. The cottage is right on the sea, they'll love it there. Of course, we'd have to let the agents know so they don't rent it out.'

'Why did you never sell it?' she asked.

'I don't really know. I just never got around to it.'

Jennifer continued the therapy and once or twice when she tried to get some input from Dr Thornton he'd answer her with, 'Precognition, it's not my field. Anything's possible, but Jennifer, you've got to let them go. The girls, they're gone.'

'I know they are. Philip and I have been discussing going

to England this summer and taking the boys there. What do you think?'

'It might be a good idea; might erase the imprint you have of it, but Jennifer, we're not really finished until we talk about Melanie.'

'I know,' she said wearily. 'I'm not sure I can talk about her.'

'I've read all the newspaper accounts so I can save you some questions, but we do need to get it out in the open.'

She sighed deeply. 'I was on so many pills, anti-depressants, tranquillizers ... it's all very fuzzy. I did a curious thing that night. I cut off all my hair.'

'Cut your hair? Do you know why?'

'No. I cut it off in big hunks with the hedge-shears. You remember, I told you I would bring them up to the bedroom, and I often daydreamed about cutting off his penis.'

'It could have been a transference of some kind.'

'No, I think I was defying him. He always told me I wasn't allowed to cut my hair, and earlier that night he was holding it, my long hair, twisting it and hurting me while he made me—' she stopped. 'Made me suck his penis.'

'The night Melanie died he made you do that?'

'Yes. It went on for hours and hours – he couldn't get hard.'

'Impotent men are often like that – cruel, compensating for their lack of virility.' He checked his notes. 'You're sure that this was the same night?'

'Yes. I can never forget it.'

'But you've said how many pills you were taking.' He leaned forward. 'Yet you're certain. What happened then?'

'It took hours, but finally he did—'

'He climaxed?'

'Yes.'

His fingers flew into the tent. 'Try to remember clearly what happened then, Jennifer. It's important.'

'I checked on Zachary, he was coughing. I rubbed his chest with Vick's. I checked on Melanie. She was asleep.'

His voice was so quiet she almost didn't hear. 'What did you do then?'

'I washed the dirt off my hands then I cut off my hair with the hedge-shears and went to bed.'

The tent collapsed and she heard him tapping his pen.

' "Washed the dirt off your hands"?' he questioned.

'Oh, I don't know why I said that. Probably I was thinking of the garden.' She began again. 'I checked on Melanie, she was asleep, then I cut off my hair with the hedge-shears and went to bed.'

'Let me understand this. What time was this, when you had finished doing what he wanted you to do?'

'Two o'clock or almost.'

'What time did you wake up?' he asked.

'Seven, when the alarm went off.'

'What did you do then?'

'I remember screaming over and over. Oh, Dr Thornton, I had so much to scream about. I thought I would never stop.'

'Jennifer, think! Were you screaming before you saw the empty crib?'

'I don't know, I'm not sure. I had taken so many pills.'

'So you're telling me that between two and seven Bobby Lee got up, went to Melanie's room, put his penis in her tiny mouth and on her little body—'

'*No!!*' she screamed. The horror of that image was too much for her.

Jennifer started crying and couldn't stop. 'That bastard, no, no, he never touched her.' She looked up and through her tears she saw him, a look of disbelief on his face.

'He didn't kill her either,' she whispered.

Dr Thornton swivelled in his chair, and she knew he was hiding from her and finally she heard him say, 'That's between you and God, Jennifer. Our conversation in this room is privileged.'

He turned, his face white with shock, but she could see

274

he had regained his composure. 'You're going to have to face it some time. Get it out, to somebody somewhere. You have to start at the beginning, Jennifer, and tell it like it really happened, or your dreams are never going to go away!'

EPILOGUE

'Philip, is it possible to do something that's very important for me?'

'Of course, what is it?'

'Could you take off one day at the shop and drive me up to Jeff City? I haven't driven on the highways very much.'

'Well, sure, but what's in Jeff City?'

'The prison. I need to see Bobby Lee.'

'Is that wise?'

'It might not be wise, but it's necessary. There is something I need to tell him.'

'Maybe you should check this out with Dr Thornton. It could make the dreams worse. It might be a good idea to see what he thinks.'

'It's his idea.'

'You mean he told you to see Bobby Lee?'

'Not exactly, no, Philip. He didn't say I should see him, nor did he say I shouldn't. He just said I need to tell someone about that night.'

'Why him? Why would you want to talk to him?'

Jennifer turned and clutched her stomach. 'Oh Philip, it stays in here, twisting and turning like a mass of angry snakes. There's something I really need to tell him. I have to, or it will never go away.'

'All right. What day would you like to go?'

'As soon as possible – tomorrow?'

'I'll call Betty now and ask her to mind the store. What about Zack and Scotty?'

277

'I'll call the sitter.'

Jennifer barely slept that night. She went over it, again and again. The imagined dialogue almost satisfied her, but not quite. She rose early and went to the drawing board and drew it in thick crayon; it was so perfect it could have been the original. She folded the paper and carefully put it in her purse, and she felt light, like someone going to Confession, knowing she'd feel better afterwards.

The car sped smooth as glass over the highway. 'Wanna talk about it?' Philip asked.

'No. Could we just listen to the radio?' She fiddled with the dials till she found the FM station and soft music bathed them with soothing sound.

They located it easily, the prison. It stood perched high on a hill, an ugly sprawling stone building, with barred windows like the house, and vicious barbed wire tangled on top of the sturdy brick walls.

'Are you sure about this?' Philip pressed. 'Can I go in with you?'

'Yes, I'm sure, and no, I need to go alone.' She got out of the car and walked straight towards the intimidating doors.

In the search, the female security guard only shuffled the piece of paper in her purse; she did not unfold it.

Sitting in front of the mesh screen, Jennifer's heart hammered with fear and elation. She almost did not recognize the thin, gaunt man who walked towards her. He looked puzzled, searching the other cubicles He squinted. finally saw her, and sat down barely feet away behind the screen.

She noticed the naked-looking forehead where his hair had receded. Black circles ringed his blue, blue eyes. Bobby Lee had aged a great deal.

'I didn't recognize the name,' he said. 'You changed it, huh?'

'I've remarried.' She said it quietly.

'Oh. What brings you here? Georgia get in touch about my appeal?'

278

'No.'

He sat staring at her through the mesh.

Jennifer opened her purse, unfolded the paper and held it up against the screen so he could see it.

'She didn't know how to spell hate, Bobby Lee. She forgot the "e".'

He stared at the crude childlike drawing.

'What is this?' he asked, and she could see a nervous twitch begin about his mouth.

'It's Tammy's; she drew it. Don't you recognize yourself?'

'Oh jeez, Jeanne – kids do that funny shit all the time. It don't mean nothing.'

'My name is Jennifer,' she said harshly.

'That's class, real class, but I still like Jeannie with the light brown hair,' he said, in a feeble attempt to charm her.

'When I found a picture like this, that's when I knew you had killed her, drowned her in that awful lake.'

'Look, I don't know what the hell this is all about,' he said. 'I didn't kill nobody. I'm filing an appeal.'

Jennifer folded the paper and put it back in her handbag. 'I didn't come here to talk about this picture. No, I came to talk about the night Melanie died.'

Visibly, his anxiety flared. 'I didn't kill her; as God is my witness, I never touched her. You've gotta believe me, Jeanne.'

'I do.'

'You do? You believe me! Then why weren't you at the trial? It might have helped me, you being her mother and you believing I was innocent.'

'We're getting out of sync, Bobby Lee. I wanted to tell you about that night. What really happened.'

He nodded and was quiet, his face puzzled.

'You remember you were pulling my hair, sticking your fingers in my ass, cussing me out 'cause your little prick wouldn't get hard?' He flinched at her words. 'Well, it was then I heard it, a sound, a funny sound. I didn't know exactly what it was, but that useless thing was in front of me, and you were worrying me to get it hard. Do you know how long it took before you came? It was two and a half hours! And right under the bed I had them, the sharp hedge-shears. That was the night I was gonna cut it off, your prick. I was gonna do it for you, Bobby Lee, so you wouldn't be worrying about it all the time. But Zachary saved it. Is it still there between your legs?'

He looked at her with pure hate, and she saw his murderous daydreams blooming, just like hers had done.

She went on: 'Zack was coughing, and I realized he needed a mother, one that wasn't in prison, and I figured too you needed to keep Dickie after all. Yes, Zack's coughing saved it for you.'

She saw him put his hand involuntarily down towards his crotch.

'But that wasn't the highlight of the evening. Oh no, Bobby Lee, it was just the beginning. After tending to Zack, I went to see about Melanie, and you know what? She must have left us when I was doing my wifely duties, all two and a half hours of it. I told you about that strange sound. I still don't know exactly what it was, but now I'm sure it was her gasping, taking her last breath. Regardless, I found her cold, her little hands set and clutching each other. I took her right up against my big tits, the ones with the purple nipples, and I tried to warm that cold little dead baby. "Crib death", or "cot death", I think they call it. I saw it once before when I was a candy-striper at the hospital. They just die in their sleep. But I was so sorry for her. You took all the love out of me and I had none left for our little baby. I could only pity her 'cause she didn't have a little Dickie.

'I cried and cried and I kissed her, apologized for giving her life, and blew into her little mouth, but I knew that nothing I could do would ever warm her again. Cot death . . . I only hope it was easy for her.'

Jennifer stopped talking. It hurt to say it, and the rest would be worse. So much worse, she had to relive it, that terrible night.

Bobby Lee was breathing hard now, his eyes fiery with disbelief.

'When I went to her room, I had it in my hand, that gown of Tammy's. It was wet with sperm, and may God forgive me, that's when I did it. I forced those blue little lips open and desecrated her tiny pink tongue, and on her lips I smeared it thick, like an ointment that would cure, making sure they were coated with sperm.'

Jennifer stopped and breathed slowly, pushing hysteria away. Finally she went on: 'Next I undressed her, spread those tiny legs wide, and smeared YOU ALL OVER HER.'

'You bitch! You fucking bitch!' he screamed, and lunged at the screen, shaking it so hard she thought it would break. Two guards rushed over to him.

'He'll be okay,' she said calmly. 'It was just some bad news I had to tell him.'

The guards pushed him down firmly in the seat and walked away.

'You know the rest, Bobby Lee. I'm sure you know it all by heart.' Changing tactics, she said, 'At the Mission, you never came inside, did you? Well, sometimes they play with the scriptures a little. They change a word here, move a bit there. This kinda thing they'd call "An Eye for an Ear".'

And in a low voice she began singing it:

> *'The Devil is a sly ole fox.*
> *If I could catch Him I'd put Him in a box.*
> *Lock that box and throw away the key,*
> *And that would be the end of He.'*

She wasn't sure he heard all of the words, for he was screaming and banging on the screen. 'You bitch! You fucking bitch!!'

The guards were pulling him away, and Jennifer turned and walked out, and the snakes were quiet; and she knew for sure they were all dead.

A selection of quality fiction from Headline

THE POSSESSION OF DELIA SUTHERLAND	Barbara Neil	£5.99	☐
MANROOT	A N Steinberg	£5.99	☐
DEADLY REFLECTION	Maureen O'Brien	£5.99	☐
SHELTER	Monte Merrick	£4.99	☐
VOODOO DREAMS	Jewell Parker Rhodes	£5.99	☐
BY FIRELIGHT	Edith Pargeter	£5.99	☐
SEASON OF INNOCENTS	Carolyn Haines	£5.99	☐
OTHER WOMEN	Margaret Bacon	£5.99	☐
THE JOURNEY IN	Joss Kingsnorth	£5.99	☐
SWEET WATER	Christina Baker Kline	£5.99	☐

All Headline books are available at your local bookshop or newsagent, or can be ordered direct from the publisher. Just tick the titles you want and fill in the form below. Prices and availability subject to change without notice.

Headline Book Publishing, Cash Sales Department, Bookpoint, 39 Milton Park, Abingdon, OXON, OX14 4TD, UK. If you have a credit card you may order by telephone – 01235 400400.

Please enclose a cheque or postal order made payable to Bookpoint Ltd to the value of the cover price and allow the following for postage and packing:

UK & BFPO: £1.00 for the first book, 50p for the second book and 30p for each additional book ordered up to a maximum charge of £3.00.
OVERSEAS & EIRE: £2.00 for the first book, £1.00 for the second book and 50p for each additional book.

Name ....

Address ....

....

....

If you would prefer to pay by credit card, please complete:
Please debit my Visa/Access/Diner's Card/American Express (delete as applicable) card no:

Signature .... Expiry Date ....